Marianne and the Mad Baron

Copyright © 2016 Kathryn Kohorst

Cover by Shardel at selfpubbooks.com

All rights reserved. No part of this book may be reproduced, scanned, or distributed in any printed or electronic format without permission.

This is a work of fiction. Names, characters, places and incidents are either the product of the author's imagination or are used fictitiously, and any resemblance to actual persons, living or dead, business establishments or events or locales is entirely coincidental.

This Paperback edition is published by Kohorst Books, LLC

For question or comments about the quality of this book or review inquiries please contact kohorstbooks@gmail.com

ISBN:10-0-9972521-2-X
ISBN-13:978-0-9972521-2-5

Marianne and the Mad Baron

Kathryn Kohorst

To my husband—the love of my life. I would never have thought to take this path if you hadn't pointed the way.

Acknowledgments

Special thanks to my critique partners—Ann Hinnenkamp, Neroli Lacey, Leanne Farella, and Nan Dixon. I wouldn't be the writer I am today without you ladies. Thanks to my wonderful editor, Sherri Hildebrant.

CHAPTER ONE

"Am I invisible?" Marianne muttered as a carrier pigeon whizzed past her so close she felt the air from the propellers at its back. The blades shifted, moving to the top of the bullet-shaped bronze body, and the device accelerated upward. If carrier pigeons could travel anywhere in the world or even the aether, and if they could avoid objects as large as planets, why couldn't they avoid a woman who was barely five feet tall?

She touched the necklace at her throat. She called it Snake, for it looked like a snake made from tarnished copper, but it was so much more. It slithered from around her neck, coiled around her hand, and back to her neck. The reminder that her mother's gift was still there steadied and soothed her. Her anger dissipated and she drew her cape back over Snake, hiding it from the world again. She was headed toward Barrow's department store and the gossips were sure to be present. No one would understand why the daughter of a viscount would wear such a tarnished old thing.

Barrow's was London's largest department store. It was the place to be for anyone who was anyone, and its high membership fees kept it exclusive. Even Queen Victoria shopped there.

All she wanted was a new notebook and some ink. She would have been much happier at a smaller shop farther down Bond Street, but her father insisted that she keep up appearances.

She stopped in front of the enormous gilded doors. Intricately engraved brass panels hid the gears and levers used to operate them. Society members might love technology, but that didn't mean people liked to look at it.

She hustled up to the globe-shaped kiosk next to the door and pulled on a lever.

The domed lid opened to reveal a number pad also made from brass plates. Punching in her code took mere moments and she stepped back to wait for the doors to open.

Nothing happened.

Her dues should have been automatically withdrawn from her bank account. She had plenty of funds; why wasn't she allowed inside?

Frowning, she tried her father's number.

A deep groan echoed through the metal and the ponderous doors slid wide.

Pushing her worries aside, she ducked through and made her way past the counters full of cosmetics and jewelry.

A man bowled passed her and Marianne stumbled into a low shelf full of books. She glared at the retreating man's back and quickened her pace. The sooner she got out of here the better.

Around her, conversation buzzed. Men and women came here not to shop but to converse, to see and be seen. Why anyone would want to come into a crowded building to talk baffled her. Most of them would be going to balls and parties later on, too. How exhausting.

Get in and out. That's what she intended to do.

Grabbing the items she wanted from their shelves, she walked up to an automated cashier machine. She placed her items on the counter in front of it. Everyday technology made life easier and better for everyone. She reached up and touched Snake. If only father would understand that. Shaking away the thought, she turned her attention to the ACM itself.

It was a humanoid-shaped mechanical, with a cylindrical body sitting behind the glass countertop. The spherical shape on top looked roughly like a head but it had no features other than a keypad, a speaker and a cone shaped light that rested on top like a hat.

She typed in her membership code and the light flashed yellow.

"Would you like to make a purchase?" it asked in a light musical voice that reminded Marianne of a wind chime.

Marianne leaned into the machine and spoke into the speaker on the head. "Yes."

"Please repeat your answer."

"Yes," she said again, slowing down and elongating the word even as she resisted the urge to roll her eyes.

The counter under the ACM flashed and a light traveled from left to right and back again. "Items counted. Do you have further purchases to make?"

"No."

The mechanical tucked its head down into its neck. After a few moments, the light on top flashed from yellow to orange before the head popped back up. "This transaction has been denied."

Conversation quieted. Marianne wrung her hands. "Denied? What do you mean? The account held ten pounds just yesterday."

"I do not understand the inquiry."

"Please explain why this transaction is denied." Marianne carefully enunciated each word. Her gaze darted around the room, and she clutched her arms around her waist.

Conversation stopped as people inched closer.

She wanted to curl into a ball and hide. The small snake curled around her throat, dropping its head so it rested on her breastbone and over her heart. It began to heat, sending warmth to her core. Then it began to purr, its soothing vibrations easing her fear. It always seemed to know when she needed it. She pressed her hand to the back of its head and took a deep breath. She could get through this.

"Please repeat the inquiry." The ACM repeated.

"May I be of assistance, miss?" A tall, gangly man in the uniform of a Barrow's department store clerk walked up to her.

"This ACM won't let me buy these." Marianne waved her hand at the pile on the counter. Snickering erupted behind her and she tucked her shaking hand back under her arm.

"Please inquire why the purchase was denied." The man told the machine.

The mechanical's gears whirred, producing a low buzz that rattled in her chest and shook her resolve further.

Marianne wished people would stop staring. They weren't even trying to hide their interest. Her cheeks heated and she glanced at her toes. Where was the invisibility she'd hated earlier?

Chimes blared from the ACM and its head popped up, the light flashing an angry red. "No funds, no funds, no funds."

Marianne staggered back. The mechanical's voice wasn't loud and only the clerk nearby could hear it, but it might as well have been shouting. That flashing red light meant only one thing to anyone who saw it, and the blaring chimes would make sure everyone would look.

"Do you have any other form of payment?" the clerk asked, his tone respectful, even understanding, and somehow that made the humiliation worse.

Of course she didn't have another form of payment. No one carried physical money around anymore. Why would they, when every business of note had an automated cashier with direct access to the banks? Her cheeks flushed, and she cast a quick glance around the room. Some people were grinning outright. Others at least held handkerchiefs to their mouths. Not that it mattered. The message got across. The room began to spin and she clutched her throat.

Snake's purr intensified. It reached out and eased back the panic.

"No." Her voice was barely a whisper as she looked back up at the clerk.

"I see." He typed a command into the automaton's keypad.

A mechanical arm appeared out of a compartment on the ACM's torso and pulled her purchases into a box behind the counter.

"I'm sorry, miss, but you're making a scene." The clerk ushered her toward the door. "I'm afraid I'll have to ask you to leave."

Marianne flinched but she managed a jerky nod. Now she understood why her membership code hadn't worked on the door. No funds. She swallowed. She had to get home as fast as possible.

She tried to avoid eye contact with anyone in the throng of people gathered around her. It was impossible.

There was tight-lipped scorn on the faces of several of them and soft sad eyes full of pity from others. Those faces turned, following her as she walked down the aisle toward the door as if they were watching a condemned prisoner walking to the gallows.

"Isn't that Lindstrom's daughter?"

"Oh, the poor dear."

"Cut off her funds, did he?"

"Worthless girl."

Not all of them were nasty, but all of them stung. No matter how hard she tried to ignore those whispers, they all hit, every one piercing like tiny shards of glass. No single cut was too damaging, but she felt bloody and broken by the time she finally reached the doors. They hurt all the more because by nightfall, all of society would assume that Viscount Lindstrom had cut off his daughter's funds.

The street was buzzing with activity. People were hurrying about. Flying carriages whizzed past above her head and horse-drawn carriages clomped along the street. It seemed every person there took a moment to stare and accuse.

Dizziness threatened to topple her but she swallowed it down. Don't break down here. Get home.

It was only a few blocks to her father's house but it felt like miles. Every person who passed her stared as if he or she knew of her disgrace. Marianne tried to clear her head but even the wind taunted her. It blew through her hair, echoing the cutting words of the crowd.

"Worthless."

"Worthless."

She bolted across the street just as a mechanical curricle came racing by. A second and then a third followed the large wheeled monstrosity with its tiny seat and stinking diesel engine.

The men on top laughed and pointed at her cowered form as they circled her. "Little mouse caught in a trap!"

Her heart leapt to her throat and tears stung her eyes. She pushed them away. Crying never did any good. It only made it worse. She hurried up the front steps of her father's townhouse, and the butler opened the front door. Never had she been so grateful. She couldn't bear another moment under the scrutiny of the outside world. All she wanted was to curl up in the parlor and hide.

"Thank you, Hendricks. Is Papa in?" she asked.

The butler took her cloak, hat, and gloves. "No, miss."

Marianne nodded. "I'll be in the parlor. Please have some tea brought in."

"Of course, miss." The butler bowed.

Ensconced in her favorite chair, a hot cup of tea in her hand, Marianne tried to understand why her father would publicly humiliate her. He was never shy about letting her know his displeasure, but he usually spoke to her in private.

What had she done to deserve this? It was clear her father had emptied her pin money account. He was the only one who could. But why? And if he was going to do it, why hadn't he warned her? He had to know she'd find out at Barrow's. Now she would be ostracized at every event she went to.

Her father was a stickler for propriety. What had she done this time to provoke him? She was a good daughter, and she kept his household running smoothly. What more could she do to please him?

Nothing worked. Nothing. She tucked her feet up under her skirt and swallowed back a lump in her throat.

The front door opened and muffled sounds came from the hall. Slipping her shoes back on, she hurried out.

Her father stood next to the hall table. His left hand grasped a dispatch tube so tightly his knuckles had turned white. New lines were etched into his face. He looked older now than he had that morning at breakfast, as if he'd aged a decade or more over lunch.

"Papa, what happened? Are you all right?" She touched his arm, her own cares forgotten at the sight of his worn face.

He looked at her with sunken eyes.

"Can I help?" she asked.

"Ha," he snorted. "What could you possibly do?"

"I..." Her ribs squeezed and the tea she'd had earlier threatened to reappear. "I..."

Lord Lindstrom stared, the dark light in his eyes accusing her, no, blaming her for his failure. "Why couldn't you have been born a boy?"

Marianne stumbled back as if she'd been slapped. She'd spent her whole life trying to please him. Her whole life trying to be what he wanted. Pain seared her heart, and her breath came in shallow gasps. Her father had never made any attempt to hide his dislike for her, but she'd always believed there was something she could do to make it better. The truth hit her like a hammer, sending jagged fragments of her heart spiraling away.

She grabbed her father's arm. He couldn't mean it. He was tired, worried about something. Surely even he wouldn't go so low. "Papa?"

"Lily, why did you have to leave?"

He shrugged Marianne's hand away and paced down the hall to his study, slamming the door. The lock clicked.

Why was he asking after her mother? She'd been dead for twenty-two years. She shot a quick glance at Hendricks.

The old butler frowned, his eyebrows pinched together and his hands clasped in front of him so tightly his gloves wrinkled, revealing his wrists. "Should I get him some tea, miss?"

"I think he might need something stronger." Marianne hurried toward the study. Something must have happened. He wouldn't have said such a thing in front of a servant if he were himself. She knocked on the door. "Papa? Can I get you something?"

She turned back to Hendricks. "Maybe we should go—"

A sharp crack reverberated from the study.

Marianne jumped, her hand moving to her throat. She pounded on the door and twisted the handle. "Papa?"

No answer.

She tried again, desperation making her hands sweat. Her heart sank into her chest. That couldn't have been what it sounded like. Not possible. Not her father.

"Let me, miss," Hendricks said, putting a hand on her shoulder.

She barely heard him through the ringing in her ears.

"Miss," he said again. "Let me."

She looked over her shoulder at the man who had led the staff since before her birth. His kind eyes were strained with worry and she let him push her aside.

He rattled the handle. "My Lord?"

No answer.

Hendricks motioned to a couple of footmen. Shoulders slammed against the solid wood, one, two, three times. The frame splintered by the lock and the door flew open.

The two footmen stopped dead. The taller of the two turned a pitiful glance her way. "You might want to step back, miss."

"Why, what's happened? Papa?" She peeked under the arm of one of the footman and gasped.

The lamp on the desk blocked most of her view but her father's hand, limp and bloody, dangled over the edge. Blood dripped slowly onto the floor.

Coldness seeped from her core, chilling everything, even her bones. Her legs went numb and she sank to the ground. Her mind screamed at her to look away, to run away from that horrid image but she couldn't. Her gaze remained locked on that growing pool of blood. Her father's blood.

Suicide.

Such an ugly, horrid word.

Marianne took a deep breath, trying to calm her racing heart. Even saying it to herself was hard. Oh, the official report, filed last week with the court, stated that Lord Lindstrom had been killed in a tragic accident while cleaning his guns, but everyone knew the truth.

How was she to get on now?

She reached up and touched the small, coiled snake around her neck. The feel of its cold metal skin comforted her. Settled her mind. Happiness seemed so far away but at least she had Snake. No matter how far away happiness seemed, she had proof that it existed.

Looking around the room, she took in the stark masculine decor from the dark wood wainscot to the short balding clerk sitting behind the single large desk with its cubbyholes full of documents. The law offices of Flink, Fauler, and Franklin were devoid of anything mechanical. They specialized in serving old-fashioned clients who disliked the mechanical trend of modern society. Her father, a Luddite to his core, had hated mechanicals. He'd only suffered through the few interactions, like the ACM's at Barrow's, that were required to maintain his place in society. Otherwise their very existence sent him into a rage.

It hadn't always been that way. She remembered a happier father. Brief glimpses of joy. Mother. She closed her eyes and brought up the image of her mother. Smiling. Laughing. She'd died when Marianne had been six. Snake had been her final gift.

"Mr. Flink will see you now," the clerk said.

"Thank you." Marianne rose, holding her hat in a death grip.

He led her down a well-lit hallway that gave off an ambiance of cheerful tranquility at odds with the somber business of law. Marianne was grateful for that. She was tired of darkness and death. Tired of tears.

The clerk opened a door at the end of the hallway and after bowing her through, shut the door behind her. Mr. Flink sat behind his desk but rose as she entered. He extended his hands to her in greeting, his expression grave.

"Miss Lindstrom, my condolences." He grasped her hands tightly before motioning her to a chair before the desk.

She sat, taking a moment to arrange her skirts and fuss with her hat. "How bad is it, Mr. Flink?"

The solicitor sat back behind his desk and rested his clasped hands on the blotter. "I won't try to hide it from you, my dear. Things are really quite bad."

Slivers of ice pierced her. "How—"

The clerk returned bearing a tea tray. He placed it on the desk and Mr. Flink waved him away. "That will be all, Wilbur. You can go."

Wilbur left and silence settled on the small office.

"The thing is," he began as he poured her a cup of tea and passed it to her, "your father left you nothing."

Her body went numb, but she reached out and took the offered tea, grateful to have something warm in her hands. Taking a sip, she tried to remain calm even as her emotions boiled inside of her. Somehow through that jumble of thoughts she found the composure to speak. "I see."

"As there is no direct male relative, the title will revert to the crown but the estate was not entailed and he left all he had to his first cousin twice removed, a Mr. Grubber." The solicitor continued. "Not that there will be much to leave."

Mr. Grubber had fawned over her father. Had, in fact, done his best to ingratiate himself. And since her father had shown nothing but contempt for her, Mr. Grubber had followed suit. She'd find no help in that corner.

It shouldn't surprise her that Papa had left everything to the only male relative he had. And it didn't, not really. But it still hurt.

"So, I have nothing then?" she asked. Her voice came out strong and clear as if someone else was taking over her mouth and speaking for her.

"I'm afraid so." The solicitor said, regarding her though a set of bushy eyebrows. But his eyes were kind and she was grateful for it.

"Well..." There really wasn't anything she could say. Nothing she could do.

"Your mother, on her death, left you funds. It hadn't amounted to much but it would have been enough to survive on."

"Would have been?" Marianne forced her eyes up to look at him. Despair hovered above her, an oppressive cloud ready to smother her.

"It seems that your father, as your guardian..." The solicitor frowned. "He spent it."

"He could do that?"

"Actually, no."

"So, is there some way I can get access to it through his estate?" Marianne asked, the cloud lifted but didn't disappear.

"Normally, I'd say yes, but I'm not sure it would do any good to try in this case." Mr. Flink met her eyes levelly.

Even knowing what was coming, she felt compelled to ask. "Father was heavily in debt, wasn't he?"

Mr. Flink nodded. "Yes, and it pains me to say it, but the men he owes money to will get first call on his estate. I doubt there will be anything left to give you when it's over."

Marianne's jaw clenched but she forced it to relax. It all made a sick sort of sense. Her father had been Chancellor of the Exchequer. Financial distress... It was the only explanation for her father's final act. The only reason he would put a bullet in his head. "And if I were to fight for those funds in court it would only sully my father's name further."

"Yes."

Even after all the pain he had caused her, Marianne couldn't do that to her father. "I..." she swallowed. The cloud fell down. Heavy and dark, it smothered her hope. She wanted to cry. Wanted to feel the cool cleansing rush of water down her cheeks. But the well was dry. There were no tears left in her. Not for her father and not for her.

She rose. "Well, I suppose I had better return home and pack up my things. I doubt the creditors will waste much time in kicking me out."

"What will you do?" His brow wrinkled as he peered at her over the rims of his thick glasses. "Your father's creditors have already contacted me. You likely have only a single night left in your home."

Marianne barely managed a shrug. She didn't like thinking about it. The ever-present shadow of despair hovered again, held at bay by the thinnest thread. She had twenty-four hours at most to find a job and a place to live. If she didn't, she'd be out in the street.

CHAPTER TWO

Marianne's stomach rumbled. But it wasn't just any rumble. It was the kind that starts deep in your abdomen and vibrates outward and up your spine. The kind not meant to merely nudge a person's awareness but to slap them awake and demand attention.

She'd never been this hungry before.

Two and a half months since her father's creditors had forced her from her home and she still had nowhere to go. No job. No prospects. No future. All she wanted was food, and even that was denied to her.

When was the last time she'd eaten? Yesterday? The day before?

What was she going to do?

The window rattled and then snapped open. The lingering winter chill blasted through her hair and thin cotton shirtwaist. Climbing up on the rough straw mattress, she closed the window. The mattress was the only furniture in her small rented room.

The four wooden walls, black with soot and years of dirt, were all that kept her from the cold, but at least there weren't any fleas.

She rubbed her arms and glanced at the empty coal furnace. She hadn't had a piece of coal to put in there since she moved here.

A sob caught in the back of her throat, and she placed the back of her hand on her mouth to fight it back.

Snake purred, piercing through her sorrow, telling her she wasn't alone. Her gut twisted into knots and the tears fought harder to fall.

How was she going to sell him?

Did she have a choice? She needed food.

The workhouse was out of the question. She shuddered to think what they would do to her, a debtor's daughter. The tales of shaved heads, beatings, and sackcloth clothing had kept her awake into the night as she struggled to find employment.

But if not the workhouse, what? She closed her eyes and curled her fingers around Snake.

Through the tough months, the disappointments, and the fear, Snake had been there, somehow getting her through the worst of it.

She gently pressed the underside of Snake's head; it uncurled from her neck to wrap around her hand. A tear trickled down her cheek, leaking through the bedrock of her heart. "I'm so very sorry."

Snake glided its way up the salty path left behind by her tear to purr against her moistened skin, sending its message of love. The only message it could give.

The single tear was followed by another and then another. Her chin dropped to her chest as a tidal wave of sorrow crashed over her, crumbling the walls she'd erected to contain her burden of fear and loss. Gasping sobs thundered through her body, ripping her apart and leaving her shattered. Smaller.

With shaking hands, Marianne wiped her tear-stained face and rose. Shoulders slumped, clutching Snake to her chest as if by pressing it to her heart she could embed its memory forever.

The stairs, so narrow her tiny feet couldn't fit fully on them, were as old and weathered as the walls of her room. She ran her hand along the railing to keep her balance as she made her way down to the street below. Each step sent her heart plummeting further.

Mr. Ogleman looked up from a window display as she entered the pawnshop below her rented room. He shot her a leering grin that reminded Marianne of an oil slick spreading across the Thames. His gaze roamed her body and disgust slithered its way up her spine in tempo to the movement of his eyes. "Good morning my dear, have you thought more on my proposal?"

Snake heated in Marianne's hand. She swallowed. "I must decline, Mr. Ogleman."

His smile slipped. "Then I'm afraid I will need your rent today or you will have to leave."

Marianne hesitated, looking down at Snake. It looked up at her, its head cocked to one side as if to ask her how she could sell it. A lump caught in her throat but she placed it on the counter. "I have come to sell something."

"Is that so?" Ogleman sneered at the tarnished lump of metal. "I couldn't sell such a trinket. It's worthless."

"It's a mechanical." She touched Snake's head and it stretched to its full length and then curled into the shape of a necklace. "It can be polished up."

"That is something. Hmmmm… " Mr. Ogleman rubbed the stubble on his triple chin. "I'll give you half a crown for it."

"Half a crown?" Marianne couldn't keep the incredulity out of her voice. The tiny mechanical was worth twenty times that. "I won't sell for less than a sovereign."

"Nothing is worth that much." He snorted.

"It is to me."

"Half a crown, my dear, and a week's stay in the room upstairs." He countered, a grin spreading across his face. "Come now, this little ticket isn't worth you starving over."

Her stomach warred with the tightness in her chest. Her only friend sold for half a crown, but she had to eat. "Half a crown and two week's stay."

He held out his hand and shook hers. His sweaty palm left a smear on her hand.

Holding Snake up, he popped a looking glass in his eye. It bulged like a sore on his round head. "How does it work?"

With trembling fingers she showed him how touching certain links on its body made it do different tricks.

She refused to show him how to imprint the machine to its wearer. Snake would always be hers, even when another owned it.

Satisfied that he knew everything, Ogleman walked over to the register and pulled out the required sum. "Don't spend it all in one place."

She tucked the money into the purse hidden beneath her skirt. The single coin felt heavy in her pocket—a heaviness in strong contrast to the bareness of her throat. Covered to the neck in her cotton shirtwaist, she felt naked without Snake.

At the door, she turned back to watch Mr. Ogleman put Snake in one of his display cases. "Good bye," she whispered.

Snake raised its head and stared at her.

She swallowed and hurried out the door. She didn't want to think about Snake, or about what she would do when this small sum disappeared. It was a reality too difficult to face. She had to focus on the now. Food first.

Winter still clung on with its chilly fingers, despite the arrival of spring. Hugging her arms around her for warmth, she made her way down the alley toward Commercial Street.

She was here in Spitalfields, a place she'd never have dreamed of visiting before her father's suicide, but it was better than Whitechapel. Even thinking the name of that place in her mind sent chills down her spine. Jack the Ripper had visited horror on that neighborhood only weeks before, and nothing short of a forced march at gunpoint would get her to step foot there.

Footsteps echoed behind her. She paused.

The footsteps paused.

Her heart raced.

She glanced around. The thick, morning fog rolled off the Thames and down the narrow streets. She was trapped in a maze. The pounding in her chest reached a crescendo. Which way to run?

Her breath came in short gasps.

Two rough looking men approached out of the mist.

"Hello, lovey?" A large man in a bowler hat and muddy brown coat stepped forward. "How 'bout a bit o' fun?"

"Show us a good time. We'll treat ya nice." A second man appeared out of the fog.

The second man reached for her and grabbed the sleeve of her shirt.

Blood rushed from her head as she wrenched free, her hat flying off her head. Her hair tumbled down her back. "Leave me alone!"

"Blimey! Will you look at that hair?" The first man said, his voice laced with wonder.

"Wouldn't mind a fistful of that," The second added.

"Come now, miss, show us what a lady does."

Marianne didn't think. She ran.

"Circle around," the larger man shouted.

Was she going the right way, toward the busier streets, more witnesses, and safety? Her legs were like soft rubber, hardly holding her upright as she raced away.

The crash of boot heels on cobblestone continued behind her and she screamed in terror.

"What's wrong with that man, Mama? Is he a monster?"

Tavish tried to ignore the child's words. She was innocent. Didn't understand.

"Ssh," the mother admonished. "Just ignore it."

It? Tavish fisted his hands and kept his eyes on the streets. The child was an innocent; the mother… He closed his eyes. She was right. It was better to ignore him. Better not to see.

He was too exposed. He needed to get this blasted errand done but there were too many people about, too much risk.

He darted into an alley.

People always stared. How could they not? It wasn't every day that a person got to look at a cyborg. He gritted his teeth and longed to return to Sheba. Life aboard the aethership was exciting, and isolated. Just the way he liked it.

The sooner he posted the job for a new cook, the sooner he could get back. With luck, he'd do it without having to converse with any actual people. At least the agency the captain preferred had a mechanical clerk. Mechanicals he could deal with. He wasn't that far from one himself.

A woman's scream ripped through the air.

His pulse quickened, but he continued forward. "Don't get involved," he growled. "It's not your concern."

A second scream erupted, echoing along the narrow streets. He grimaced as he heard his mother's voice in his head.

"A gentleman looks after those weaker than himself."

He could see her now as if she were standing in front of him.

"Help her."

"Hell," he grumbled, stopping to gather his bearings.

He reached up and adjusted the dial on his artificial ear, drowning out background noise.

There.

He dashed toward the sound and rounded a corner.

Two large men, one with a wicked scar and the other squint-eyed, pressed a petite woman against a soot-covered alley wall.

Her eyes were wide above her trembling chin as she clutched the two halves of her shirt together.

Tavish roared, ripping scar face off his feet. Gears in his shoulder whirred to life and he slammed his left hand into the man's temple.

A sickening crunch and the assailant crumpled to the ground.

Squint-eyes spun around. Snarling, he dropped into a fighting crouch.

A grin spread across Tavish's face.

He circled his opponent, waiting for an opening.

Squint-eyes struck first, reacting faster than Tavish expected.

His hat and wig flew off his head. The chilly morning air blowing across his baldhead left him charged, and Tavish bowled forward, knocking the other man down.

Tavish wrestled Squint-eyes to the ground.

Pulling free of Tavish's hold, he punched him in the gut.

The air rushed out of Tavish's lungs, but he managed to dodge the follow-up punch and landed a fist to the man's jaw. Bone shattered and teeth flew out of the gaping wound. With a haphazard gesture, Tavish threw the now unconscious man on top of the other.

Then he circled, taking in his surroundings. There would be a third man, someone on watch.

"Behind you," the woman cried out.

He dodged to the side but a fist crashed into the metal covering his left temple.

Tavish barely felt a thing.

The assailant howled in pain and clutched his hand. His fingers jutted out in unnatural angles.

The man hobbled away, backward, his gaze darting between Tavish and the woman.

Tavish waited until he'd fled before turning back to the lady he'd rescued.

There was no doubt she was a lady.

Her diction was delicate and refined. Not the sort of voice he'd expect from this neighborhood. He forced himself to look at her——to really see her. Her eyes, a pale green that reminded him of spring, were a match for the unruly mass of strawberry blonde curls tumbling down her back.

On most women her tiny beak-like nose would give the impression of a stiff-necked spinster, but on her it merely gave her face character and kept the lovely heart shape from being too perfect.

And she was skinny. Too skinny. When was the last time she'd eaten?

She didn't belong here. She stood out from the impoverished immigrants who lived here like a brilliant light in the dense fog. Questions flooded his brain and refused to leave. What was a girl like her doing in a slum like this?

Even in her worn, tired-looking clothing, clothing she still clutched together with one hand, her posture screamed lady.

Damnation!

He ripped off his greatcoat and dropped it around her shoulders. The ends of his coat pooled at her feet but she was covered.

A blush blossomed across her lovely cheeks. "Thank you."

Her simple words sent a knot to his throat. "You're welcome."

They stared at each other for several moments. He was unable to look away. She looked like a delicate flower growing out of the cold, hard ground——a fresh splash of color in a drab world.

She bent down and retrieved his hat and wig. "Are you hurt?"

He blinked at the coarse black wig and tricorne hat. His face heated and he rubbed the top of his baldhead. He must look frightening to her. He quickly turned so his right side was facing her and slammed the hat and wig down on his head.

Very few people ever saw him uncovered. Now that the adrenaline from the fighting had eased, awareness crept back in. The woman was too beautiful, too delicate for him. What was he thinking standing here staring at her? She shouldn't have to look at something as ugly as he was.

"Well, I can see that you're well." The woman looked away, her eyes darting down to look at her feet. "I'll just continue on my way then."

Whether he was thinking clearly or not, there was no way he could leave her here alone.

A gentleman didn't do that sort of thing and, as much as he hated society, his mother had worked too hard to instill duty and honor into his brain for him to just walk away. Sheba, his haven of solitude, dimmed into the distance. He was stuck with her at least for now.

She turned to leave.

His hand reached out to stop her. "Why are you here?"

The question was rude and in his gruff uneven voice it must have sounded even worse, but he was incapable of much speech. Just looking at her made his head fuzzy. Maybe the punch to his temple had damaged something. Screwed up the wiring?

She looked over her shoulder at him. "I live here."

"Can I get you something to eat?" he asked.

She stiffened "I'm fine."

He softened his expression, tried to look less frightening. "It's obvious that you're hungry."

A soft rumbling noise erupted from her. She blushed and clutched her stomach.

"Come along. We'll get you something to eat."

"I can—"

"Please, let me help you. I can't just leave you in the fog with unconscious ruffians."

She bit her lip and glanced down at the prostrate men. "All right."

He led her out of the mist. His goal of reaching the ship before most of London was awake floated in the back of his mind but he pushed it away. Maybe it was the way she looked at him without judgment, or the fact that she so clearly needed help but was determined to have her own way. Whatever the case, he was going to see her to a good meal and then he'd part ways. That wasn't too much involvement. He could survive that long in her company.

Who was this man and why was she following him around blindly? He probably meant to lead her deeper into the alley, and then? Marianne snorted. She was being ridiculous. If he wanted to hurt her he would have done it already. Yes, she was following a strange man but she really didn't want to be alone.

Safety.

It was something she hadn't felt in a long time. She wanted to cling to it for as long as she could, and she really couldn't turn down a free meal. It would help her stretch the measly amount of money she'd gotten for Snake.

Her heart constricted and she closed her eyes. She couldn't think of that now. Stay focused.

"I didn't catch your name," she said. Conversation would help and she really had to stop thinking of him as *the man*.

"I didn't offer it." He laughed

It nearly sent her to her knees. The deep-throated chuckle reverberated through her whole body.

"My name is Tavish."

Struggling to regain her equilibrium, Marianne stopped and shook his hand. "I'm Marianne Lindstrom. Pleasure to meet you."

He stopped and glanced down at her hand, his face puzzled.

She dropped his hand and resumed walking. She'd taken four steps before she realized he hadn't followed. Turning, she cocked her head. "Aren't we going to get breakfast?"

He coughed. "Of course... I just—" With a brisk shake of his head, he followed her.

What an odd exchange. As they walked, Marianne risked a glance up at him.

She had to tip her head up to see his face. He was taller than she was by at least two heads.

He walked with his right side to her, but she could still remember the sight of him in the alley, face red with exertion.

The left side of his face was almost gruesome in appearance, with an ugly scar that ran from his chin past his left temple, broken only by a glowing, opalescent bionic eye. The eye, encased in a bronze setting, dug into the skin around his eye-socket extending up and over his left temple.

Where his left ear should be was a small spherical, knoblike protrusion. Marianne guessed it was an artificial ear but she had no way of knowing.

His tricorne hat, charmingly out of date, fit him. As did the black wig that sat below it. If she hadn't seen it fly off his head during the fight, she never would have guessed it wasn't his natural hair.

She'd been so relieved to have someone help her that at first she hadn't noticed his appearance. He'd looked fearsome, but then he'd dropped his coat around her shoulders to hide her torn clothing. The warmth reminded her he wasn't a monster, no matter how terrible he looked. She wrapped it more tightly around her shoulders, warm for the first time in months, and sent a smile of thanks his way.

He stared straight ahead.

She took a deep breath and suppressed a sigh. His scent, a mixture of leather and engine oil, surprised her. It was a workingman's scent. Yet, he acted and spoke like a gentleman. Who was he?

Tavish turned toward a tavern.

She caught his hand. "We don't want to eat here."

"They have food, do they not?"

"Yes, but unless you want to be hugging a chamber pot all day you don't want to eat it." Two months ago, those words out of her mouth would have shocked her. Now they were just part of her life. "There's better food just a bit farther on."

"How long have you lived here?"

"A few months."

He set a hand on her shoulder. It was his left; she could feel the metal exoskeleton and the reserved strength. Just as quickly as he'd placed it, he pulled it back. His cheeks turned a violet red and he coughed. "Ah..."

"Where did I live before that?"

He nodded.

"Park Lane."

"What are you doing here, then?"

"My father was Lord Lindstrom." Marianne crossed her arms and stared up at the giant. Why did he have to rub it in? Surely he realized how painful the subject would be.

Here it comes. Marianne braced herself for the set down and the scorn. It was all she'd gotten from everyone who'd heard her name. It was why she was stuck here, instead of working as a governess. Her father hadn't settled for ruining his own fortunes. He'd sold his "advice" and ruined the fortunes of others.

"Lord Lindstrom was Chancellor of the Exchequer a few years ago, wasn't he?" Tavish asked.

Marianne blinked. Really, that was what he remembered? "Yes, but..."

"Then why are you in Spitalfields? You ought to be in a drawing room somewhere."

He was going to make her say it. Of all the people in the world who'd shown her scorn this was the worst. At least they'd never made her say it out loud, didn't make her relive it. "He's killed himself. I'm destitute."

She turned away. She wouldn't cry. Her father didn't deserve her tears.

Once again his hand stopped her. "I'm sorry. I didn't know."

She whirled on him. "How could you not know? Everyone knows. Even the street sweepers know!"

Tavish glanced around them and pulled her into a side alley, away from the view of people.

Marianne's cheeks heated as she realized the scene she'd just caused. Why had she let him goad her like that? Had she learned nothing from her father? Quiet was always better. When you were quiet, no one could yell at you.

"I work on an aethership. I haven't been in London in months. We just docked."

"Of course, that explains the hat." She'd thought the tricorne hat was odd but it was standard uniform for aethershipmen, an affectation they'd developed to distance themselves from their wet navy counterparts. Or so she'd heard.

"I still owe you that meal."

"You don't owe me anything. You rescued me and I'm grateful, but why are you still helping?"

He shrugged. "I can't leave a lady stranded. My mother would never forgive me."

Marianne waved across the street to the line of women bustling by on their way to work. "Did you help any of them?"

He lifted up her chin. "They don't need help. They're a part of this world, and know how to survive in it. You don't."

She tore her chin away. "I've survived this long, haven't I?"

Tavish shrugged. "Wouldn't you like to get away from here? Somewhere safe?"

Marianne narrowed her eyes. "What are you offering?"

"Can you cook?"

Marianne started. Either his wits were addled or hers were, and at the moment she didn't know which. "Do I look like someone who knows how to cook?"

"You look like someone in trouble."

She sighed. "I don't know a thing about cooking. Nothing in my upbringing prepared me for this life."

"Of course it didn't." He tipped his head. "You were meant to get married and have children, but you're wrong about cooking. You can run a household, plan menus that sort of thing, can't you?"

"Yes..."

"This is similar. We have an autochef. All you have to do is plug in the recipe and it will make the food. You'll do fine."

A cook? Her stomach rumbled. "All right, I'll do it."

"Do you need to get anything from where you're staying?"

Snake.

Was gone. Thinking about it now wasn't going to help her.

"No, I'm wearing everything I own." She had a new profession to learn. Cooking wasn't glamorous, but at least it was a job. The poor couldn't afford to be choosy.

CHAPTER THREE

The ticking of the grandfather clock leaning against the wall roared in Draven's ears. Time slipped away with each tick. Time Nora no longer had. Sweat dripped down his forehead and he wiped it away with his handkerchief. Damn it! He needed his grandmother's will read now!

He glanced at the clock. He'd been sitting in this stifling office for half an hour. What was taking the solicitor so long? This shouldn't be difficult. All the man had to do was tell him he'd inherited everything and be done with it. All he needed was the book. That stupid book wasn't even for him, but Nora's life depended on it.

Beep Beep.

A whirring broombot, cleaning the carpet, bumped into his foot. The small round bot was barely bigger than a man's head but could clean a carpet the size of a ballroom. The bot rolled around the office on its four wheels. Its arms swooshed away as if nothing in the world mattered. Apocalypse could fall and the little bot wouldn't care as long as it had a carpet to clean. What would it be like to live that life, never worried about anything, as happy as a broombot with a dirty carpet?

He shook his head. That wasn't his life. His was much darker. Nora had counted on him and he'd already failed her. He wouldn't fail her again.

"Lord Draven, I am terribly sorry for the wait." A clerk bowed before him.

"You had better be." Draven rose and straightened his jacket. "I can't imagine what has taken so long."

"I don't know, my lord."

"Hrmph." Draven brushed passed the clerk. It was clear the fool knew nothing and would likely never rise higher than his current position. It was the solicitors he needed to deal with. And they would answer for wasting his time.

He entered the office without knocking. Two solicitors were hunched over a desk.

The taller one looked up and with a smile, held out his hand. "My lord, I apologize for the wait. There was a small matter with the will that needed to be cleared but all is in order now, and we are prepared to read it at your pleasure."

Draven looked down at the solicitor's outstretched hand and turned up his nose. "I do not appreciate being kept waiting."

The tall man bowed. "Of course not, my lord. If you will have a seat, we will proceed."

Draven took a seat, reclining back in elegant ease. He reminded himself to keep his agitation to himself. He had to remain calm and collected and mustn't let anything show. Tugging on the lace cuffs of his sleeves and straightening his signet ring, he kept up the charade. "Let's get this over with. I have things to do."

The man behind the desk nodded as his partner shut the door. "As you know, you are the only living relation of the late Mrs. Attewater, and as expected, you are the main beneficiary of her will."

"You mean the sole beneficiary?" Draven raised a quizzing glass, and peered at the stout little man.

The partners exchanged a look Draven couldn't read. "Well, there are the usual bequests to trusted staff—"

"What nonsense," Draven grumbled. Why did they bother him with such trivialities? A tick started in his left cheek. He clamped down hard on his emotions. He couldn't afford to lose it now.

"—and a small bequest to a Miss Marianne Lindstrom." The solicitor continued over Draven's interruption.

"Did you say Marianne Lindstrom?"

"Yes, my lord."

Draven was familiar with the late Lord Lindstrom and had been introduced to his daughter. He wracked his brain, trying to pull up a mental picture of the chit. Petite and mousy were the words he would use to describe her. It had been several years ago but he was certain his grandmother hadn't known her. So, what had the old bat been playing at?

Unless.

The tick intensified and he was forced to squeeze the arm of his chair to keep from pacing.

No, she wouldn't have done it. Couldn't have. Not after he'd said he wanted it.

Draven's stomach rolled even as his pulse quickened and heated. He had to force himself to speak. "What did she leave the lady?"

"Apparently, it was a book. A..." The solicitor looked down at his papers. "A Brief History in the Time of Ancients."

His heart stopped beating and his mind froze. All he could do was stare at the solicitors, first one, then the other. His composure was gone, his social mask slipping.

"My lord, are you well?" the taller man asked.

Draven shook his head. "Excuse me, I was trying to remember where I'd heard that book title before. It's not at all common, but it is familiar."

"Of course." The solicitor's tone was polite but the two men shared a quick look. A look he had no trouble identifying. It was clear they thought him a lunatic.

Not that he could blame them. He'd questioned his sanity many times. Usually when Nora was involved.

Nora.

How would he save her now?

He cleared his throat. "Was this the cause of the delay?"

The taller man smiled. "Yes, we couldn't find the book amongst the items left at our offices." The solicitor chuckled. "Turns out the book is in a foreign language of some kind. We had it all along. Simply needed the former housekeeper to point it out to us. It's all rather embarrassing."

"Has the book been delivered to Miss Lindstrom?" A plan began to formulate in Draven's mind.

"It has not. We wanted to read the will first. We will deliver the item to Miss Lindstrom after our meeting has concluded."

Draven leaned back in his chair. "I can deliver it to Miss Lindstrom. I am acquainted with her. She's a second cousin I believe," he lied.

"That won't be necessary. Thank you for the offer, but Jacobs and Hodson will handle the delivery. It is as Mrs. Attewater wished." The stout man grinned. "Now on to the important bits, eh? Mrs. Attewater has left you a large sum in the Funds, her airship…"

The solicitor droned on and Draven ignored him. Damn, he needed that book. What did he care about the rest? That book was the only reason he'd been nice to the old bag. To think of the hours he'd wasted reading to her and calling on her.

God, how was he going to tell Nora?

He wanted to rip out his hair in frustration, to beat the solicitor until he admitted he'd lied. Anything but think about what this news was costing him—costing her.

Why had his grandmother given the book away?

How the hell did she even know Miss Lindstrom?

"Excuse me, my lord. Did you say something?" The solicitor asked.

Draven's head jerked up. Had he spoken aloud? He waved his hand. "No, I was just clearing my throat. Do continue." He took a calming breath and plastered a smile on his face. This was only a minor setback. If the rumors were true, Lord Lindstrom had left his daughter destitute. The woman wouldn't know what she had. She wouldn't understand its importance. She would be glad to part with it for any amount of money and he was prepared to be generous.

Nora's soul was in the balance. With the book he'd be able to set her free. He couldn't fail her now. One way or another Marianne Lindstrom was going to give him what he wanted.

Crack! The door slammed against the wall and Draven snarled. He'd spent the rest of the morning and most of the afternoon searching for the Lindstrom girl, but she'd disappeared. No one knew where she'd gone after the creditors had kicked her out. Surely there weren't many places a gently bred girl could go. How the hell had she just disappeared? He reached for the door, slamming it again.

A gilded mirror crashed to the floor, shattering. Shards of glass flew across the polished marble. If he hadn't already been having such rotten luck he might have cared. As it was, all he saw was one less piece of useless frippery in his house.

All that time wasted.

He kicked the now empty frame, sending it twirling across the floor.

It spiraled outward, not stopping until it bumped into the shiny black shoe of his butler.

"Is everything all right, my lord?" Stiltson stood at attention, ignoring the frame resting next to his foot.

Draven bit down on his anger. While he had few qualms about upsetting servants in general, the anger would be wasted on Stiltson. The butler had been with him for years and had survived all that he could throw at him. "Everything's fine."

"You slammed the door, sir."

Draven plastered a smile on his face. "It must have been a gust of wind."

"Of course." Stiltson waved a maid over and she began to clean up the broken glass.

"I'll be in my study. I'm not to be disturbed."

Stiltson bowed, his lips compressed in a thin line.

Forcing a contrite smile on his face, Draven nodded to Stiltson and the hovering maid. "I apologize for the outburst. It's been a trying day."

The butler bowed. "I'll see to it."

With another nod, Draven stormed down the hallway and into his study, careful to shut his door gently. Loyal servants were hard to find, and he didn't want to irritate Stiltson further by throwing any more tantrums. He took a deep breath.

He had more to think about than servants.

He must be calm for her.

Nora didn't need the added burden of seeing him upset.

When his blood pressure had cooled he locked the study door and headed toward the wall behind his desk. Inside a glass case rested three first-edition copies of the King James Bible. Two of those copies were still intact but the one on the right was merely a beautifully preserved facade.

He opened the cover to reveal a number pad. With careful deliberation, he entered the proper code. The sequence was long, fifteen numbers to be exact. A grin spread across his face as he thought of the disaster waiting anyone who typed that code in incorrectly.

Draven couldn't afford to have anyone stumble on his laboratory. Anyone who failed to type the number in correctly would fall thirty feet into a pit of spikes when the floor opened up beneath them.

A soft click, like the priming of a gun, was the only indication that his code had been accepted before the glass case moved aside, revealing a spiral staircase leading down into a dark passageway.

He glanced back at the locked study door one last time before stepping into the dark. The glass case slid over the top and sealed him in. He knew the way to his lab by heart. A light source was unnecessary and the dark was further protection against unwanted intrusion. Nora had to be kept safe.

A large heavy door stood sentinel at the bottom of the stairs. It had no handle, only a wicked-looking metal spike the size of a lady's hatpin that glowed with irradiated light. Without hesitating, he reached up and pricked his finger on the point. Blood seeped down the spike until it reached the door.

The screeching of stone against stone sounded through the small chamber as the large door opened to reveal a lab illuminated by flickering electric lights that swung from cords in the ceiling.

Yellow light danced from corners and crevices and bounced off tables full of his tools and half-built machines. He ignored it all and headed straight for a table draped with a Holland cover in the back of the room. With loving care, he pulled back the cloth to reveal the head of a mechanical.

Unlike most mechanicals, this one was truly beautiful. The head was covered in ivory. Long, blonde human hair draped gracefully over a satin pillow. The mouth was lined with tiny rubies and the optic sensors trimmed in sapphires. He'd built her to look like Nora and someday she'd be more than a mere lookalike. With the help of his grandmother's book, he'd bring Nora back. With this new body, she would live forever.

"Soon, my love." He petted her hair, stroking back the blond curls. "I had a minor setback today, but nothing will keep us apart."

He reached for a spanner and screwdriver. He may not have the book but he could see to it that his wife had a perfect body to return to.

The lights over his head began to flicker and a chill wind crept through his bones.

"No, not again," he whispered.

The lights sputtered and died one by one as smoke billowed from their sockets.

Draven dropped the tools as his heart began to race.

The temperature in the room plummeted. Ice crystals grew on workbenches and tables and his breath came in misty gasps.

His eyes darted about, watching the smoke pour into his laboratory. He was imagining this. "It's not real."

A sinister chuckle echoed through the darkening room. "I'm real enough. Where is my book?"

Draven swallowed. "There's been a complication."

"Complication?" The smoke seeped around him.

A cold caress sent ice storming up his spine.

"I do not like complications."

A heavy weight settled on Draven's stomach making it difficult to breath. He stared into the yellowish green glow emanating from the smoke. "It couldn't be helped."

A dark, roughly humanoid figure coalesced from the smoke and stood on the other side of Nora's table. "Everything can be helped."

"Not this." He willed his mind to focus. It was just a shadow; it couldn't hurt him.

"I'm not going to hurt you." Shadow stroked Nora's hair.

Draven's legs began to tremble and he clutched the table edge. *God not this, anything but this.*

"You cannot fight me." Shadow touched Nora's head and her eye sockets glowed a sickly purple.

"Nicholas?" Nora's voice called out in pain. "Please make it stop."

Agony pierced him with each gasp of pain that escaped Nora's lips. He ran around the table and inserted himself between Shadow and Nora. "Please don't make me relive this."

Shadow laughed and shifted to the other side of the table. Red eyes glowing brightly, it touched Nora's abdomen.

She screamed.

Tears racing down his face, he gripped the table edge. "No, no, no."

"Nicholas, it hurts so much... the baby... Oh, Nicholas."

Nora's eyes blazed up at him. He was no longer looking at the mechanical's face. His dead wife was lying on the table, her body writhing in agony. Her grotesque, distended belly arched into the air. The walls of his laboratory changed to his wife's room at his estate. Every detail exactly as he remembered, down to the gold embroidery on his wife's coverlet soaked in blood.

He clutched her hand and bent to kiss her forehead. "Nora... I..."

Tears clouded his vision but he could still see her. Still hear her. He was forced to watch his beloved die again. She'd died because of him and she suffered now because of his failure.

"We had a bargain," Shadow whispered.

"I haven't failed, please."

"Her soul is mine." Shadow reached forward and pressed his hands into Nora's body and ripped out her heart.

An inhuman scream erupted from her.

Draven fell to the ground, covering his ears and shutting his eyes. "Stop. Stop."

Shadow's breathless voice smothered him. "Do not fail me again or her torment will last for eternity."

The light returned and Draven opened his eyes. Shadow was gone but in its place sat a still beating heart.

He waved his hand through it and the heart disappeared in a puff of smoke. If only he could banish the image from his mind so easily. But it would remain—a reminder of the price of failure.

CHAPTER FOUR

"Wait here." Tavish led Marianne to a bench and waited for her to sit down. "The shuttle won't depart for another hour. I'll be right back."

He was probably being presumptive but she couldn't go aboard in a torn shirt.

Marianne's eyes darted around the busy shuttle dock. Her hands twisted in her lap. "Are you sure I'll be safe?"

Tavish noted the harried passengers running between the shuttles but Marianne sat in a bubble of tranquility.

"No one will bother you and I'll just be through there." He waved at a nearby shop. "I won't be long."

Her eyes looked doubtful but she nodded.

It amazed him she'd managed to survive alone so long. An image of her standing in the alleyway holding her torn shirt together sprang unbidden into his mind. His gut twisted and he growled.

Marianne's head snapped up, her eyes grew into round orbs, and her mouth fell open.

He coughed. "Ah... Just wait here." He hurried off. He had to get her to the ship fast. The sooner she was handed over to someone else's care, the happier she would be. She deserved better than the constant reminder he presented. The constant fear she must be feeling every time she looked at him.

He winced at the sting in his own thoughts. He should be used to the fear now. He'd lived with his deformity long enough to have grown numb to it. Or so he'd thought. He gritted his teeth and headed toward the nearby shop.

Sitting high above the city, the three grand towers of the London Air-docks serviced the near constant travel of people and goods between London and the large aether platforms that housed the space-going aetherships. As with any such place, businesses had popped up. A person could find anything they needed at one of the shops lining the towers.

Shops like the general store he'd just entered.

"Can I help you?" A gray-haired woman in a neat waistcoat and trousers looked up from the book she was reading. A grin spread across her face. "Tavish! What brings you back here?"

He coughed and held out the piece of paper with his list of items on it. "I need a few things."

"Interesting selection," she murmured, after a quick glance at his list

"No questions, just get me what I need," Tavish snarled. "I have to catch the next shuttle back to Sheba."

"Crisp white shirtwaists and trousers," she began.

Tavish ground his teeth.

"Corsets and knickers." Her eyes danced. "Got a lady love?"

Tavish shot a glance out at Marianne. She still sat were he'd left her. The sight soothed him. "Get on with it, woman."

The shopkeeper chuckled. "You've got it bad, son."

Tavish crossed his arms in front of his chest and glared. Why couldn't the woman keep her thoughts to herself? He was having enough difficulty with his own.

"I ran into a girl in trouble. She doesn't have anything and—"

"And you're playing hero. Always out to rescue other people." She spoke over him.

Somehow her simple words settled him. He was just helping the girl out. Hadn't his mother taught him to care for others? He was doing his duty as a gentleman. Now if only he could tell the inner bear in him to back off. Marianne didn't need his protection, just his help.

"I'll get these for you." The shopkeeper entered a curtained doorway.

"Wait," Tavish said. "I just need one of the shirtwaists now. Send the rest on to Sheba."

She nodded and ducked behind the curtain.

Tavish let his eyes wander around the shop, taking in the changes that had been made since his last visit. From snuffboxes to bars of soap, people could find just about anything in her shop.

Soap.

He looked at the selection. They came in several different scents with options for both genders. Without letting his mind dwell on it he reached out and grabbed a lemon-scented bar.

The shopkeeper returned. She snorted when she saw the soap, but blessedly, only named a price.

Tavish reached into his pocket and pulled out the required sum. "Wrap the soap, too, if you would."

"How long are you going to be gone this time?" She wrapped his items up one at a time in brown paper.

Tavish fisted his hands and bit back a growl. "Not sure. Just a few weeks hopefully. We're headed out to New Richmond."

"New Richmond's a nice island. Have any leave?"

How long did it take to wrap up two items? After the shopkeeper's all-too-accurate insights, did he dare risk a glance outside again? He turned his head. Marianne was sitting chatting to a young man. Was he bothering her? His nostrils flared and it was all he could do to remain standing where he was.

"If you're headed out there, you stop by my friend, Lola's. She serves the best kidney pie you'll ever eat."

Tavish glanced out the door. Kidney pie, really? "I'll make sure to do that."

"Good." She handed him his package. "Well, take care now."

Package in hand, he hurried out. The central square was busier then when he'd left. Others had joined the single man he'd seen earlier. A crowd of men now surrounded her.

His body tensed, and his blood pulsed in his neck. Something feral grew in his gut, erupting from his mouth in a roar. Conscious thought fled. He rushed forward, ripping the first man he reached off his feet.

The man yelped in surprise. "What the...?"

"Mr. Tavish, it's all right." Marianne put her hand on his left arm.

The pressure of her touch barely registered on his mechanical arm.

"They weren't bothering me," Marianne continued.

"We were just talking." The man dangled from Tavish's fists, his hands tugging at his throat.

Tavish glanced around. An even larger crowd had gathered. What had gotten into him? How had he? Cold eyes stared back at him from the crowd. A mother grabbed her child to her breast and turned away. A father tucked his children behind him and stood facing Tavish, legs spread, hands fisted at his side.

A little boy tugged on his father's leg. "Papa, what's the monster gonna do now?"

Monster.

Tavish's heart constricted. God, what had he done? He dropped the man he held. He had to get away before he made another scene. Before he hurt someone. Plowing through the crowd, his mind raged at his actions. This had been a mistake. He couldn't be trusted around people. Why had the captain let him out?

"Mr. Tavish." A strong soprano voice rang out over the din of the crowd.

He closed his eyes and stopped moving, dropping his chin to his chest. The captain.

"That was quite the show you put on back there." Captain Henrietta Ridgewell sauntered up to stand next to him. She was a tall woman. The only woman he didn't have to crane his neck to see.

"It was nothing," Tavish muttered.

Ridgewell snorted. "Did you put the advertisement in for my new cook?"

"I..."

The crowd had moved to surround him again. The captain regarded the group under an arched brow. "Move about your business."

People started to head off in other directions. The few who had opted to stay were soon greeted with the captain's full attention. She didn't say a word but the temperature seemed to drop several degrees. Soon, the stragglers left. All, that is, but Marianne.

"I said there's nothing to see here." Ridgewell's tone could have frozen lava.

Tavish's chest tightened. How could Marianne bear to even look at him?

"I'm the new cook, ma'am," Marianne said, holding out her hand. "Miss Marianne Lindstrom."

Tavish stared and snapped his mouth shut. After what she'd seen him do she was still willing to come on board what was essentially a closed bronze can with him?

Lips pressed together in a tight line, Ridgewell glanced down at Marianne's offered hand but didn't take it. "I see."

Silence spread like a thick blanket over the small group. The crackling of the brown paper in Tavish's hands echoed between them. He glanced down at his feet and thrust the package out at Marianne. "I... ah... picked up a few things up for you. You won't have time to change before the shuttle leaves but well... ah... you can wear my coat until then."

"Thank you," Marianne's voice trembled. "I... "

He looked up. For a brief moment everything else faded away and they were the only people standing on the platform.

Marianne's eyes were rimmed with tears as she clutched the package to her breast.

The shopkeeper had been right. He was in trouble.

"I see," Ridgewell repeated. Her voice was like a Damascus steel blade cutting through their moment with brutal efficiency. "Freddy, please escort our new cook to the waiting shuttle. Mr. Tavish and I will be along shortly."

Like a ghost, the captain's steward appeared from behind her, arms laden with packages. The wizened little man reminded Tavish of a garden gnome, complete with baldhead and a pointy white beard. He'd lost an eye a few years back but the eye patch he wore only added to the appearance.

"Aye, ma'am." Freddy bowed to Marianne. "Miss, if you'll just follow me?"

Marianne glanced at Tavish, a question in her eyes.

"Go ahead, Miss Lindstrom. Freddy will see you get to the right shuttle." Tavish nodded at Freddy.

Ridgewell stood with hands on hips watching them leave. When they were out of sight she turned back to Tavish. "Care to explain what this is all about?"

"You wanted a new cook, and I found one." Tavish crossed his arms and fought the urge to squirm like an errant schoolboy.

"Why is the daughter of a disgraced viscount coming on board as our new cook?"

Tavish shrugged his shoulder, hoping to appear nonchalant. "She needed help."

"Can she cook?"

"No, but she knows how to run a staff and manage menus."

"It is customary for a paid cook to have some knowledge of the culinary arts." Ridgewell arched her brow.

"She'll learn what she needs to know. Freddy could teach her. He cooks your meals."

"You'll do it," Ridgewell ordered.

His hands slipped to his sides and he had to snap his mouth shut. "Freddy is more qualified and—"

"Freddy could teach her but she's your rescue project. You must make it work."

27

"But, ma'am—"

Ridgewell turned to walk away. "You're responsible for her, Mr. Tavish. If she fails, it's your fault."

Tavish followed behind her. He couldn't be responsible for her. How could a monster ever hope to help a lady?

Tavish dropped into the chair behind his desk. Ripping his hat and wig from his head, he threw them at the hat stand across the room. They hit the wall behind and crashed to the floor.

He spread his gaze over the desk. A pile of correspondence sat unread on the blotter. Work he'd neglected to do before heading off to find a cook. When he'd set out this morning he hadn't imagined the day would end as it had. He'd lost control in a crowd.

Endangered a man.

How had he let it happen? People made him nervous, crowds even more so, but never before had he been anything but aware of his surroundings, careful of what he said, did.

Not this time.

When he was around her, Marianne flooded his brain and befuddled his senses. Now he had to spend time teaching her a new profession. A profession he knew nothing about. He rubbed the top of his baldhead. She probably knew more about what to do than he. He enjoyed the food put in front of him, and if he were out in the field alone, he could prepare simple camp fare. What did Ridgewell expect him to do?

He wasn't even sure how to use the blasted autochef. He'd be learning right along with Marianne. It was preposterous.

He slumped in his chair. Preposterous it may well be, but the captain was right. He'd made the mess; he had better clean it up. He shouldn't have offered the job to a woman who wasn't qualified. He knew that.

But he'd had to act. He knew that too. It didn't matter that Marianne was unqualified. He couldn't have left her in the situation she was in.

He didn't like people, but his mother had instilled in him a sense of right and wrong. He might be a monster but he understood honor. He protected women.

Marianne didn't belong in that squalor and wouldn't have lasted another month. He rubbed his hand down his face. She didn't belong here either, but at least here she wouldn't starve—or worse. He shuddered again at the image of her pressed against that dirty wall with two men crowding toward her. Even thinking of it sent his pulse racing.

Once he'd set his feet on the path to her rescue, he had to see it all the way through.

Which meant he was going to have to learn to cook. He needed to find a manual for the auto-chef and somehow squeeze learning how to use it in with his other myriad duties.

CHAPTER FIVE

"Don't worry about getting lost, miss. I'll give you a map."

Marianne clutched the package to her chest and barely managed a nod in Freddy's direction. She was too overwhelmed and too nervous to worry about getting lost. The ship was huge. It looked like a copper-plated copy of any ocean-going ship she'd seen. Only it was at least three times larger with sails that dwarfed the largest smokestacks

"How many people does it take to crew a ship this size?" she asked.

"About 600." Freddy shot her a smile.

She shriveled. Freddy hadn't meant to frighten her. He was likely only being honest, but the sheer vastness of the task before her looked insurmountable.

"Here we are!" He pressed a button next to the hatch.

Stamping down her trepidation, she stepped into her future home and froze.

Her breath caught. The bronze room shone so bright it blinded. The walls in the halls she'd passed had been a dull matte hue that made the corridors seem almost eerie, but here they were polished to a shine. It was as if someone had deliberately set out to dazzle whomever walked through the door.

"Oh, my," she breathed.

"The previous cook liked things clean." he replied.

"I see that." Marianne resisted the urge to roll her eyes.

The wooden countertops on the long central island had been sanded and oiled to a gleaming finish that would have made any housekeeper proud. The cupboards lining the back wall were made from the same material as the rest of the ship, but like the walls, floor and ceiling, they shone with spectacular brilliance. Pots and pans hung from rungs above the island counter and the stove with its giant, black smokestack rose like a mountain.

Marianne walked into the room and turned around, trying to take it all in. There was another hatched door just next to the stove and a large open passthrough along one wall that looked out over a sea of benches and tables. Across from that window sat what she could only assume was the autochef. It covered the entire wall. It had several doors, multiple "heads" and more dials than Marianne had ever seen in a single place.

The idea that she could manage all this seemed laughable. How on earth was she to make that thing work?

Freddy laid a gnarled hand on her shoulder. "You won't have to worry about cooking a meal until breakfast. The crew was expected to eat while on shore leave."

Unable to tear her eyes from the massive mechanical, she couldn't even nod at him.

"Your room is just through here." Gently steering her toward the rear hatch she'd seen earlier, he hit a button and propelled her inside.

"Just take a rest. I'm sure everything will work out fine. Here's the map I promised." He hurried into the room and grabbed a folded piece of paper from a shelf on the wall. Then, pausing, he grabbed a thick bound book as well. "And this is the manual for the autochef. Just take some time and read it. You'll catch on quick enough."

"Mr. Tavish said the rest of your things would arrive in a few minutes. You'll feel better with your own about you." He placed the book and map on the bed and left.

She barely heard the hatch close behind him.

The enormity of what she faced closed in around her. She couldn't move. Couldn't breathe. Couldn't focus on anything.

She hugged her arms to herself, heard the crinkle of paper.

The package.

She glanced down at the brown paper package Tavish had given her. Walking to the edge of her bed, she sat, fingers idly twisting the string that tied the paper together. His scent, rich and masculine, still clung to his overcoat, reminding her of what he'd done.

For her.

For no other reason than that he could.

She took a deep breath and with trembling fingers attacked the string. The paper fell open and the scent of lemons rushed out—a hint of summer. A crisp white shirtwaist sat on the paper and nestled on top was a bar of soap.

She fingered the gift. A soft smile curved her lips. She grabbed the bar and holding it to her chest she let Tavish's kindness soothe her. She would make this new job work. Fate had sent her a guardian angel, and she would not disappoint him.

The trunk arrived fifteen minutes later along with a note, and Marianne didn't know what to think.

Tavish hadn't just bought her a new shirt. He'd bought her an entire new wardrobe.

She wrung her hands, crumpling the note.

She tried to understand the unease that settled on her the moment she'd seen that trunk. She was grateful to Tavish. She'd had to sell all her clothes save a single outfit. Living with only a single dress was hard for a lady like her, used to changing her clothes several times a day. Having clean sets of clothes was… She wracked her brain, trying to come up with a word that fit.… Wonderful.

Yet she couldn't shake the idea that every stitch she owned came from him.

Her cheeks heated.

While on the streets she'd managed to avoid becoming a kept woman. Now what was to become of her?

What did Tavish expect?

Was she to warm his bed now? Did she need to repay him with services? She shuddered and then closed her eyes.

She pressed her lips together. It didn't matter what he expected. Only what she was willing to give.

If the clothing was a gift, all the good, she'd pay him back by proving he'd been right in offering her the job. If he wanted more, she'd just have to set him straight.

With a new resolve she looked at the note.

If it would be convenient, please repair to Navigation at 1700 hours. –H. Ridgewell

It was phrased as a request but she had no intention of refusing.

The captain's aura of command was unmistakable. When she'd first met her, it had been all Marianne could do not to curtsy. Deeply.

Something in the way Ridgewell held herself reminded her of the queen, royal, proud and radiating authority.

Grabbing her new her coat, she snatched up the map, and headed out the door.

After only one wrong turn she made it to what she hoped was the bridge hatch.

"Would it hurt anyone to label things around here?" She stared at an odd-looking doorway. It was different than the other hatches she'd seen. This one was flush against the ceiling above her. If it hadn't been for the large hand crank on the wall beside her, she'd have walked right under it. Three lights blinked from a panel next to the hand crank.

She turned the crank.

It wouldn't budge.

Hands on hips, she stared up at the door. She couldn't turn back now. She'd never make it in time if she had to find another way to the bridge. She pressed the panel with the three blinking lights. It gave and the door clicked.

Her stomach did a giddy leap as the door slid into the ceiling above and a ladder clanged to floor in front of her.

"What the… " A man's foot slipped into the hole made by the retreating door.

Marianne's heart sank. What had she done now?

The foot disappeared but was shortly replaced by a man's head. "Which idiot opened the hatch?"

Marianne sank back against the bulkhead but the black-eyed man found her.

"Don't you know anything?"

"I… I…" Marianne stammered.

"That's enough, Mr. Galveson." The captain's cool soprano broke into the corridor but it didn't make Marianne feel any better. "Let the girl up."

Girl? Marianne shivered at the contempt she heard in the other woman's voice. She'd already failed, and she didn't even know why. She started climbing up the ladder but stumbled and nearly fell.

"Come on you, get up here." Galveson seized her by the shoulder and yanked her up the rest of the way.

She rubbed her shoulder and backed away from him, taking in the room. The bridge was full of a bustling array of mechanical devices. The noise was enough to send a sane woman to Bedlam.

With spine stick straight, the captain stood next to a chair in the center of the room—the calm in the center of a storm. If it weren't for the braid draped over her shoulder or the gentle curve of her hip, she'd look the perfect model of an aethership captain, one straight from a picture book. Her gaze was locked on a small screen next to her chair. "I'm glad you could join us, Miss Lindstrom. In the future, I would appreciate it if you used the main deck hatch to access the bridge."

The captain's voice was the same tone she always used, no inflection, no pitch change. Yet, the very fact that she hadn't raised her voice made Marianne want to crawl back to the galley.

"What is she even doing here?" Galveson asked.

"She's here at my invitation." The captain kept her gaze focused on her small screen "Now, Mr. Galveson, please take your place."

Galveson scowled at her but made his way to a chair along the opposite wall, directing his attention to the displays.

A door to her left opened and Tavish stepped out. He nodded in her direction before crossing to the captain.

"Mr. Tavish, so glad you could join us. Please take Miss Lindstrom to the quarterdeck. She should have a good vantage point for her first aether launch."

"Aye, ma'am." Tavish waved Marianne toward another hatch. "This way."

She turned. Her foot caught on a cord and sent her sprawling forward.

Strong hands caught her, steadied her.

Her pulse leapt. She looked up, gazing into the steel gray of Tavish's eye.

He stared at her lips, his own set in a firm line.

Moments stretched and time slowed.

Then, he set her back on her feet. His fingers peeled back from her shoulders, one at a time, as if he were forcing them to comply.

As the last finger lifted from her, she took a breath. The world rushed back in. Alarms blared and she whipped her head around.

Galveson's voice rang out from the din. "Someone figure out what's causing the problem and get that alarm off."

Marianne flattened herself against the wall, making herself as small as possible.

Slipping away from her chair, the captain walked back to where Marianne was standing. In a single graceful movement, she reached down and plugged a cord back into the wall.

The alarms went silent.

Ridgewell paused before her, arching one eyebrow. "You must be more careful while moving about, Miss Lindstrom."

Marianne swallowed and ducked her head before turning for the door.

Tavish held the hatch open for her and she stumbled through. What had she been thinking? All she'd do was cause more problems, more trouble for everyone. She was utterly useless.

"That cord shouldn't have been there in the first place. You were on a walkway," Tavish interjected.

Marianne tried to smile, but failed. "I'll be more careful."

Tavish led her up a set of stairs. "You'll figure yourself out. Give it time."

"I came through a hatch in the floor. Was I not supposed to do that?" Marianne asked.

"You what?" Tavish stopped moving and stared open-mouthed at her.

"It was the shortest way to the bridge on the map."

"It's an emergency hatch. Unless the lights are flashing red, no one is to use it."

Marianne's chin sank to her chest. "Oh."

"You'll learn." He placed his flesh and blood hand on the small of her back. The heat of it seared into her.

She pulled away and fingered her bare throat. "I need to know what you expect of me."

His face went slack. "I don't follow. You're to run the autochef."

"The clothes you bought for me." Her voice squeezed and she cleared her throat. "I need to know what you expect for them."

He scowled. "I expect you to be warm."

"Oh," she put a hand on his arm. "I'm sorry if I offended. It's just... Well, a lady doesn't get gifts like that from men unless..."

"I don't like the tenor of that question." Tavish's face turned to stone.

She stumbled back, her hand stilling on her throat. "I..."

"Your virtue is safe from me. Don't worry." He grimaced and took a deep breath. Anger dissipated from his face like smoke in a breeze. "Sorry, a man doesn't like to have his honor questioned."

Marianne shrank into herself and dropped her head. "Of course, I'm sorry I even thought it."

Tavish let out a heavy sigh and tipped her face up. His gaze locked on hers. "It was a valid concern and you showed courage in asking it."

She gave him a tentative smile. "Thank you.

"You're welcome." He rubbed the back of his neck growing pinker by the moment. "Ah... The best place to watch the ship is on the starboard side."

"The what?" Marianne asked.

"Starboard is the right side of the ship, facing forward. Port is on the left."

Tavish walked a ways and then continued. "For ease of use, the same terms for a wet-navy ship are used for aetherships. Less confusing that way."

Marianne nodded. "That makes sense."

They stopped by the railing and she looked out into a sea of stars so striking they took her breath away. On an aethership, starboard took on a whole new meaning. It literally faced the stars. "Beautiful."

"Wait until we're clear of the platform's atmosphere. It gets even better."

A long purple tail flicked out from below the ship. She stepped back. "What's that?"

"The aetherwhale. It allows us to breath up here."

She reached out to touch a tentacle but paused. "Can I touch it?"

Tavish shrugged. "Don't see why not."

Her hand connected with the soft, pebbly skin. It rippled under her touch. Giggling, she looked back at Tavish. "I think it likes me."

"Most people ignore them." He took off the glove on his real hand and ran it over the tentacle. "It never occurred to me to pet it."

"What an odd creature...." She continued to stroke it.

"It was discovered some fifty years back, and now humanity rules the stars." Tavish's voice became almost wistful as he gazed out over the ship's railing

"You love it up here, don't you."

Tavish looked down at her. "I do, and if you give it time, you'll learn to love it too. Very few people can resist the aether's call. Once you hear its song, it never leaves."

Marianne turned her gaze back over the canvas of stars as she mulled over Tavish's words. Her future was so unsure. It wasn't her choice to be on this aethership. Not really. When Tavish had offered her the job, she'd had to take it. It was either this or starvation.

Mixed in with all of it was the problem of whether she could do the job she was hired to do. Would she get fired? Would she find herself stuck on some out-of-the way island worse off? It was hard to imagine she might someday find herself in a position to choose where she lived, or what she did.

Tavish rested a hand on her shoulder. "Let yourself enjoy the moment. You only get the first time once. Forget everything else."

His words settled her and she obeyed. Letting herself enjoy the vista, she pushed her worries away.

A blanket of silence wrapped around them as the giant ship moved. The aetherwhale's purple tentacles waved gracefully out from the center of the ship. They danced through the starlight like trees blowing in a gentle summer breeze.

The sails took wind and the ship shuddered.

"Watch those lashings!"

Marianne and Tavish whipped around just in time to see a crate shake free from its stack and topple over the side of the ship.

"Stay here," Tavish yelled, leaping toward the tower of crates.

Marianne stood still, her hands twisting in knots as the men scrambled around the cargo, tossing ropes.

A rope caught on her legs, ripping her feet out from under her. She screamed as she was dragged up and over the edge.

"Man overboard!" Tavish bellowed, his stomach plummeting as Marianne's scream ripped through the air. Racing to the railing, he leapt up and over, following Marianne in her descent toward Earth.

The crate and Marianne were tiny specks growing ever smaller in the distance. He'd never catch her in time.

He tore off his boots exposing the metal exoskeleton of his cyborg lower limbs. He lifted his big toe, initiating the transformation. The tops of his feet unhinged from his heels and tucked up against his calves. Nozzles appeared from his heels. Fire belched forth, accelerating him forward at three times Earth's gravity.

He only had two minutes of power. He had to catch her, slow down, and return to the ship, but she was already only a speck in his vision.

He grunted as the acceleration hit his body, but then he let out a whoop as her image grew. He was catching up.

For once, his monstrosity wouldn't be a hindrance. He'd save her.

He calculated how much longer he needed to reach her and a chill crept up his spine.

He was going to overshoot her.

He dropped his big toe back to rest, pulling it out of his calf and shutting off the rockets. A second grunt escaped his lips at the rapid deceleration.

He was still closing too fast. What if he passed her?

He shook the thought away, forced it to the back of his mind. He couldn't distract himself.

Extending his arms, he tried to grab her but he was just out of reach.

Sweat dripped into his eyes.

He stretched. The fingers of his right hand skirted over fabric. He pinched, and pulled.

Caught her.

She was nearly pulled from his grasp but his fingers tightened on her coat. With straining muscles, he hauled himself toward her.

Her eyes were shut but her arms clamped like vises around him. Her heart, racing in time with his own, began to slow as she realized he had her.

"I... I... " she stammered.

"Breathe," he ordered as he reignited the boots. The boots flared but they didn't stop falling.

He added propulsion but they only inched away. What was the problem?

Glancing down, he cursed.

The damn crate.

His jaw locked. He had to cut the rope. Get her free.

He pried her arms from his back. "Please Marianne, I have to cut you loose."

She whimpered.

The soft sound pierced him.

"I won't let you go," he soothed. He pushed her over his shoulder. Flexing his left hand, he pulled back his thumb. Out shot a three-inch knife.

He turned off the rocket boost. With a clean swipe at the rope, the crate hurtled away from them

Hauling her back down, he pressed her to him. Without cyborg enhancement the rapid acceleration would harm her. He flipped the switch knowing she'd be protected while cocooned in his arms.

The fire flared and they raced upward. He held her tight. Giddiness rushed to his head. Now all they had to do was get back to the ship.

The boots sputtered and his heart skipped a beat.

No.

Only a few seconds more and he'd reach the hull.

The flames sputtered one final time.

Died.

Earth was calling them back.

He'd failed.

CHAPTER SIX

He'd failed her.
　Marianne held tightly to him, her head buried in his cravat. The rapid beat of her heart pounded through him. Reminded him again that he was to blame. He'd taken her from the safety of the ground and brought her up here to die.
　Below them the platform bustled with activity. People moved about looking like tiny grains of sand. They were unaware of the disaster befalling the Sheba. To those people below, Tavish and Marianne was mere specks indistinguishable from the stars.
　He took a deep breath and resigned himself to his fate.
　Their fate.
　Wind rushed passed his ears as they picked up speed. The atmosphere created by the platform's aetherwhale was strong enough to allow them to breathe, even up here, but it only meant they'd die on reentry. Even his enhanced cyborg body wouldn't be able to handle the heat and pressure the Earth could dish out.
　Holding her close, he rested his cheek on her hair. "I'm sorry."
　She pulled away, just enough to look up at him. "It's not your fault. I was the one..." She swallowed. "I was the one who fell. You've been nothing but kind."
　"I should have—"
　"Should have what? Left me in that horrid place. At least you gave me hope." Her voice trailed off and she stared at his throat. "It's been a long time since I had much of that."
　He squeezed her. "At least you're not alone."
　"Thank you," Marianne cupped his left cheek.
　The gentle massage of her fingers on his scars both soothed and pierced him. How long had he dreamt of a woman touching him so reverently? Yet, here they were, falling to their death. Fate was a cruel mistress.
　He closed his eyes and tried to fight the upwelling of despair. Those people at the air-docks, hell, all the people who'd pointed at him and accused him over the years, had been right. He was a monster. It would have been better for everyone, better for her, if that explosion years ago had simply killed him.
　Marianne's lips brushed his.
　His eyes snapped open.
　He pulled back and stared at her. "What?"
　"Thank you." Her face flushed and she glanced down at his throat again.

They were falling to their death. Otherwise, he'd never dream of being so bold. Tipping her chin up, he pressed his lips to hers.

The feather light touch of her lips on his sent gentle warmth flowing through him. He wanted more of it. He angled his head to better meet her embrace. Taking what she offered and nothing more, he gently tasted.

She was honey and summer. A sweetness that shook him. He couldn't save her and hadn't protected her, but he could give her this, a distraction from their fate. A distraction for them both.

The kiss enthralled him. Pulled him under. Distracted him as no other thing could.

Wrapped in his arms, she was a soft, warm reminder of what fate had taken from him. What could have been flooded his mind. The thought should have angered him, but for the first time since the accident that robbed him of his legs, he felt whole.

His heart constricted. Fate had given him a taste of what could have been. What he could never have. He held her close and savored her nearness—allowed himself to finally admit what his heart had yearned for. A closeness like this. A woman to love him. He would never find such a woman, but in this moment, he could pretend, maybe even believe that this woman could.

Now, as they faced death together, he could feel complete. He swallowed back a lump caught in his throat. If only she were safe.

Something cinched around his waist and jerked them backward.

Instinctively, he squeezed Marianne tighter. Pulling from the kiss, he glanced down, and saw the purple end of an aetherwhale tentacle wrapped around them both.

Her eyes grew round and her mouth dropped open. "Is that what I think it is?"

"It appears so."

The aetherwhale, with its fifty-meter-long tentacles, could reach them as no rope tossed from a ship could. He never imagined the creature would do that: protect them.

A weight lifted from his chest and a single, crystal clear thought grew out of the chaos of his mind. She was safe.

Relief so strong it made him giddy washed through him.

The tentacle snapped taught, and they were whipped up and over the edge of the ship.

Tavish twisted in the air, cushioning Marianne before they slammed into the deck.

They were surrounded before he could rise and help her to her feet. Voices rose in a cacophony.

"Who would a thought it?"

"The aetherwhale! If I hadn't seen it with me own eyes, I wouldn't have believed it."

"You all right, missy? Took a scare, I'd wager."

"Here you are, miss. Let me help you up." Freddy pushed his way through the crowd and pulled Marianne to her feet, wrapping her in a blanket.

Tavish rose. Practiced eyes scanned the ship, taking in the unfurled sails, now clearly full of wind pulling them away from Earth.

The crew hadn't had time to furl and unfurl the sails in the time he'd been falling. The captain must have ordered the engines fired. It was the only way Sheba could have gotten close enough.

It would have burned a lot of fuel. Not all captains would have done so. Yet, the quickness of their rescue indicated that Ridgewell hadn't even hesitated.

"Well done, mate." A rail thin airman slapped him on the back.

Tavish grunted but turned his attention back to Marianne. She avoided his gaze, looking instead at her feet.

He looked down at his legs and swallowed back a curse. His cyborg exoskeleton was there for all to see. The now bare, metal legs shining with reflected sunlight. "Freddy, take Miss Lindstrom back to her room, get her a cup of tea and sit with her a while."

Freddy nodded and ushered Marianne away.

While Freddy opened the hatch, she turned and locked gazes with him. Confusion and something else he couldn't identify swam in her eyes.

His whole body locked, fighting the urge to walk over and comfort her. But she needed quiet and space away from him. Away from the fear and danger he offered her.

Freddy whisked her below decks.

Tavish tried to breathe easier. He'd hoped that with her away he could focus again, and redirect his thoughts back to the matter at hand. Even separated by meters of corridor and metal he could sense her. It was as if part of her lingered with him, refusing to let him go.

No other woman had ever had the power to move him the way she did. He'd tried to lie to himself. Tried to tell himself he was only protecting her because of her station. Because, as a gentleman, he could do nothing else.

He'd been wrong.

Some primal part of him, some part he'd long since thought dead had roared to life the moment he'd seen her. Now the beast refused to be caged. He couldn't—wouldn't—return to the way he'd been.

Which left him grappling with his new reality. How was he to face each day with this feeling tugging at his heart? How was he to control it and make sure it didn't push to the surface? He had to protect her, even from himself. She deserved that much.

Clenching his fists he looked away, out over the starry vista, and frowned. They had to work together. Which meant he had to fight whatever this was. If he couldn't control it, then he had better learn to ignore it.

"Here you are, miss."

Marianne looked up and took the offered tea from Freddy's hand. She didn't drink it. Instead, she set it down on the counter next to her.

Freddy patted her hand like she'd was a frightened child. "You'll be all right. Danger's past now."

"I think I'll just sit here for a while." She offered him a faint smile. "You have other duties. I'll be fine on my own."

"If you're sure." Freddy looked into her eyes. "Yes, I suppose you'll do all right. The shock seems to be easing."

He rose and walked to the hatch. "Just make sure you rest. The full impact of what might have happened will hit you eventually. When it does, just let it out. It gets better after that."

Marianne heard the click of the hatch. Freddy assumed her shaken nerves were due to her near-death experience. Any other woman and he might have been right.

Her time in the slums of London had already forced her to acknowledge her own mortality. Spitalfields had given her that much.

Still, she might have had some lingering terror if it hadn't been for the kiss. She'd kissed Tavish.

She hadn't meant to. Not to the extent she had. She'd meant it as a thank you. Just a peck to tell him that she was grateful. What she'd gotten had been so much more.

Her tongue dashed out and licked her lower lip. She could still taste him there, could still feel the way his lips had firmed under her touch. A hint of the power behind the man.

A shiver raced through her but she wasn't cold. That kiss had been her first. It had taken all of her expectations and sent them hurtling away, leaving behind confusion and something else she couldn't identify.

What happened now?

Her duties on the ship hadn't changed because of that kiss. She would need to work with him. Yet, how was she to act around him? She didn't know how a lady reacted to a man she'd just kissed.

Shaking her head, she stared at the autochef and frowned. She was a novice at... well... everything. It was as if for the twenty-eight years she'd been alive all she'd done was exist. She'd learned little. Certainly nothing that would help her in this situation.

Glancing down at the teacup, she sighed. Here she was, a full teacup that had never been sipped. A life wasted. If she had died today, no one would have mourned her. No one would have cared. She'd never taken chances. Never reached for anything in her life.

Tavish made her feel... cherished. Even desired. He was rough around the edges but the soft center of him drew her like nothing ever had.

Rising from the bench, she walked to her room. She could sit here and tremble, doing nothing but reliving the terror of the last few minutes, or she could put her life together and take a grasp at happiness.

No longer would she let her life be driven by others. From now on, she would drive herself. When Tavish came to help her learn to cook, she'd let him teach her something else. She'd be bold and demanding. For the first time in her life, she would reach for something she wanted.

Him.

Death.

Tavish had faced it so often it hardly registered anymore. Death haunted him, ready to strike at any moment. Its constant, looming presence had become a friend of sorts over his long years of self-banishment.

Not until today had Death actually touched his soul. The day's events had shaken him as nothing had before. Because of her. Because of Marianne.

He had to remember that he was dangerous. That Death's infatuation with him could threaten others.

He couldn't let her be hurt. He wouldn't let it happen. He had to get this infatuation with her out of his head.

Once again ensconced behind his desk, Tavish glanced over the pile of work, trying to force his mind to work again. Even now he felt the tug of his awareness of her. She didn't even have to be in the room to distract him.

He ground his teeth and refocused on a readiness report from the chief engineer. His eyes narrowed as he took in the insensate yet subtle complaints about Mr. Galveson, the second mate.

Reaching behind him, he flipped open the veemitter control box and typed in a code.

"Engineering." The chief engineer's usual cheerful voice seemed to drag through the speaker.

"Sam, can you spare a few minutes? I'm poring over your report and there are a few things I'd like to go over in person," he said.

"Sure thing, boss, I'll be right up."

Ten minutes later a knock sounded on his door. "Enter."

Samantha Quinn strolled in. She was a short, stout woman with close-cropped, dirty-blond hair and a round, well-worn face that always appeared smudged with oil.

Tavish wasn't even sure the woman could clean the oil off at this point. "Have a seat, Sam."

She pulled out the chair and plopped down. Unbidden, an image of Marianne swam into his mind. Her straight posture, elegant and graceful movements, all in stark contrast to Quinn's petulant, teenager-like actions. Marianne looked more mature and sophisticated despite the fact that Quinn easily had a decade on her.

He grimaced. Now he was comparing women. What the devil was wrong with him? He cleared his throat. "This report about the spare parts?"

Sam flung her hands in the air. "That bastard wouldn't order the parts I need and now I've lost the only box of 'em he'd let me order."

"I assume the bastard you are referring to is the second mate?" Tavish raised an eyebrow in gentle rebuke.

Sam slouched further. "I can't keep this ship running smoothly if I don't have the parts I need. Why can't he let me do my job?"

"Sam," Tavish scolded. "He's the logistics officer. It's his job to make sure that we only order what the ship really needs."

The engineer was a brilliant woman, but she had the unfortunate habit of ignoring anything that didn't pertain to her "'chinery," as she called it.

She crossed her arms. "I don't see why the captain gave such an important assignment to that little weasel."

"You know very well why he has that assignment. You're the senior officer in your department and the staff will follow your lead. You can't act this way aboard ship. I can't let it continue."

She looked ready to argue but sighed. "You're right. I shouldn't let myself get so worked up, but I'm serious about needing these spare parts. If we break down out here, I won't have anything to work with. It'll be jury-rigging and prayer."

Tavish understood her dilemma. He didn't like the idea either.

He glanced at the framed merchant mate certification hanging against his wall. Everything he'd been taught and everything he'd learned in his years up here screamed that Quinn was right. Galveson was playing with fire. If it had been any other situation he would have let the fool fail, but it wouldn't be Galveson alone who would burn if things exploded.

"All right, in your opinion as a department head, has Galveson failed to take into consideration pertinent facts regarding your request?" Tavish kept the question formal. Galveson's family had political clout. Clout enough to make it all but impossible for the Sheba to continue sailing the aether under the British flag. If he screwed this up, it was the whole ship that would suffer.

Quinn straightened in her chair. "Yes, and I formally request that you intercede on this matter. It has gone beyond my ability to fix."

Tavish nodded and rummaged in a desk drawer. Pulling out a sheet of paper he handed it over to Quinn. "Very well. I will need a written report for the file."

Quinn ripped the paper out of his hand. "I have evidence of each of these occurrences. I can get them if you need."

"That will help. Bring back the report and evidence for a meeting in say... " He glanced at the clock. "One hour."

Sam sprang from her chair with all the excitement of a rabbit that found the lettuce patch.

As the door shut behind her, Tavish glanced back down at the report she'd filed earlier.

How had he let it get this bad? He was supposed to keep an eye on things like this. Wiping his hand down his face he pulled out a piece of paper and wrote down a quick summons.

He headed toward the door. The bustling noise of navigation washed over him as he scanned the area. "Mr. Hardy?" He waved a young deck cadet over. "Have this delivered to Mr. Galveson."

The deck cadet nodded and fled.

Tavish smiled after the young man but the smile quickly faded as he thought back over his problem. How to talk Galveson down without setting the man off?

He needed a walk to clear his head. The deck would be quiet now that they'd finished launch. He grabbed his great coat. Throwing it over his shoulders, he froze.

The soft scent of woman still clung to its folds. Was it just his imagination that he still felt lingering warmth? With an irritated huff he headed out of navigation. Would he never get the woman from his mind?

Stepping out on the main deck, Tavish took a deep breath, inhaling the scent of apples and freshly fallen leaves.

One of the aether's many wonders.

The air smelled different to each person. Some believed it brought out what a person most desired. Still others felt it simply fed on happy memories. As far as Tavish knew, not a single person ever smelled something rotten up here. It was as if the aether wanted visitors to hunger for its vastness.

Each time he inhaled the smell he thought of Summerfield. His birthright. His home. It didn't matter that he hadn't stepped foot there in more than a decade. He could still smell the orchard, ripe with fruit, where he'd played as a boy. Autumn had always been his favorite time of year. It was a time of plenty for both the estate and its tenants. They had the Autumn Fair, the harvest, and fresh apple cider to look forward to.

If anything had the power to bring him home it would be the apples. Many times over the years he'd longed to return just to see the apples plucked from the trees. But reality would gallop in and trample his dreams. No one wanted him there.

His mother's letters always confirmed it. She'd done her best to keep him up to date on estate matters. Since his father's death three years ago, he'd been the one with whom ultimate authority over the lives of the estate and its workers fell. Yet, every letter just proved how little they needed him. Even less that they wanted him to return.

Hands behind his back, he walked toward the quarterdeck. He'd long since realized that Summerfield, his by law, was not his by right. Those who lived there deserved to live free of the reminder he represented. When he closed his eyes, he could see the pain on his mother's face and the horror on Lucy's.

Lucy Bridges, a woman he hadn't let himself think about in a long time. The woman who'd promised to wait for him until he returned from his service in the army. The woman who, on his return, after taking one look at him, had run straight into the arms of his first cousin.

She was one more reason why he belonged up here. When he died without issue, his cousin would get Summerfield and Lucy would finally have her prize.

And though the thought hurt, he also understood it was for the best. His cousin was a better landlord than he ever would be. If Tavish could do it, he'd give Summerfield to him now.

He stepped on to the quarterdeck and instantly knew that Marianne was there. She was a lodestone, drawing his attention no matter what path his mind was on.

No one had ever had that power. Not even Lucy.

He paused on the top of the steps and drank in the sight of her. She'd changed again. She wore trousers. The supple fabric hugged her curves and sent his heart racing.

He knew he'd bought them for her because skirts weren't practical aboard ship, but he hadn't factored in how the sight of her in them would affect him.

Keeping his arms locked behind him, he approached. He couldn't trust his hands not to touch.

"After what happened, I thought you'd avoid the open deck." He tried to keep his voice to a conversational tone but it came out rough and husky.

She turned around and smiled as if she'd expected him. Welcome danced in her eyes. "Good evening."

A lump caught in his throat. It had been longer than he cared to remember since a person had looked at him with such genuine welcome. "Ah... Good evening."

Marianne turned back to look over the edge of the rail.

"What happened doesn't bother you?" Tavish moved to stand next to her.

She took a deep breath, the fabric of her blouse pulling over her breasts. Petite, round breasts that were still large enough to be a handful.

He had to force his gaze off of them and back to her face.

"I won't let it bother me." She stroked her throat as she stared out over the starry scape.

Admiration bloomed in his chest. She didn't shrink from a challenge. It was one more reminder that other than their upbringing, Lucy and Marianne had little in common.

He sensed more than saw the delicate shiver that ran through her body before she wrapped her arms around her chest.

Slipping out of his great coat, he threw it over her shoulders.

"Thank you." She clutched it tight.

Tavish grunted in reply, unable to say in words how much her acceptance of him meant. She wasn't cringing in fear. She hadn't run for the hatch. It seemed she was content to stand here next to him, even knowing the deformities barely hidden by his clothing.

He stood and let the moment be. His worries disappeared. Galveson, Lucy, even the captain faded from his mind. For the first time in the presence of another he let down his guard and relaxed. It was a feeling he could all too easily get used to.

He felt her gaze shift to him and he looked at her, arching a brow in question.

"I want to thank you again for saving me." She rested a hand on his.

Pleasure rippled through him at the gentle touch. He reached over and covered her hand with his left. A part of his heart shifted, moved into place, and locked.

"There's no need to thank me. I'm just happy you're all right."

He didn't know how long they stood there gazing at each other, hands clasped. But eventually, she pulled away and took off his coat.

"I should get below decks. I have an early morning tomorrow."

"I'll walk you back." He turned to leave but she stopped him with a hand on his arm.

"I'll be fine, and you came up here for a walk of your own. I won't trouble you further."

He gazed into her eyes.

Her eyes sparkled back at him, showing no signs of fear or trepidation, only acceptance and contentment.

Warmth spread through him, covering him like a blanket. Unable to stop himself, he raised her fingers to his lips and kissed them.

She gasped, her eyes becoming large pools as she blushed and tugged her hand back.

"Until tomorrow." He purred.

She nodded and hurried away down the steps.

He watched until she disappeared below decks. With a sigh, he turned back toward his office. He had a meeting to attend, a certain officer to reprimand, and he had to figure out what to make for breakfast tomorrow. But none of those things worried him any longer. The relaxation he'd felt around Marianne hadn't left him. The contentment still remained. Perhaps it wasn't such a bad thing he'd have to stay so close to her.

Perhaps he needed her.

CHAPTER SEVEN

A bright incandescent bulb shone onto the subject of Draven's newest experiment. He never understood the dreary atmosphere of the scientists in books. How did one do such delicate work in a poorly lit laboratory?

Draven liked light. He grinned down at his newest machine—a brain extraction device. Its purpose was to remove a human brain for preservation. If he misaligned the device by even a millimeter it would fail in a bloody mess that would take hours to clean and completely destroy the subject, rendering the brain useless.

He smiled at the dock porter strapped tightly to a chair, his head completely immobilized by large metal clamps and wire. After tracking the Lindstrom girl to the air docks he'd hit a dead end. No one would tell him what he needed to know. Porters saw everything that happened on the docks. Properly motivated, the man would tell him everything he needed.

Shadow was growing impatient and Nora was suffering for it. Time for drastic measures.

He glanced around the room, taking note of every crevice, every hint of shade in the otherwise well-lit room. All he had to do was wait for the drugs he'd used to subdue the larger man to wear off before he could interrogate, and Shadow wasn't known for patience.

The man groaned and his eyes flickered open.

Draven rolled up his sleeves and pulled out his shaving kit. "What's your name?"

"Ace." The man's eyes were cloudy and unfocused. "Where am I?"

"You're my guest." Draven lathered Ace's head with shaving cream.

"Wait... What?" Ace's eyes began to clear and he struggled in his chair. "What are you doing?"

"Shaving your head." Draven continued his methodical work. Making sure every inch of Ace's head was covered in cream. He'd never shaved anyone before. Not even himself, but it didn't look too hard. "Hair clogs up the machinery."

"What do you want?" Ace's eyes darted about the room, still unfocused; his gaze didn't linger on any one thing.

"I'm looking for a young lady." Draven dipped a knife in water and pulled it over Ace's head.

Ace's head twitched in his binds. "I don't know no lady."

The knife skimmed across Ace's head, removing hair and pushing the shaving cream like a shovel pushed snow.

"But you might have seen something," Draven soothed.

Ace tugged at his binds. Glaring at Draven in a mixed look of fear and anger. "I'm telling you, I don't know nothing."

Smoke billowed from the lamp. The temperature in the room plummeted and ice crystals formed on the edge of the machine.

Draven suppressed a shiver.

The smoke wrapped around Draven, swirling around him before it formed the shape of a man on the other side of the chair.

"What are you doing?" the ice-cold, raspy voice asked.

"He has information you need," Draven replied. His hand holding the knife started to shake and he put it behind him. "He refuses to share it. I was starting the extraction process."

"Who are you talking to?" Ace's voice rose in pitch. He struggled, the veins in his temples bulging.

"Quiet," Draven ordered.

"He cannot see me... Interesting." Shadow flowed over to stand before Ace. One long, shadowy appendage reached out to caress the man's face.

Ace froze, his eyes darting around the room, his face chalk white. "What's that? Who's there?"

"He can sense you." Draven returned to his work, bringing the knife back up to the fool's scalp. "Perhaps you should stand aside. It would be unwise to kill him before we have the information we require."

Shadow didn't say a word but swooshed away, hovering behind the machine. Its red glowing eyes bored into the back of Ace's head.

Ace shrank back into the chair and tried to turn his head. A whimper escaped his lips and his gaze locked onto Draven. "Why are you doing this?"

"I told you that. I need information," Draven purred.

He relaxed into the motions of his work. Shadow was distracted by fear, and as long as the potential of that fear remained intact, Draven was free to work uninterrupted.

"I can't help you. I don't remember. I... I... don't know." Sweat dripped down Ace's head, smearing shaving cream and leaving a trail of white stripes down his face.

"Properly motivated, you'll remember." He nicked Ace's head. Blood seeped out of the wound and down the earlobe. The copper scent of blood mingled with the almond shaving soap and Ace's sweat. Draven inhaled deeply. A grin spread across his face. So, this is what fear smelled like?

Reaching behind him, Draven pulled a piece of plaster and slapped it over the wound.

"Why stop it?" Shadow asked.

"Blood interferes with my machinery. Too much and the gears will stick shut." Draven put the plaster away and walked to stand in front of Ace. "Before we begin, I'd like to give you another chance to talk."

"I see lots of ladies on the platforms. I can't tell them apart." Tremors danced across Ace's body. His gaze clouded and his head jerked.

Draven was reminded of a startled lemur he'd seen at the zoo.

"This particular lady was accompanied by a cyborg," Draven proved.

"Lots of cyborgs on aetherships," Ace pointed out.

"Not helpful, Ace." Draven shook his head. "Not helpful at all."

Foamy spit sputtered out of Ace's mouth. "I'm telling you everything I know."

Draven ignored him, picking up a toolbox from the floor. He placed it next to Ace on a small table. "I want to wait to use my machine on you. It's new, and I would rather not kill you too soon. We'll start with something tried and tested."

He placed a diode attached to a wire to Ace's neck. Then he attached a clamp to the middle finger of Ace's left hand. Pulling over a portable generator, he attached the diode to the machine and the wire from the finger clamp to the ground. "Do you know what this is?"

Ace's hands convulsed, the diode clamp on his finger clattering against the chair arm like it was using Morse code. "No."

"It's a generator. It provides electricity and can power any device I plug into it. I can make it produce a shock strong enough to hurt but not so strong it kills."

"I'm telling you everything I know," Ace repeated, his eyes darting between the Draven and the machine.

"Good, I see you've gathered my intent." Draven patted Ace's hand.

Shadow shifted and the smoke in its body rippled. It looked like an excited child waiting for a treat.

Draven adjusted the voltage and grabbing the hand crank, turned the engine until it caught. Diesel smoke permeated the air around the machine like thick fog.

With a sputter the machine whirred to life. A wheel turned on a belt. Arcs of electricity jumped to diodes set atop the wheel.

With the generator running, Draven could control it at will. He flipped a switch on the side and the electricity traveled down the wire attached to Ace's neck.

Ace jerked in the chair, a low grunt emanating from his lips.

"Care to enlighten me about the girl's whereabouts?"

"I don't know."

"Good, I like it when you resist. It means I can learn more." Draven increased the voltage but kept the amperage low.

A stronger jolt bore down through Ace. His left arm convulsed and his head jerked against the restraints. This time instead of a grunt, he got a scream.

Shadow grew darker. "Continue. I need more."

Draven flipped the switch off. "Care to tell me now?"

Ace's breathing came out in short gasps. "I can't tell you nothing."

"You keep using double negatives." Draven upped the voltage again and flipped the switch.

He left it on longer after each refusal.

Shadow changed from a dull, sickly green to a deep, disturbing purple.

"There was... a cyborg... Made a scene," Ace breathed, finally.

"Do continue." Draven's hand hovered over the switch.

"Stop... Pain...." Ace's breath was haggard. "I... I'll talk."

Draven kept his hand where it was, but nodded. "If you tell me what I want to know, I won't flip this switch again."

"The cyborg works aboard an aethership named Sheba. I carried a tr... trunk for him. Ladies trunk... Might be who you want."

"Anyone tell you what the girl looked like?" Draven asked.

"Pretty, young," Ace stammered. "Long, blonde hair."

"Is that her?" Shadow asked.

"Could be, and it's easy enough to check." Draven ground his teeth. "Where are they going?"

"That's all I know," Ace whimpered. "I only say what I heard."

Was he going to have to harry off to some fool aether island? Draven took a deep breath. At least he had a lead. And if he had to sail off to an island, at least he had an aethership to do the chasing.

Draven looked up at Shadow. "I'd say we've gotten everything we can from him. Do you wish to watch as I use the brain extraction device?"

Ripples radiated through Shadow. "Yes."

"Wait, who are you talking to? You said you'd let me go."

Draven tightened a strap. "I said no such thing. Your brain will be useful to me for research."

"Wait, no!" Ace pulled and shook, his frantic movements not budging the tight straps that held him down.

Draven dropped the large wire covered device over Ace's head and screwed it into the restraints that held him in place.

He stepped back and flipped the switch. Hopefully, the man's screams would satisfy Shadow long enough for Draven to get the book. Shadow grew impatient far too fast and the long aethership voyage would be unbearable if he had to hear Nora's screams every night.

CHAPTER EIGHT

Tavish trudged down the corridor toward the galley. It was an ungodly hour to be up, and after the night he'd had wrestling with his own demons he'd have preferred to stay abed.

One kiss, that's all it took to render him witless. He'd thought himself immune to those needs.

How wrong he'd been.

Last night, he'd tossed and turned, unable to keep thoughts of Marianne from his mind. And then when he had fallen asleep, the dreams—her long hair spread over his pillow, eyes dark with passion. He bit off the thought and stopped to readjust his trousers. Damn! He hadn't embarrassed himself like this since he'd returned from Eton.

He ground his finger into his right palm, using the pain to redirect his thoughts.

Breakfast had to be ready by the end of watch, and he couldn't leave Marianne to figure it out on her own. Since he had to teach her, he couldn't be daydreaming about her.

He fingered the recipe card he'd found. It should work and it was simple enough that he could limit this exchange to only a few minutes.

He opened the hatch into the galley and stepped in.

Marianne sat behind the island, her hand idly stroking her neck as she perused a book open on her lap. She brought a cup to her lips, sipped, and turned a page. Her tongue dashed out to lick a spot of tea from the corner of her mouth.

Desire raced through him. He shifted where he stood. Coughed.

Marianne looked up and her eyes gleamed. "Good morning. I was just reading through the manual. I think oatmeal shouldn't be too hard."

"I was thinking the same." He bludgeoned his wits back into place.

"Would you mind checking my work?" Marianne rose and walked to the autochef, her shapely legs shown to advantage in trousers.

The sight sent him reeling. He couldn't help but stare at her, watching the simple fabric move across her skin. He shifted again.

"Tavish?"

He wrenched his gaze back up to her face. "Ah, of course."

Standing next to her, so close he could feel heat radiating from her body, he actually found it easier to think. Her nearness soothed him.

Taking a deep breath he inhaled the scent of her—woman, with a touch of lemon.

He wanted to grab her in his arms. He wanted to hold her until his wayward senses returned and let him be. He wanted to kiss her until both of them were senseless—to take from her the comfort that she alone could give him.

Instead, he leaned forward and checked her work against the recipe card he'd brought with him. "Looks fine."

She beamed up at him with her radiant smile and pressed the big green button next to the code pad.

The recipe rattled to life.

"It should take an hour or so." She smiled. "Would you like a cup of tea?"

He should go. He knew that, but he was reluctant to leave her. Besides, he actually liked tea, and shouldn't he wait to see if the recipe worked? He was as much novice at this as she was. "That would be pleasant." He turned to get a stool to set next to hers and ran right into her.

She rested her hands on his chest. Her eyes searched his.

He tensed and forced his hands to stay at his side. The weight of her was enough to drive any sane man wild. He was close to exploding, his desire a fast rising tide ready to wash both of them out to sea. She couldn't know the danger she courted. If she did, she'd run from the room.

Her gaze dropped to his lips.

His hands came up to grip her shoulders—to push her away or draw her closer, he couldn't tell.

She solved it for him by leaning in. "I've been wondering since yesterday if…" She raised her gaze back to his face. "If… "

Her arms slid up behind his neck and she kissed him.

Tavish's world tilted.

His mind wrestled with this new direction, but his body didn't hesitate. His lips firmed under hers and took control of the kiss, demanding far more of her than was wise.

Fire, hot and insensate, rose between them, engulfing them both in a heady dance.

He should stop, but that meant pulling away from her, sitting her down and physically leaving. He couldn't do it. Couldn't bring himself to deny the heat that flared between them.

Her desire blindsided him. Took away conscious thought and left him acting on instinct. He was at sea on a course he didn't recognize.

Her lips moved along his. Tentative and untutored, the innocence of her kiss only set the flames inside him roaring higher.

The heat was familiar, one he'd danced with before, but the intensity, the all-powerful hunger that she elicited, was new… something he'd never before guessed was possible, let alone something he would get to taste.

He scooped her up and set her down on the counter. He needed to taste more. Feel more. It was as if her lips had stripped away his last barrier of civility and unleashed a beast.

Her lips opened on a gasp.

He surged in. Plundered. His tongue waltzed with hers and he pulled her further into the inferno they built—an inferno spiraling out of control.

Her arms dropped from his neck and traced reverently over his shoulders and chest.

He cupped the back of her neck and let his right hand roam over her curves. A growl, deep and guttural, reverberated through his throat. His body screamed to take her, claim her.

It was all he could do to keep his exploration gentle as his hand brushed the underside of her breast. He wanted to squeeze and knead, feel the firmness of her flesh in his hand.

She arched her back, pressing her body into him, urging him on.

The image of her naked, skin flushed, head tipped back in ecstasy took hold.

If he didn't stop soon, he'd take her right here on the galley counter. He'd ravage her like the animal he was.

That thought pulled him out of passion as quickly as a bucket of iced water.

He stepped back. With his pulse raging in his ears and his fists balled at his sides, he battled for control.

She was leaning on her arms, her head tipped back. Her shirt stretched tight over her breasts as they rose with each deep, panting breath.

Her lips— red, bruised by his kiss—stirred him, urging him, even more than her bright, desire-filled eyes, to continue the kiss, to take them further.

He shook free of the spell she'd cast. He'd only hurt her if he succumbed. He couldn't let that happen. "This was a mistake."

"But—"

He stormed to the door. "I'll return to help with lunch."

Like a coward, he ran from the passion she'd ignited within him. He couldn't ignore or even control his own demons. Couldn't keep them leashed or contained. How the hell was he to control hers? That he had to was a given. She was a gentle lady. A creature he should protect. A woman he had no right to even dream about, let alone taste.

What had she done wrong now? Marianne's head swirled in a daze as she tried to wrap her senses around what had happened? Why had he left?

She'd meant to kiss him. And oh, how he'd responded. The kiss had stolen her breath and ravaged her senses.

His abrupt departure was the bit she didn't understand. It had left her confused, cold, and—she swallowed back a lump in her throat—hurt.

She never should have been so bold.

How long had she dreamed over a prince to rescue her from the walls of her father's castle, or a tall handsome knight to slay the dragon and wrap his arms around her?

Ever since the first kiss and the way he'd held her as they fell, she'd wanted to learn more. He was someone she trusted. The first man to treat her as a woman.

The first man to show he cared for her. Standing next to him, alone, with his lips so close to hers, it had seemed like the perfect opportunity to explore.

He'd taken her on a journey through pleasure so wonderful it lingered in her mind. It was a drug, heady and inciting.

No wonder ladies fell to lust so readily. Tavish's kisses could lead to addiction.

She'd been so engaged in that kiss, she'd have let him take her where he willed.

She cupped her breast. Her body still tingled with pleasure. He'd done this, stripped away her inhibitions, and left her wanting something she didn't understand.

He'd been attracted too. He couldn't deny that he'd enjoyed the interlude. His breath had been as ragged, his face as flushed as hers.

So why did he leave?

She gazed unseeing at the door, her chest a hallow cavern that echoed with each breath. Somehow she'd come up wanting.

How could she have let herself dream that a man like Tavish would ever want her? She was a useless girl who couldn't even take care of herself.

Later that night, Marianne walked up to the quarterdeck. She'd been inside the galley all day keeping the autochef running, learning how the machine worked, and planning meals for the next day.

The oatmeal had come out slightly burnt but the crew had eaten it, and the other meals she'd made had turned out fine. She was getting the hang it.

Tavish hadn't made another appearance, but he'd sent a note with a recipe attached.

She'd ignored it. She was capable of doing that on her own. She could read and it didn't appear that Tavish was doing more than picking something from the manual.

As cook, she should know how the machine worked. How was she to do her job properly if all she did was plug in a recipe code? A good cook should be able to improvise and prepare her own dishes.

She'd acted so brazen that she'd scared Tavish away. She would have to learn everything on her own now.

She walked over to what was quickly becoming her favorite spot on the starboard side of the ship. She could get used to these walks. It was as if the blanket of stars cloaked her in calm and stilled her mind.

She took a deep breath and inhaled the delicate sweetness of peonies. The smell reminded her of her mother.

She didn't have many memories of her, but she remembered the peony beds that surrounded the house. The soft scent would permeate the house every morning. Mother loved those flowers.

After her death, Daddy had the beds ripped up and refused to allow another peony to grow on his properties. To this day the scent reminded her of Mother.

She closed her eyes and let the smell transport her back to her mother's bedside. Mother had been ill for several days. Ever since giving birth to her baby brother. He brother had died, but Marianne didn't understand why her mother was still sick.

"Come here, poppet." Mother patted the bedspread. Her skin was a sickly yellow, and her lovely blond hair drooped around her head.

Marianne crawled up and cuddled near. Peony blooms rested on the bedside table, chasing away the scent of medicine.

Mother stroked Marianne's hair. "I'm going on a journey." Her voice was garbled as if coming through a closed door.

Marianne snuggled closer. "When will you be home?"

Mother's had stilled on her head. "I won't be coming home, poppet."

"Is it something I did?" Marianne sat up. "I'll be good. I promise."

Mother reached toward the bedside table. "I don't want to leave you, but I must. God is calling me home."

Tears trickled down Marianne's face and she sniffled. "But I still need you."

Mother wrapped something around Marianne's throat. A necklace shaped like a snake.

"I won't be far from you, whenever you wear this." Mother raised Marianne's hand to touch the Snake's head. "I love you, poppet."

The memory faded and she was once again standing on the deck of the ship.

She reached up to touch her neck. Empty.

A lump caught in her throat and she closed her eyes. How was Snake doing? Had it found a good home or would it still be at the pawnshop when she returned from this trip?

"You touch your throat a lot." Tavish stopped to the left of her, his hands resting on the rail.

Her pulse leapt. She'd thought she'd ruined everything, pushed away the only person who'd shown her kindness.

He still sought her out. He was still watching.

"I had to sell a gift from my mother. The aether makes me think of her."

"You smell her perfume." Tavish nodded.

"No, her favorite flower." Her eyebrows pinched together. "How did you guess?"

"I smell apples from the family orchard." Tavish took a slow, deep breath as if he were inhaling the essence of the aether. "I figured you smelled something to remind you of your mother."

"Is it different for everyone?"

"The scent?"

She nodded.

"I believe so. The captain says she smells chocolate. Our chief engineer smells lavender honey." He shrugged. "It's part of the aether's allure. It helps us remember happier times."

"No one ever thinks of bad memories?" Marianne asked.

"Not that I've ever heard."

Once again she turned to gaze out over the stars. Only now, the sight wouldn't calm. Her nerves tingled and her mind raced. She wanted to reach out and touch him—to lean into his strength. Some part of her had awoken when she'd met him, and now it sang whenever he was near.

She knew she shouldn't hope for anything. He'd been avoiding her all day. She couldn't risk his friendship on any foolish advance, but she could dream.

His hand rose and rested on top of hers. Confusion and longing etched his face.

"This morning... Ah." He ran a hand through his hair.

"I'm sorry. I was thoughtless and stupid. I promise it won't happen again." She tried to pull her hand away.

He didn't let her go. "You did nothing wrong. I was a fool."

"Why did you leave?" she whispered.

"I liked it too much."

"I don't understand."

"You won't. You're an innocent." He gave a soft snort. "I should have known better."

"You're not mad at me?" Hope burbled through her veins.

"No," he sighed and looked away. "But, it would be best if we have limited contact."

Hope turned to sludge. "Why?"

"Because I'm not sure I can keep from kissing you again, and once I start, I won't be able to stop."

Marianne frowned and looked at their joined hands.

He pulled away. "If you don't see me around much, it's because I'm keeping my distance, but please understand that it's not you I'm afraid of."

He left before she could reply.

She watched him go, feeling even more confused than when he'd arrived.

CHAPTER NINE

Draven sat in his study and brooded. A glass of brandy swirled in his hand. He had to get that book, and soon. Shadow was getting more and more demanding every day.

A commotion echoed from down the hall and he frowned.

"My lord." Stiltson bowed from the door. "There's a young boy who claims to have some information for you."

A scrunch-faced urchin stepped out from behind the butler. He was hopping from foot to foot, energy radiating from him like a roaring fire.

Draven crossed his arms. "Spit it out, child."

"That place you asked me and m'boys to watch. The toffs left." The boy's arms waved wildly. "We followed 'em to the air docks. They boarded a ship to New Richmond."

Draven bit back a curse. How had the solicitors found out that the girl had left? His mind raced. Was this a good thing or a bad thing? Damn it! This whole business was getting out of hand.

"I told them." Shadow breathed down his neck.

Draven jumped.

"Why would… " He shook his head. He couldn't ask that question now. If Stiltson could see Shadow, he'd have said something. He turned back to the boy. "Are you sure they left for New Richmond?"

"Yes, milord. Said so on the boarding ramp." The urchin stuck out his chest. "I can read."

An urchin who could read was a valuable asset. "Good. Stilton, give the boy an extra shilling and have my carriage brought round."

The boy's eyes grew round. "You need anything else from me or m'boys, you just ask, milord."

Stiltson bowed and waved the lad down the hall. "This way, young man."

Shadow hovered next to him causing a constant chill to creep through his body. Cursing in three languages, he headed toward his bedroom. Once there, he slammed the door and glared at the entity. "What were you thinking?"

Shadow, now a dark purple, stood in in a beam of sunlight and stared out of the window. "It has been eons since I last saw the sun."

"You didn't answer my question. Why did you tell the solicitors?" Draven threw his arms in the air. "How did you tell them?"

Shadow shifted.

Was it just his imagination or was it gaining a more substantial form? Draven could just make out a pointy chin and elongated head. The arms were longer than most men's, but not grotesquely so. This being was slowly growing more human-like.

Silence stretched across the room.

"Why did you—"

"Because it's the book I want, not the girl," it hissed.

"Why didn't you just have the solicitors give me the book instead of sending them off after her?" he retorted.

"I can't." It shrank against the wall. "My power lies with dreams and souls. I can suggest but I cannot force."

"But you manifest to me." Draven pinched his brows together.

Shadow seemed to grow more substantial. "You are different. You can see me when most cannot. That makes you useful to me."

It cocked its head to the side, a wicked grin parting the smoke of its face and making it look more like a being from a Bosch painting then a smoky apparition. "But not indispensable."

Tremors started up his Draven's legs and he locked his knees to keep them still. "You shouldn't have interfered. Better for the book to remain in London."

"I don't follow." Its grin disappeared.

"I'd just have to marry her. As her husband, I'd be able to get the book directly from the solicitor's office."

"But what of dear Nora?" Shadow teased.

Draven's heart shriveled and then hardened again. He'd have to tell Nora when she woke, but she'd forgive him. "I only need to be married to the chit long enough to get the book for you."

"I hadn't thought of that."

"Now, I'll have to convince her to part with it." He crossed his arms and glared. "And we can't even be sure she'll still be there."

"She will."

"How do you know that?" Draven narrowed his eyes.

"Do not question me." Shadow grew, the smoke billowing outward to block out the sunlight.

The electric lighting sputtered and died, sending the room into darkness so deep Draven couldn't see the hand held before his face.

Draven backed up to the bed and collapsed on it. His breathing came in short started gasps and he fisted his hands at his sides to keep from calling out.

A wailing cry echoed beyond the darkness.

A child's cry.

Draven froze. His mind refused to work as each cry pierced his heart. *Not my boy. Not my son.*

"Need I remind you who I have in my power?" Shadow hissed.

The baby, his Henry? Draven wilted. Surely such an innocent would have gone to heaven. How had it gotten him?

"I have my ways. You will not question me again."

Draven's jaw firmed. He had power here. Shadow needed him. "I am not being disobedient. I am being practical."

The wailing grew louder.

"Are you now?" It purred. The sound was chilling, like the howling of a north wind.

"Yes." He swallowed and blocked out the sound. "You need me. If you didn't, you'd have simply taken the book."

Shadow remained silent.

"When I torture others, I make you stronger?" Draven asked.

"Yes," it wheezed.

"Then let me be. I can't do this job if you continually interfere."

For what seemed like hours, the wailing of the child was the only sound in the room. Each wail dug a nail deeper into Draven's heart.

Then it spoke. "I will speak to you before I interfere again and I will see to it that the girl is there when we arrive."

Draven breathed easier. "How?"

"I am a being of elemental fury forged in chaos. I have my ways." It shrank back, letting light return to the room. "You may not see me for a few days. I will need to recover."

The wailing baby grew louder and a small bundle appeared on the floor before them—bloody from birth and squirming in agony.

Draven's heart constricted and he reached out to touch the child. His child.

It disappeared in a puff of smoke.

A strangled cry escaped Draven's lips and his body shook. He looked up at Shadow through teary eyes.

"Do not think I am weak because I cannot act without you," it warned. "Do not think that because I am absent you are free of me. Remember. I control those who have passed. I can torment them at will."

Draven closed his eyes. He didn't need the reminder. He knew who would suffer if he failed.

Nora.

Henry.

"I won't fail you, Nora," he whispered. "I won't fail either of you. Never again."

CHAPTER TEN

Tavish glanced down at Marianne's note and cursed under his breath. What was the fool woman about? Tavish tried to keep his mind focused on anything but Marianne, but that was becoming all but impossible. Every little sight of her heightened his awareness.

It had been three days since their last hot kiss, and she was driving him demented. It wasn't anything she did overtly. It was the little innocent touches and her perfume that sent his head spinning.

Avoiding her wasn't working either. All that did was make him yearn more.

It was bloody distracting.

"Bad news?" A navigation tech asked.

"The autochef isn't working," he growled.

"What is the captain thinking, hiring a woman like that to cook?" Galveson asked.

"She didn't." Tavish looked up from the navigation console. "I did."

Galveson slouched back in his chair—the central one—the one for the officer of the watch. Tavish was senior to him and he should have vacated it the moment Tavish had walked in. A sign of insubordination he'd have to address later in private.

A good leader inspired his people. He didn't make them fear him. Ridgewell had taught him that. It was a lesson Galveson had yet to learn.

"She's unfit for her office," Galveson continued.

"How?" Tavish asked.

"No training."

"Everyone has to start somewhere." Tavish gritted his teeth and reminded himself that Galveson's maternal grandfather was First Lord of the Admiralty. They had to put up with him if they wanted to maintain their letter of marque from the British government. As insufferable as the prick was, he kept them on the right side of the law. Sheba was armed enough to put even a battleship to shame. Without a national flag to fly at her mast, no respectable port would let her dock.

Tavish forced his body to relax and he looked back at the console. "I'm surprised you care. It's not like your breakfast was burnt."

"I'm not worried about my stomach."

"Turns out I don't much care about it either. And here I thought we'd never find something we had in common."

Galveson narrowed his eyes and rose, looking over Tavish's shoulder. "You could show a bit more compassion for the crew."

Tavish ignored him, frowning down at the ship's course laid out before him. He didn't like the look of the shifting islands. Despite it being the wrong time of year, Tavish had a growing suspicion that the movement was due to powerful aether winds. That heralded an aether storm in Sheba's direct path. It was never wise to take the full brunt of what the aether could dish out.

"Aren't you going to answer me?" Galveson asked.

"No." Tavish switched his gaze to Galveson and pitched his voice so only the second mate could hear. "You are walking a fine line. I don't care who your grandfather is, step over that line and I will swat you down so hard you'll need a medic to get back up."

Galveston's chest bloomed out but fear danced in his eyes. "Are you threatening me?"

"No, I'm warning you. I am first mate aboard this vessel, and you will remember it."

Galveson made a strangled noise but said nothing further.

Tavish returned his attention to the plot. A small change to course now and they'd miss the worst of it. Tavish made a few adjustments to the console's directioner. The display changed to show the projected course and he breathed a sigh of relief. They'd just skim the edge of the storm.

He walked to the veemitter and punched in the code for the helmsman.

"Helm," the bright, young voice of a deck cadet answered over the speaker.

"Ms. Haversham, please tell helm to alter course according to my new heading." He pushed a button, and with a whir, the new course zipped up to the quarterdeck and waiting console next to the wheel that steered the massive ship.

"Aye, aye, Sir. Altering course now," Haversham replied.

The great ship heaved as the rudder was adjusted, and Tavish walked back to the navigation console. The plot now showed the new projected course locked in over his adjustments.

Galveson leaned over him. "You're going to cause a delay with that course change. The captain said she wanted us to make New Richmond Island in four days."

Tavish rose, forcing Galveson to step back. "She also said she wanted us there in one piece. Can't guarantee that if we hit an aether storm."

Galveson sniffed. "Wrong time of year for that."

"The Lords of the aether do not bow to the whim of mortal man." Tavish shrugged.

"Humph." Galveson crossed his arms.

"I'll inform the captain of the change. Just stay on course and we should be fine."

Galveson lifted his nose and crossed to look out of the open starboard window.

"You can't watch where we're going from a porthole." Tavish heard Galveson's disgruntled outcry as he shut the door to the navigation room and walked down a hall to the captain's office.

He knocked.

"Enter."

"Good afternoon, ma'am." Tavish walked in.

Ridgewell was bent over a box of files. Wisps of hair had come loose from her braid and she wiped them away from her face as she rose. "What can I help you with?"

He frowned. "Is everything all right?"

She laughed. "I seemed to have misplaced last week's ledgers. I could have sworn I put them away with the others."

He glanced around the immaculate office. Everything about her was neat and tidy. Ridgewell didn't misplace things. "Do you want help?"

"I'm sure they'll turn up." She shuffled some papers together and placed them under her logbook. "Now, what can I do for you?"

"I made a slight course change. It will add a half day to our travel time, but we'll miss most of an aetherstorm that's brewing off the Gordian strait."

Ridgewell frowned. "Are you sure we'll miss it? Storms from that straight tend to be nasty."

"As certain as we can be in this business," Tavish replied.

The word strait wasn't the same thing as on Earth. It was simply a word human kind used to differentiate different areas of the aether. It was just one more way humanity brought the aether's vastness into terms they recognized. In the aether it was a path between two celestial bodies that was equal to a lunar unit, the space between the Earth and her moon.

Ridgewell nodded. "If you manage to keep us out of a gale, then that half-day will be worth it." She waved a hand at the book on her desk. "I'll make a note of it in the log. Anything else?"

"No, ma'am." Tavish, sensing the dismissal in her tone, left her to her worries. He had his own to muddle through.

Like a broken autochef and a certain cook.

His jaw locked as the image of what she'd look like after he'd ravaged her flooded his brain. He shoved it away. That was the third time that afternoon. It was getting impossible to think. He was going to have to start wearing his great coat to hide his arousal.

God, that was a humbling thought. He was a grown man. He shouldn't be having this much difficulty keeping his mind focused.

He looked at the clock. Three hours until watch change. He had better get his arse down to the kitchens and find out what was wrong with the autochef. Avoiding it wouldn't make the problem go away.

Standing before the hatch in the galley, he squared his shoulders. It shouldn't be that difficult to keep his distance. Just go in, help her fix the problem, and leave. With luck, he wouldn't get closer to her than a couple of meters.

Snorting at his dithering, Tavish pressed the button and walked in. Marianne's round derrière was aimed right at him as she stood bent over the autochef.

His fingers itched to trace along her curves, to gently cup. Squeeze. He remembered the lush feel of her in his hands.

Unable to stop himself, Tavish let his eyes roam over the gentle sweep of her hip and down her long slim legs. It was enough to make his groin ache.

Marianne turned around. "Tavish is here."

A mumbled reply came from the autochef.

Tavish peered around Marianne to see Quinn buried to the small of her back in the autochef's innards. "What's wrong with it?"

"It's busted." Quinn popped up and wiped her hands on a towel.

"What do you mean, busted?" Tavish asked, not wanting to hear the answer.

"Broken, out of order, not working—take your pick." Quinn shrugged. "You'll have to do things the old fashioned way. I don't have the necessary parts and I can't fabricate them from what I have on hand."

"When do you expect to get it fixed?" Marianne asked.

"Well, I doubt New Richmond will have the parts we need. The island's too small and won't have a need for an autochef of this size. Our best bet would be one of the larger islands farther along our route. Gregoria might have what we need."

Quinn started muttering about possible places to stop but Tavish ignored her. How the devil were they to keep the crew fed?

He looked at Marianne.

Her eyebrows were pinched together and a slight frown curved her lips. "What do we do now?"

"I don't know, maybe—"

"If that idiot had let me order the parts I wanted, this wouldn't have happened," Quinn grumbled.

"Please tell me those parts weren't on the crate we lost at launch." Tavish fisted his hands and fought the need to punch something.

"No, it was on the list that Glav—excuse me, Mr. Galveson refused to order."

A growl echoed deep in Tavish's throat.

Marianne twisted her hands. "Is there anything we can do in the meantime?"

Quinn looked up from where she'd been packing away her tools. "Cook the old fashioned way I suppose."

"That's not an option," Tavish bit out.

Quinn frowned. "I don't see why. There's an oven, a stovetop, plenty of counter space. Seems that was how it was done before 'chinery."

"One person couldn't possible cook for six hundred people that way." Tavish crossed his arms and glared at the chief engineer.

Marianne sank into a chair. "Six hundred people?"

Quinn's mouth opened but she shut it again with a snap. "I hadn't thought of that."

"I don't know how to cook." Marianne clutched the chair arms as if they were the only things keeping her upright. Her voice was frantic and her gaze darted between Tavish and Quinn. "If the machine doesn't work I won't be able to do my job." She swallowed. "I'll fail."

Marianne looked ready to collapse and Tavish racked his brain trying to come up with something, some way to make it all better. He couldn't stand seeing her look so lost.

Quinn patted her arm as if she were afraid to break her. "I'm sure we'll think of something."

"Can the officers' autochef work as a stand-in?" Tavish asked.

"No, it's not big eno… " Quinn's voice trailed off as she stared open-mouthed at the broken autochef. "Of course, why didn't I think of that before? I'd have to do a bit of jury-rigging, but I should be able to make it work."

"Make what work?" Tavish growled.

"I'll cannibalize the officers' autochef to make this one work. It won't be pretty, but it'll get the job done."

"Won't the officers be upset?" Marianne asked.

"Well, speaking as one of the officers, we'll just be happy the crew is fed. A hungry crewman is not someone I'd like mess with." Quinn grinned.

"Do it," Tavish ordered.

"Aye, aye sir." Quinn gave him a mock salute.

Marianne shook Quinn's hand. "Thank you for coming so promptly. When the third meal in a row came out burnt, I knew there was something wrong. I'm just glad it wasn't me."

"My pleasure," Quinn shook Marianne's hand with gusto, nearly unseating her. "Besides, it's my job to keep the 'chinery running."

With a nod to Tavish, she headed out the door, humming an out-of-tune version of Londonderry Air.

"She's a character."

Tavish nodded. "We'll still need a meal in two hours."

"There's a cookbook of sorts in my room. I'll go get it." Marianne turned and ran right into him.

Cursing under his breath, he scooped her onto the table.

"You're making a habit of this," Marianne muttered. "I'm not a doll you can just move around as you will."

"Just stay put." Tavish rested against the table, his two hands on either side of her, his body locked, refusing to leave her side.

"You are being beastly," she breathed. Her cheeks flushed and she parted her lips.

The word pierced him. He stiffened and backed away. "You're right. I am a monster."

She grabbed his left arm. "I would never call you that."

"You just did." He couldn't look at her—couldn't face the disgust he knew must be etched on her face. And yet, he couldn't leave, his body even now craving her touch.

"No, I called your *actions* beastly." She stroked his arm as if he were a skittish animal she needed to soothe.

He swallowed. A skittish beast.

"Perhaps my choice of words was poor. Your actions... " She squeezed his arm. "They're driving me mad."

"I can't help it." He inspected the floor tiles.

"Look at me," she demanded.

He obeyed, but still couldn't meet her eyes.

"Tavish, what will it take to make you see that I don't care about your metal parts? They're part of you, but they don't define you. What are you afraid of?"

How to answer? *That you'll leave. That all the people in my past were right. That I truly am a beast.* He couldn't say any of those things. "That I'll hurt you."

She tugged on his arm until he shifted closer, then she tipped up his head. "You'll never hurt me."

"How can you stand to be near me?" he whispered.

She touched his cheek. "If you can stand to be near a lady who's failed at everything she's attempted, then I don't see why I should have a problem with you."

He met her eyes, caught and held her gaze. "If you promise not to call yourself a failure, I won't call myself a monster."

"I suppose it can't hurt. Who knows, maybe if we keep at it, we'll eventually believe it." Her lips turned up in the corner in a gentle smile that sent his heart racing.

Tavish looked at the broken autochef. "Time for a confession. I can't cook."

"Me either," she chuckled. "We'll have to do our best. There have to be some simple recipes in that cookbook. Surely between the two of us we can manage, and Quinn will have it fixed or at least working again soon."

"We still have to have a meal prepared in two hours that can feed 600." Tavish arched a brow.

Marianne swallowed. "Will the crew mutiny if we serve them more cold meat and cheese? I think there's cold chicken from last night, and I was baking more bread when the autochef broke. We might have enough."

"That should be fine." He shrugged. "With luck, Quinn will have the autochef working by next watch."

Marianne rested her hands on his chest. "Will you kiss me again?"

Tavish sucked in a breath as his body instantly reacted to her words. It was all he could do to keep the small distance between them. "Marianne, this is madness."

"Please." She cupped his cheek. "I need to learn why I feel different around you. Why you and only you make me feel like I can conquer the world. I need to discover more of how I feel around you. More of what could be."

She gripped the back of his head and tilted it until his lips hovered over hers. "Teach me?"

He couldn't move away—couldn't disengage like he felt he should. He wanted her. God only knew how much.

He took hold of the reins of his desire and pulled back. He couldn't do it. He wouldn't let himself hurt her.

"There's no future for you with me." He managed to say though gritted teeth.

"So you say." Her lips firmed. "I disagree."

He drew back. Each step agonizingly slow. Each step pulling him away from what he really wanted. "I won't risk hurting you."

"I see." Her gaze shuttered and she turned away. "We'd better get that simple meal ready then."

She'd shut him out. The sparkle in her eyes was gone. The light that drew him inexorably toward her, died as she turned, and slipped away to the hatch that led to food storage.

He reached out. "Marianne, I… "

She shrugged off his hand. "You've said enough. Let's get this done so you can tend to all the other obligations you have."

He wanted to resist and fight back. He wanted to tell her she was wrong, but he didn't have the right any longer.

In silence, they pulled out cold chicken, slightly burnt bread, and wedges of cheese. With each trip to gather food, he felt her shut herself further away.

With a heavy heart he left the galley. He was doing the right thing in protecting her. She may be upset now, but she'd thank him later. His own heart? There was no help for it. That was already breaking into tiny pieces.

CHAPTER ELEVEN

How could she have been so stupid? Marianne splashed water on her face and stared into the mirror. How could she think that any man would be interested in her?

She was mousy and inconsequential.

A nobody.

She sighed and headed over to her trunk. More than a day had passed since his rejection and it still stung.

For one brief moment she'd dared to reach for something she wanted and had been smacked down.

She should be used to it by now.

The room tilted and she stumbled against the bed. The pitcher of water crashed to the ground, sending shards of glass darting along the floor.

Before she could right herself she was thrown across the room, her head smacking against the wall. She saw stars.

She shook her head, trying to clear it. What was going on? The candle on the bedside table fell and rolled to the floor and under a towel.

It went up in flames.

Marianne grabbed a blanket from the bed and put the fire out.

The kitchens!

The autochef had a coal furnace that was always lit. If it were disturbed it could light the whole place up. Most of the hull was made from metal but there was enough wood in there to be a real danger. With the ship shuddering around her she struggled to her bedroom hatch. The door swung open and she stumbled into the galley.

Grabbing the edge of the counter, she took stock. The pots, pans, and everything that hadn't been bolted down or shut tight littered the floor. The cupboards holding the dishes were still secure, one more thing to thank to proper ship design. At least she didn't have to deal with more broken crockery.

The autochef stood tall, seemingly untouched by the chaos.

That didn't mean a fire hadn't started inside.

She picked her way between fallen debris as the ship heaved violently again.

Shouts and the pounding feet of airmen sounded above her. The cacophony made it hard to think.

The ship tilted nearly sideways and she flew, landing hard against the main galley hatch. Her head smacked into the hand wheel and she sank to the floor.

Blackness closed in, seeping from the edges of her vision, slowly clouding everything.

The coals.

She had to get to the autochef.

"Watch that beam!" Tavish bellowed.

Aether lightening crackled across the darkness, revealing the airmen swarming the masts like army ants on the hunt. Men and women trained by the very best worked as one, securing the loose beam and scurrying to check the ties on the others.

Tavish watched with no small amount of pride as the crew under his command worked with such perfect precision.

The captain was below decks. Her skills and knowledge were better suited to the navigation controls.

For Tavish, there was nothing better than staring the wind in the face, ignoring the storm as it unleashed its fury.

"Watch those life lines!" He shouted down at the peg-legged airman stationed by the tall mainmast and the bundles of lines tied to it. "Make sure they're tight. I don't want to lose a single man tonight."

The airman saluted and dutifully checked the ropes.

The wind changed.

It nailed the Queen of Sheba hard on her port side, sending the ship plummeting starboard. Tavish reached out with lightening reflexes, grabbing the guardrail next to him, holding on as the ship tilted.

A scream rent the air. The helmsman, ripped from the wheel by the sudden wind, dangled ten meters from the ship, a tiny dot nearly lost amongst the stars and raging wind.

"Man overboard!" Tavish bellowed. "Haul him in!"

With a grunt, he pulled himself level with the wheel. Letting go of the rail he fell into it. Using all the strength of his synthetic arm, he hauled the wheel around, stabilizing the floundering ship.

With trembling arms he locked the massive wheel in place, defying the very wind that threatened to destroy the ship.

Sheba steadied.

"Captain says to turn hard to starboard and unfurl the mainsail, sir," Miss Haversham said from her post by the veemitter.

"What?" he asked.

Her voice had barely registered above the wind.

"Hard to starboard and unfurl the mainsail, sir!" Haversham repeated.

"Unfurl the mainsail!" Tavish's deep voice carried over the whining wind.

The crew didn't hesitate as they moved to perform their ordered tasks.

Tavish spun the wheel hard to starboard, harder than he would have thought wise. The ship pitched, shuddering as the full brunt of the gale hit her again, and then the sail was unfurled. It caught the wind, hurling Queen of Sheba forward.

The fallen helmsman crashed to the deck with bone-breaking force. He screamed in agony as other men swarmed to help him.

The wind howled past Tavish's head, but the tug on the wheel eased and the ship moved with the wind, sailing off on her new course as if the aetherstorm raging around her was nothing more than a light spring zephyr.

The energy of that storm still set the hair on his arm standing up, but the ship remained calm, steady on her new heading.

"Captain says to maintain course, sir," Haversham said. "We should leave the storm system in a few minutes."

"Take the helm, Rogers," Tavish ordered the airman stationed behind him.

Rogers, a small, wiry man whose job was to man the signal light at the stern of the ship, obediently stepped forward.

Stepping away from the wheel, Tavish headed to the veemitter. "Ship is steady on her heading, captain."

"Excellent, repair to the navigation at your earliest convenience, Mr. Tavish."

"Aye, aye, ma'am."

The faint whiff of smoke hit his nostrils.

His stomach churned. There was nothing more terrifying on an aether voyage than a fire on ship.

He followed his nose, peering over the edge of the stern rail. Tendrils of smoke rose from the galley portholes like dancing snakes.

The fear that clenched his stomach, moved to his heart. Dear God, he thought. Not that. Not now.

"Fire!" His body was in motion before he'd realized he'd shouted.

"Where?"

Tavish didn't know who had spoken and didn't care. "The galley."

He ripped the stern hatch open, and dropped the two meters to the floor below, not bothering with the ladder.

He had to get to her—had to make sure she was safe.

The storm had taken all his attention, but he should have had someone warn her.

Damn his stupidity. She could be dead and it would be his fault. He hadn't warned her. He hadn't taught her enough.

Dizziness threatened to send him falling to the floor. He shook it away. He couldn't panic. He had to stay calm.

He reached the galley door, airmen with buckets right behind him.

"Marianne." He slammed his hand on the galley hatch panel.

Nothing happened.

He turned the wheel and pushed against the door.

It budged open a crack.

Something had fallen in front, blocking him form opening it further.

"Marianne," he called again.

No answer.

He pushed harder, shoving the door open despite the weight holding it shut. He saw her.

She was folded over, her body now wedged between the hatch and the nearest bench.

A fire raged, not ten feet from him, but he didn't care. All he could think about was helping her. Getting her to safety.

The tangy smell of copper, barely noticeable over the acrid smell of burning wood, assaulted his nose and he looked down at his feet. Blood.

Her blood.

He knelt down next to her. Her head had rolled to the side, revealing an ugly read gash just behind her left temple.

His throat clenched shut.

He couldn't breathe.

"Please don't be dead," he whispered.

He ripped his glove off his right hand, and pressed his fingers to the base of her neck.

The soft thud of her pulse tickled his fingertips. Her chest rose, shallow but steady. All around him chaos loomed but he only saw that small, soft breath—all he heard was the sound of air escaping those delicate lips.

She was alive.

Praise to God.

She was alive.

He scooped her up, careful to protect her head from further damage, and carried her out of the room, not bothering to give orders.

The men didn't need them.

They would fight the fire.

They would win.

But Marianne?

Her breath was too shallow, her heartbeat too faint.

He had to get her to the doctor. His heart was racing, speeding as if no end was in sight and the race had yet to be won. If only he could give her his own heartbeat. If only he could lend her his strength.

"Starting without me?"

Tavish winced as Captain Ridgewell walked into the room. Her usual neat braid was fraying, her coat torn at the shoulder and she was favoring her right leg.

"No, ma'am, just making sure we had all the information you needed." He rose and pulled out a chair for her. "We don't want to waste any of your time."

Ridgewell took the chair and sent him one of her rare smiles. "How are we doing?"

"The ship's in fairly good shape, all things considered." Tavish took his seat and nodded at the six other people at the table. Of the senior officers, the only one missing was Quinn. She was too busy keeping the ship running. "I'm sure you're aware of the sail damage but it looks like Sam's original estimates on the engine damage might have been off."

"Just like her to jump to conclusions," Galveson sniffed.

"Miss Quinn isn't one to cry wolf, ma'am." Mitchell Owens, the ship's sailing master jumped in.

Ridgewell held up her hand and shot a quelling glance at Galveson. "I know, Mitchell. You don't have to defend her. I'm just glad they aren't as bad as they looked. After what I've seen, some good news is pleasant."

Doctor Starrett squirmed in his seat. "It's not all roses, ma'am."

Tavish shook his head at the doctor. "What Doc's trying to say is that while the ship is indeed in better shape than we thought, we will need to make port as soon as possible."

Ridgewell wiped a hand down her face. "Just tell me what happened, gentleman."

"The aetherwhale was injured," Tavish said.

"At some point, one of the port-side air tubes came loose. When it did, at the speeds we were traveling… " Starrett's voiced trailed off, his face ash white. He swallowed. "As can be imagined, the tube severed the tentacle it housed. It took me nearly an hour to get the bleeding to stop, and despite everything I did, it doesn't look good. I suspect there's internal damage but we don't know enough about whale anatomy to know for sure."

"I see." Ridgewell's face remained rigid, her voice cool. Only someone who knew her well would notice the pain etched in her violet eyes.

"The crew is likely to take the news hard. The bleeding was intensive and not easy to hide. So, rumors are already spreading. The sooner we make the announcement, the better, I think." Tavish spoke over everyone's grief, saying what had to be said even though the words lanced his heart. The aetherwhale had grown with the Sheba. Inserted as a tiny infant before the hull had been completed, in many ways the whale was the Sheba.

Replacements could be found but it wouldn't be the same. The crew wouldn't be the same.

"Can we make it to New Richmond?" Ridgewell asked.

"That's what Sam's up to. She's coaxing as much power as she can from the engines. We're burning a hell… " Tavish coughed. "Sorry, ma'am. We're burning a lot of fuel, but we should make it to port before our air runs out."

"A necessary expense under the circumstances," she replied.

"We're going to have to get a new whale before we can leave New Richmond." Tavish leaned back and placed the biggest burden yet on the captain's shoulders. He had no idea how to fix this. He'd racked his brain trying to come up with a solution, but he just didn't know what to do. "New Richmond won't have the facilities for that."

"I know." Ridgewell tapped her fingers on the table. "I have a few contacts I can call on."

She leaned back in her chair. "Well, I hope that's the worst of it. What else can you tell me?"

Galveson picked up the report. "The rudder had minor damage but that's something we can fix with what we have on hand once we reach a port. The main mast is dangerously splintered and will need to be replaced. We lost three sails... "

Tavish tuned him out. He had the report in front of him and could read it for himself. For now, he stared at the captain. He was curious as to how she was going to solve their problem. She seemed so certain. So calm.

He hadn't slept in more than 24 hours and he knew the captain hadn't, either. Yet despite her rumpled appearance she was still coolheaded—a rock standing in the middle of rapids, unwavering in the onslaught of raging water.

She had to be as tired as he was but she wouldn't admit it. She'd work until she collapsed.

"Ma'am, as we seem to have everything under control, I think you should rest," Tavish interrupted Galveson.

"I'm not tired."

"Liar." Tavish shook his head. "Captain, you're no good to us dead on your feet. If an emergency crops up, we'll call you."

She narrowed her eyes at him. "You aren't any more rested then I am."

"No, but my orders won't be the ones we rely on in a crisis. Go rest, we'll keep Sheba running for you."

That captain yawned. Then, looking around the table, she blushed. "Fine, but I want to be informed the moment something happens."

Tavish couldn't hide his smile as he all but pushed her toward her cabin. "Go."

He watched her leave and then turned back to the assembled officers. "Galveson, take over for Mr. Burshe in Navigation. You're the most rested of us."

Galveson nodded and left. The storm had rattled him. He'd been pale-faced and quiet for most of the meeting. Even the quip at Quinn had been half-hearted. Perhaps the storm was a wake-up call for the pup.

"Oliver, take watch at Helm. The rest of you get some rest. We all have a busy day ahead of us."

"I need to check on the infirmary," Starrett said.

"Doc, same rules apply to you as to everyone else. You're no good to us if you fall over from exhaustion," Tavish warned.

"I have to check on Miss Lindstrom and Mr. Alleyway."

Marianne.

A pang hit Tavish in the chest. "Check on them and then rest."

Starrett nodded. "I will."

The other crewmen filed out of the meeting room and Tavish sank into his chair. Was Marianne doing so poorly that she needed such constant attention? He rubbed his temples. He had a million things to do. He should help Quinn in Engineering, or Freddy down in the storerooms making sure their food supplies were covered.

"Aw, hell," he muttered. He wasn't going to do any of that until he'd checked on Marianne.

He grabbed his hat from the hook on the wall and stormed out of the room.

Navigation was silent, so many of the consoles having been gutted for parts needed elsewhere. A single directioner was doing the load of five. Galveson and two airmen were all that was needed on watch now. Every other hand was either catching some rest or working on repairs.

Or injured.

He gritted his teeth. Too many of the crew had been hurt. He'd been so certain they'd miss the storm. He hadn't even thought about it again after he'd changed their course. Now all those people were hurt because he let himself get distracted.

He should have been paying better attention. He'd failed everyone—the captain and crew.

And Marianne.

He'd failed her most of all. He'd taken a young woman who had no experience up here and thrust her into a job she wasn't qualified for. And to top it all off, he'd hurt her.

It had radiated in her eyes as she'd dismissed him. She hadn't called him back to the galley after that. If she needed anything she'd gone to Freddy.

She hadn't woken since the fire and that worried him. It worried Doctor Starrett, too. What if she didn't wake up? What if the last words to her had been his rejection?

Doctor Starrett was standing over the helmsman's bed as he entered the infirmary.

"I thought I told you to rest." Tavish kept his voice low as he approached. Sleeping, injured airmen lined the cots, the floors, even the examination tables. He had to step around them to reach Doc. The more injured patients he kept nearer his office.

Starrett shrugged. "I will. I wanted to do another round of checks first."

"Any change in Mr. Aleyway?" Tavish looked over at Miss Lindstrom's bed. She looked so small and pale against the stark, white sheets, so fragile.

"Mr. Alleyway's fine. The fever is down and his leg is setting nicely." Starrett moved to stand next to Tavish. "Miss Lindstrom hasn't changed since the last time you checked on her."

Tavish blushed. "I ahh… feel responsible for her."

Starrett slapped him on the shoulder and shook his head. "Sure you do. Her breathing is getting better, less shallow."

"Shouldn't she have woken up by now?" Tavish wrung his hands.

"Sometimes, especially with head wounds, the body forces sleep. She'll wake when she's healed enough. In the meantime, we feed her broth and watch."

"Are you sure?"

"As sure as I can be." Starrett patted him on the back again and walked toward his office. "You can sit with her a while, but be quiet. There are other patients in here who need the rest."

Tavish pulled up a stool and held one of Marianne's hands. He'd never felt so helpless, so unless. "Marianne, if you wake up, I promise I'll be the man you need. Please wake up."

For the first time since he'd joined the army, Tavish prayed.

CHAPTER TWELVE

"How'd you manage this?" Tavish blinked at the fully rigged royal navy repair ship pulling into dock next to Sheba.

Ridgewell stood with her hands behind her back watching the progress of RNRS Decker. "I called in a favor."

He snorted. "It must have been a big favor."

"Would you like me to send them back?"

"No, ma'am." Tavish laughed.

Decker was a premier navy repair ship, with the ability to completely refit a warship in the aether. For all intents and purposes it was a mobile repair slip.

Before Decker had settled into its parking orbit, a small personal craft launched from its boat bay and headed toward Sheba.

"That would be Captain Lyall. I take it you have our requirements laid out in a nice, neat report for him?" Ridgewell raised an eyebrow.

Tavish handed her the report. "Have I ever let you down?"

She chuckled. "No."

Her gaze darted across the pages. "We'll need to give the crew alternating shore leave. Decker's crew will need some of them aboard to finish repairs, but we won't have enough room for them all to be aboard at the same time."

"Agreed. I've already finished the schedule and handed it the chiefs."

"Mr. Tavish?" a deep voice rang out

"Yes." He turned to see a surprisingly short and scrawny med tech approach. "Mr. Gorse, what can I do for you?"

"Doctor Starrett says that Miss Lindstrom has woken up."

"Ah... " Tavish shuffled his feet and rubbed the back of his neck.

"Go." Ridgewell shooed him away, laughing. "I can manage well enough without you."

He followed after the med tech.

Marianne was sitting up when he entered the infirmary.

"How are you feeling?" He hurried over.

"Like I was hit over the head by a cricket bat," she whispered.

"Not far from the truth."

She eyed him warily. "Why are you here?"

"I, ah... " He fisted his hands. "I had to know you were okay."

"It's been all I could do to keep him from your bedside," Doctor Starrett said from the doorway of his office. "He'd have sat vigil the entire time you were out if I had let him."

Tavish's cheeks heated. "It's just that I feel responsible for her."

"Of course." Marianne's bright eyes shuttered.

He scowled at Starrett.

The doctor simply shrugged and walked back into his office.

"I'm sure you have other duties you should be seeing to." Marianne played with the fabric of her blanket. "I shouldn't keep you."

He took her hands in his and squeezed. "I'm happy you're awake. I was worried."

"But you don't like me." She turned her gaze to their joined hands.

"I never said that." He took a deep breath. "I didn't want to hurt you."

"You did."

"I know." He rubbed his fingers over her knuckles. "When you feel up to it, I'd like to take you up on your offer. If it's still on the table, that is."

She looked away. "You left."

"I was a fool." He patted her hand. "Don't answer me now. Get some rest. I'll visit again once you're released from the infirmary."

She nodded.

He smiled and rose, his heart lighter than when he entered. He could teach her what she wanted to know. If his heart was broke in the process, that was his fault. He would learn to deal with it.

"Can I leave yet?" Marianne squeezed her hands under the coverlet. "I'm growing restless."

It had been three day since she'd woken and still she was in bed.

Doctor Starrett pulled out a magnesium light. A bright flash went off, blinding her.

His smiling face returned. He was a handsome man. Dark skinned, with vibrant green eyes. Gentle and intelligent, he was the kind of man she should have been attracted to. Instead her heart seemed stuck on a reticent cyborg who saw her as a burden. She was pathetic.

"You seem well enough, and your eyes are dilating correctly." He put his tool down on a table. "But rest often."

She waved her hand in a throw-away gesture. "I doubt I'll have difficulty with that. I haven't anything to do at all."

"Your clothes are in the trunk by the bed." He winked at her. "Get dressed and go check out the galley. You might be surprised at what you find."

With those cryptic words he shut the screen around her bed and left.

She quickly threw on some clothes. Cryptic or no, at least it gave her a direction.

It took her thirty minutes to find the kitchens. The ship was a mess. Corridors were cut where no corridors had been before and some that should be there were blocked off completely. In the end, she'd had to ask for directions.

The galley hatch was open and she could see men scurrying about inside.

The wooden kitchen island was missing but that didn't surprise her. It had likely burned when the galley had caught fire. Around the frenzy of activity, she could just make out the gleaming bronze replacement.

Freddy ducked out of the hatch. "Hello, miss. I'm so happy to see you."

"It was a nasty bump but it seems I'm ready to work again."

"Oh, wait until you see it. I'm green with envy." He shook her hand so hard she staggered.

She couldn't help but laugh. "What has you so excited?"

"The new autochef, of course." He pushed her toward the hatch.

Stumbling inside, she caught her breath. The kitchens were gone, no more cupboards, no more stove. What she'd thought was the new kitchen island was in fact a new autochef. Sitting dead center in the middle of the room, it was at least three times larger than its predecessor with nozzles and gears, levers and pulleys jutting off in every direction.

The previous autochef had been intimidating. This one was simply ridiculous. How was she to manage it?

"This can handle a week's worth of meals in a single program. It's capable of self-sustained cooking. All we have to do is make sure it has the proper supply of raw materials." Freddy stopped beside her.

She forced a smile. "It would appear I've become redundant."

His smile fell. "I'm sure we'll still need you to manage menus and order food supplies."

"Indeed." Ridgewell walked into the galley. "I hope you're not thinking of leaving us."

"Well," Marianne hedged. "You don't really need me."

"Come walk with me." Ridgewell waved toward the open hatch.

Marianne followed her up to the quarterdeck. Airmen parted before them like waves at the prow of a ship. The captain didn't have to say a word. Each man looked up at her as if she were some mythical creature.

Marianne tilted her head. They'd never shown that sort of awe before. Respect and obedience, yes, but some of those faces were worshipful.

"Why is everyone looking at you like you walk on water?" she asked.

The captain blushed, a delicate, rosy hue that made her look years younger. "I imagine it has something to do with how a navy repair ship found its way out here."

Marianne chuckled. "Then the expressions of awe are understandable. It can't be easy to commandeer that sort of ship. Even a landlubber like myself knows that."

"Yes, well... Let's just say someone owed me a favor." Ridgewell paused by the rail, gaze resting on the stars. "Do you want to leave Sheba?"

The question, seemingly out of the blue and abrupt, made Marianne pause to think.

Over the days she'd spent on board she'd come to love life in the aether. There had been times where she'd struggled, times when she'd been outright frightened, but it had been invigorating to finally do something on her own. For the first time, she was her own woman.

But did she belong here?

The new autochef didn't require a full time cook and she wouldn't survive a day under the conditions a typical airman endured.

"I don't want to be a burden," she whispered.

"That didn't answer my question."

"In a way, it did." Marianne stared out at the brilliant waves of aether air, a colorful vision of dancing light. The aether sang to her. Called her to remain, but she needed a purpose. She had to feel like she belonged. That she wasn't charity.

"If I found a job for you, would you stay?" Ridgewell asked.

Marianne whipped her head around. "What kind of job?"

"I need a secretary."

"You do?" Marianne frowned. Was this just make-work?

"I must warn you. This is not an easy job. I have a great deal of correspondence. I will work you to the bone." Ridgewell stood with legs braced apart and regarded Marianne with a level gaze. "This will be in addition to your work as cook. You will still need to manage the meal planning, maintain food supplies, and keep an eye on the autochef."

"You're not just making up a job for me?"

"I do not do charity." Ridgewell stiffened. "I assure you the need is real."

"And you can tell I'd be right for the job after a week and a half?" Marianne asked. "Part of which I was unconscious."

"You don't flinch from responsibility, challenges, or what you believe in." Ridgewell shrugged. "I trust you enough."

Marianne lifted her hand to her throat. "You're serious?"

"I'm not accustomed to people questioning me."

Taking a deep breath, Marianne held out her hand. "Then I accept."

"Excellent." Ridgewell shook Marianne's hand. "You'll start today. We'll need to find an office of some sort for you nearby mine, but for now you can work off a corner of my desk."

Confused and lighthearted, Marianne followed behind the captain toward her office. So many people were putting their trust in her and she was not going to let them down.

"Ouch!" Marianne sucked on her injured finger."

"Slam your finger in the door?" Tavish stepped up behind her.

She jumped and held her hand to her chest. How did a man that large move so quietly? "The spring on the control panel door is tight. It snaps back fast."

He took her hand in his and gently massaged. "I'll ask Quinn if she can't fix the door so it's not so dangerous."

Her cheeks heated. "I hadn't thought to ask her."

His calloused fingers stroked her hand. "Have you figured out how to make it work?"

Marianne nodded. "I think so. The manual was detailed."

"I'm glad. Do you enjoy your other duties?" His fingers continued their slow work on her hand.

Tingles of pleasure spread up her arm at the intimate touch. "Why are you here?"

"I wanted to know if I could have a second chance." He raised her hand to his lips and kissed her wrist.

Marianne regretted the lack of a chair. Her legs were jelly, barely holding her up. "A second chance at what?"

"To teach and learn from you," he purred.

She gazed up in his eyes and saw the longing deep within. "What changed your mind?"

"Life is too short for us not to take a chance at happiness." He brushed a loose strand of hair back from her face. "I wasn't wrong when I said there was no future for you with me, but if you still want to learn, I'm willing to teach you."

Her stomach fluttered and she swallowed. "And you're here for my first lesson."

He stepped closer, tipping her head back. "If you want it."

She held up her hand between them. "I don't agree that there's no future between us, but I will agree to take things one day at a time."

His lips curved up in a smile that reached his eyes. Joy danced within the steel gray depths of his good eye. Then his lips were on hers, hard and demanding. He instantly fanned the flames of her desire. Then he stepped back, leaving her panting for breath.

"First lesson: how far just a kiss can go." He didn't even sound winded, but the rapid rise of his shoulders belied his composure.

He was as affected as she.

She smiled at him and tilted her head to the side to gaze through her lashes. "And just how far can it go?"

He traced his hand down her arm, sending pinpricks of desire shooting through her. "As far as we want it to."

She glanced around the galley. Not a chair in sight. "Shall we repair to my bedroom?"

"No, not this time." He led her to the wall and then spun her so her back rested against it.

"Here?" she whispered.

"Yes."

"But anyone can come in."

"There's a lock on the hatch." His mouth was on her again and thought disappeared.

Her hands, pressed against his chest, rose to wrap around his neck. All she could do was hold on for the ride.

And what a ride.

His tongue waltzed with hers, an intricate dance, yet simple enough to follow. She pressed her body against his, fitting her softness against his strength.

He growled deep in his throat and angled his head. Demanding more.

She complied, opening herself to his delectation. His hands never moved from the wall on either side of her head. Only his lips touched her. They trailed across her mouth, down her throat, and stopping over her pulse, they sucked.

She arched into his embrace. Her nerves tingled with raw power.

But it wasn't enough. She was putty in his hands but she wanted more. She wanted him to break, to lose control of his thoughts as easily as she did.

She kissed him back. Her tongue did the dancing. Her tongue courted his.

"Marianne," he warned, his body tensing under her onslaught. His hands shifted behind her but didn't move. They remained rigid, locked in place.

She broke from this kiss. "We've been here before. Take me further."

She trailed kisses across his lips and down his neck. Over the scar until she too found his pulse. Then copying him, she sucked, licked, and tasted the saltiness of his skin.

"Marianne." His hands moved up to cup her waist.

Her body hummed as she explored. Who knew that giving pleasure would grant her so much in return?

He groaned. "My pace."

She smiled against his skin. "I never agreed to that."

Squeezing his face between her hands, she pressed a kiss to his lips. Giving him all the heat she could muster. She wanted him to take her further along desire's road, and that meant bending his control.

He scooped her up and carried her to the pass-through counter. Stepping between her legs he tipped back her head. "You want further, we'll go further but only one step."

"One step?" She licked her lips.

He stroked her cheek. "How will you learn if we rush to the end?"

His lips covered hers again but the flare of fire was absent. Instead, a low heat infused her limbs, her blood, and her skin. It was warmth all the more powerful for its lack of flame. It covered her and pulled her under. She reveled in its glory.

His hands lifted to her face, caressing her hair, her neck. They trailed down to her chest and palming one small globe, gently squeezed.

Her world spun. Even through the boning in her corset, the contact seared her.

He stopped the kiss, his lips hovering inches from hers. "Lesson two: the power of touch."

His fingers tantalized her skin as he pulled the first button on her blouse from its hole.

Her eyes slid shut.

"No, keep them open. Don't hide your passion from me." His voice was gentle yet demanding.

She opened her eyes, gaze locked on his.

His bionic eye, normally an opalescent white, was now a stormy purple. It mesmerized her, pulling her deeper under his spell.

He worked on her buttons until her blouse was spread wide over her shoulders, pinning her arms behind her.

He stepped back, his gaze roaming over her. "Beautiful."

With her arms caught in her blouse, she was trapped, open for his enjoyment.

She shivered and glanced down. The white mounds of her breasts pressed up by the corset rose and fell with each shuddering breath.

"Don't look away from you skin," he ordered.

The feather from his hat came into view. It caressed her cheek, her neck, and dropped lower, snaking over the soft mounds of flesh.

What should have tickled, burned. Her white skin became rosy with each inhalation, each tantalizing touch of that soft feather.

A longing she didn't understand grew inside her. She wanted something. Desperately. She didn't know what it was.

"Tavish, I—" Her breath caught.

His lips, chapped and wind burned, rasped her skin, replacing the soft feather. Her eyes fell shut and she tipped her head back, letting him take his fill.

He moaned. "God, you taste so good."

His tongue dipped along the seam of her corset. The cool air caressed her enflamed skin and the pressure within her grew until all she could do was hold his head to her breast and ride out the storm.

He eased back. His tongue slowly traced along the edge of her corset and then trailed up her neck.

"A simple touch can leave you wanting." He pressed his lips to hers in a demanding kiss. "Or leave you content."

He gentled the kiss, abating the building pressure until it was no more than a dull throb at her core.

Pulling away, he lifted her shirt back over her shoulders and re-buttoned it.

His hands resting on her shoulders he gazed into her eyes. His breathing was heavy, his bionic eye pulsating with deep purple hues. "That's enough for now."

She managed a shaky nod. "Yes."

He squeezed and released her. "Until next time."

She watched him leave, her own mind still jumbled. She'd wanted to learn more, to experience all there was to know in this arena. Yet she hadn't counted on the intensity of her feelings for him.

She still remembered his straight face, the blocked expression when he told her she had no future with him—still remembered the pain those words had caused her.

As a young girl, she'd imagined the handsome hero who would rescue her from her tower. A gentle, soft-spoken man who'd whisk her off to his castle.

Tavish was as far from the handsome hero of her childhood dreams as a man could get, but he was the man she wanted. A man who hid away from the world and kept everyone at a distance.

She was a fool.

She wanted to continue, needed to understand the woman she became in his arms. But what cost was she willing to pay? If she continued, she risked more than her virtue. She risked her heart.

CHAPTER THIRTEEN

Three days since their last lesson and Marianne's body still thrummed. She stared without seeing the pile of correspondence on her desk and relived the moments in the galley.

She'd been waiting for Tavish to come to her again but he hadn't.

Should she go to him? Did she dare look so eager?

She'd come to terms with her heart. It was impossible for her not to fall for him, and if she were completely honest with herself she'd admit she'd already done so.

But he didn't have to know that.

"Excuse me, miss?"

Marianne looked up to see a airman standing in the doorway. Had he knocked and she just hadn't heard? She shook her head, to clear it of cobwebs.

"How can I help you… Carlsby, is it?"

The airman nodded. "Yes, miss."

"Well?"

Carlsby handed her a card. "There's a Mr. Jacobs here to see you."

Marianne glanced at it. A solicitor, and one from London at that. What was he doing here? She shrugged. The only way she'd find out would be to see him. "Thank you, Carlsby. Please show the gentleman in."

Marianne quickly organized her desk. She managed to finish just as Carlsby returned with a tall, thin gentleman in tow. He was impeccably dressed in a tailored suit and polished black shoes that had to come from a master boot maker. He carried an overcoat over his arm and his gloves, cane, and top hat were held next to a solid looking leather briefcase. Marianne rose and held out her hand. "Mr. Jacobs, I presume?"

The man shook her hand and smiled warmly. "Yes, and you are Miss Marianne Lindstrom?"

"That's correct." Marianne looked at the airman standing by the door. "Thank you, Carlsby, that will be all."

Marianne motioned to a chair, one of only two in her small office. "Won't you please have a seat, Mr. Jacobs?"

He sat down, placing the briefcase on the floor next to him.

"May I offer you anything? Tea perhaps? I can have some brought up." Marianne asked as she turned her desk chair to face him.

"That won't be necessary." Mr. Jacobs smiled again. "I'm here on business from a former client, Miss Lindstrom. I won't take up much of your time."

She tilted her head and leaned forward.

Jacobs reached into his briefcase and pulled out a rectangular package wrapped in brown paper and a small white envelope. He handed them over to her. "My late client, Mrs. Attewater, wished for you to have this."

"But I don't know anyone named Mrs. Attewater," she murmured, taking the package.

Mr. Jacobs closed the briefcase. "I understand she explained everything in the letter." Rising he extended his hand. "It's been a pleasure, Miss Lindstrom, and I'm glad I was able to catch up with you."

Marianne started. He was leaving? Instinct and good breeding took over and she rose and shook the solicitor's hand. "Thank you, for taking the time and traveling so far. Your dedication to your clients is commendable."

He bowed over her hand. "If you find yourself in need of legal services in the future, do not hesitate to call. Our office number is on the card."

"I'll show you out." She put the package down on the chair started to move toward the door but Jacobs stopped her.

"I can find my own way out, miss." He said. "It's just down the hall."

"I assure you it would be a pleasure." She blushed. "Besides, I really can't let you wander the ship unattended. The captain wouldn't approve."

"Of course,"

As they walked Marianne tried to keep her mind off of the mysterious package and the letter that came with it. She only halfway succeeded. As soon as Jacobs had stepped off the gangway, she hurried back to her office. Showing more restraint then she felt, she opened the letter first. It was written in a close neat hand.

My Dearest Marianne,

I know you will find this letter mysterious. For, as far as you know, we haven't met. I assure you that we have. Though I haven't been allowed to see you since you were a toddler I have kept watch over you. Despite your father's obvious neglect you have grown into a beautiful young woman. I am more proud of you then I can say.

Your mother was my niece. A lovelier, gentler lady you will never have met and I wish you could have known her. She was taken too young and I regret the consequences of her early death on you, my dear. Your mother's death hit your father harder than anything I have ever seen. He was always a hard man but with your mother around, he was tolerable. He doted on her. She died, as you know, giving birth to a stillborn son, and your father blamed you.

It wasn't fair, and it wasn't right, but there was no way to alter his mind. He was convinced that you had weakened his wife and while he couldn't disown you without dishonoring your mother, he could hate you. I tried to intervene and get him to see reason. I even attempted to persuade him to let you live with me. He refused and flat out ordered me to stay away. I decided my continual interference could only hurt you and so I kept my distance.

I wish now that this letter could reach you under better circumstances. I had wished that before I died I would have the privilege of holding your hand again and of seeing you sit across from me at dinner. However, that is not to be and I must make alternate plans.

I am quite ill. The doctor informs me that I have not long to live, and I do not expect your father to change his mind where I am concerned. Therefore, I must perform my final act as your godmother posthumously through a letter.

Your mother lingered after giving birth to little George and she tasked me with caring for you and for delivering to you a book that had been in her family's possession for as long as anyone could remember. She wanted to be sure that you would one day receive the gift. With a heavy heart I took on this burden, for your mother was my dearest friend. I was not ready to say goodbye but I knew that she would not rest easy unless her request was honored.

I have struggled to find a way to deliver this book to you since you left school but it became even more difficult for me to approach you afterward. Your father had only gotten more severe as he aged, and he became ever more paranoid where you are concerned.

I entrusted this final bequest to my solicitors. I knew they would be able to reach you where I could not. Your father would not deny them admittance.

I hope you will not think less of me for my neglect of you. I hope you will understand why circumstances left me with no option but to watch you grow from afar. You have turned out as lovely as your mother and with an equally sweet disposition if tales are true. I send you my love and best wishes for your continued happiness.

Yours,
Marianne Mathilda Attewater

A single tear fell down her cheek and she brushed it away. The letter was just one more example of how much her father hated her. Reverently placing the letter on the small table next to her, she picked up the box. She cut through the brown string and the paper folded open on her lap, revealing a book.

It was an odd-looking but expertly crafted book. Its cover was made of leather in a shimmering aquamarine blue. Covered in tiny small lapis chips, the book shimmered as if it were covered in fish scales. A large oval, lined in gold and lapis lazuli stood out from the front cover. Inside, written in black stitching were the words: *Kis Tapí À Asər À Kalò*

She frowned. What could it mean?

Opening the cover, she found thick paper, elegantly embossed and hand painted. Strange words stared back at her from the page.

It seemed she now owned a beautiful, handcrafted book written in a language she'd never seen before.

She looked at the letter from her godmother. One mystery solved, only to be given another.

Three days since he'd had any time alone with Marianne. The absence was distracting. He couldn't focus.

"Are you even listening?" The captain waved her hand in front of his face.

"Sorry, Ma'am." He rubbed his nose. "Are you sure you put the ledgers in your safe?"

"Positive." Ridgewell paced about her office. Her movements were frantic, erratic.

He'd never seen her like this. "It was just the ledgers?"

She paused in her pacing. "Do you realize how much damage those ledgers could cause in the wrong hands?"

He frowned. "No."

"If more are stolen, those ledgers could show anyone what was being shipped and where. England's enemies could use that information to stop important shipments of foodstuffs, or base materials for things like gunpowder."

He blinked. "You think there's something nefarious going on?"

She threw her hands in the air. "All I know is that someone has broken into my office at least twice and stolen documents from me. This time they broke into my safe."

"That is troubling." Tavish looked at the open door to the safe and frowned. It was sitting on the floor. The work crew had taken it out to repair the interior walls after reinsertion of the new aetherwhale. "It was locked after Decker's crew left?"

"Yes, and everything was still in there. I checked." She bared her teeth. "Damn it, I want this thief found."

Her usual cool voice was hot enough to scald.

"I'll find out." He crossed to the door. "In the meantime, have Decker install a new safe."

"Mmhmm." Ridgewell stared at the safe, her face ash white.

Something had frightened her, and Tavish didn't like that at all. Was it really ledgers that were stolen? Or had something else been taken?

He shook his head. It didn't matter. If there was a thief on board, he had better find out who it was. It was his job, after all.

Shutting the door to Ridgewell's office, he heard singing coming from down the hall. Marianne's melodious soprano soothed his agitation and he caught himself smiling. Even with the distraction, his life had been better since she'd come aboard.

It was hard to believe that in three short weeks so much of his life had changed.

His smile fell.

Three weeks?

The first documents went missing off the captain's desk two weeks ago.

It couldn't be Marianne. She was too sweet-natured, too kind to be a thief. But would he know? He was smitten with her, had been since he saw her the first time. She could easily have gotten under his skin and....

He bit back a growl. It was a possibility he had to investigate.

He strode into the room. Marianne sat back against her chair, her pen moving about the paper in front of her with practiced ease. The wall lamp cast the room in a gold glow that brought out the strawberry of her hair.

He swallowed. How did one go about a subject like this? Shutting the door, he turned the lock and leaned against it.

Marianne looked up and smiled. Joy and happiness were spread across her face like a welcome mat. But the smile slowly faded. She rose and hurried over. "What's wrong? Something happened?"

"Someone has stolen important documents from the captain's safe." His voice sounded flat to his own ears and he winced.

She shrank back. "And you suspect it was me."

"They started disappearing shortly after you arrived on board."

"That doesn't mean I did it."

He rubbed the back of his neck. "I know, but I have to investigate."

She backed away from him. "So you plan on locking me in here with you until I confess?"

"No, I… " He pushed away from the door. "You're free to go if you want to. It's just… Well, I have to ask."

"I would never steal anything." Her voice wavered. "You should know that."

"I do, but the circumstances…." He clenched his fists. "Look, I have to be seen to investigate. And if I thought of the connection, others will too."

She closed her eyes and raised a hand to her neck. "When were the first documents taken?"

"Just before we hit the aetherstorm."

"And the other times?"

"I only know of one other time. The captain seems to think there were more." He paced her small room. Which meant he took three steps and turned around again. "It happened again while Decker was repairing her office."

"I could have done it both times. I had access the second time and the first I was alone most of the day."

"Agreed." He pounded the wall.

She placed a hand on his arm. "Wait, I haven't left the ship. Anyone leaving has to inform the officer of the watch so it can be noted in the log, and there's always a guard stationed by the gangway."

"So?"

"So, if I haven't left, but I did steal the documents, then they have to be somewhere on the ship, like, say—my room."

He brightened. "I hadn't thought of that."

"Search my room. You'll find nothing."

"I'll have someone else search the room. I don't want anyone saying I played favorites."

Marianne shrugged and made to sit down at her desk again.

"Now that we have that out of the way… " He pulled her into his arms.

She squeaked, landing hard against his chest, her nose digging into his neckerchief.

"How can we waste such a wonderful opportunity? A locked room, an empty ship?" He purred into her hair. "Don't you want your next lesson?"

She looked up at him, eyes wide. "Here? Now?"

"Yes." He kissed her cheek and then her ear. "Here."

"What did you have in mind?" Marianne gripped the lapels of his coat. Her arms trembled but her voice remained steady.

His fingers trailed down her cheek and cupped her chin. "Lesson number three: Faster is not always better." He kissed her forehead and nose and finally her lips, taking the time to savor as his lips moved about her face.

She pressed her body in to him. And angling her head, pressed her lips harder, demanding more.

He chuckled and drew back from the kiss. "Today we move slowly."

"How is that moving to the next step? "Marianne's lips hovered above his.

He turned her to face her desk. "Lean your hands on the back of the chair"

Her lips turned up at the corners and her eyes twinkled. "As you wish."

Her words caressed him like a feather and he had to tamp down his roaring desire. Slow. He had to go slow. Standing behind her, his body inches from hers, it was all he could not to close the gap, press his body into her welcoming heat.

He rested his hands on her hips and leaning forward, whispered in her ear. "When you go slow you can feel everything your lover does and anticipate what he'll do next."

She shivered.

A delicate movement that he felt to his bones.

Trailing kisses down her neck he stopped at the base of her throat. "Some of this dance you know. Your body thrums. Already your mind races to figure out what I'll do next."

"What's next?" she breathed.

He didn't answer. Instead he let his hands trace up the curve of her waist. Gently brushing her breasts, he kept going under her arm and over her shoulder until his fingers rested on the buttons at her throat.

"Each touch should heighten the next. Each caress bring you closer to the edge." He nipped her ear lobe.

She gasped, pressing her chest into his hands.

He eased the first button from its hole. "If I had a mirror, I'd make you watch as I undressed you. Instead, you'll have to imagine it.

"Close your eyes, and imagine yourself standing in front of a long mirror. You are fully lit, but your lover is covered in shadow. All you see is his hands." He whispered in her ear.

She sighed, her eyes closing as his fingers released the final button. Her head leaned back to rest on his chest giving him an eyeful of her creamy skin pushed up by her corset.

"Your lover comes to you at night." He pushed her blouse over her shoulders and down off her wrists. It fluttered to the floor. Untying her chemise at the shoulders, he pushed the garment to her waist. "Every night he undresses you."

Her lips opened on a moan as his hand snaked over her shoulders to caress her back.

Savoring each small sound that escaped her lips, he unlaced the back of her corset.

"He always stops here, with you almost bare to him." His fingers hovered over the fasteners at the front of her corset. "You want him to go further but he stops again. What do you do?"

"I beg him," she whispered.

"Beg me," he demanded.

"Please, don't leave me like this."

He traced his fingers down her check and across the soft tops of her breasts. "What is it that you want?"

"More."

"Be explicit, my dear." His voice crackled with desire..

"Bare me. Undress me."

He took her hands and raised them to the front of her corset. "You must open yourself to me. But be warned. What you reveal, I will taste."

She quivered against him as her fingers opened the first fastener.

He stopped her hands.

Her creamy skin, flushed rose with passion, peeked out at him. Blood rushed from his head to his groin causing his erection to pulse against his trousers.

He dipped his head and nipped at her shoulder. He trailed the fingers of his right hand over her breasts, dipping into the opening she'd made.

Her fingers stopped, hovered over the next fastener, her breathing labored but hot.

He trailed kisses down her neck. Stopping at the base, he sucked, tasting the racing beat of her heart.

The furnace of his desire raged higher. His left hand traced her body, roaming over the curve of her hip, the soft round globe of her bottom. Heat radiated from her like she was a steam pipe ready to burst. She was hot and waiting for him, a woman on the edge.

"Please continue," his voice came out guttural, primitive, like his inner beast.

With each slip of her fingers, his erection pulsed harder, straining against its confines. He bit back a groan as the corset opened. It dropped from her lax fingers, falling to the ground. All that lay between him and her skin was a thin cotton underdress.

Her chest rose and fell with each deep, panting breath. Her nipples puckered the thin material.

"Is that all you want to reveal?" He growled, unable to keep to the urbane role he'd scripted.

"No." She untied the laces at her neck. The fabric fell open and one rosy nipple peeked out at him.

His own need was a raging beast ready to devour. He wanted to take her now, leaning up against the chair. All he had to do was lift her skirt, release his erection and he'd have her. She was ready for him. He could feel the heat of her urging him onward.

He throbbed with a pleasure so intense it was almost painful. He bit down on the onslaught of desire. His own release had to wait. He couldn't take her here. She deserved better.

"Will you taste me now?" Her voice was husky as she rested her head against his chest.

She pushed the fabric wide, over her shoulders and down to her hip. She was naked to the waist, ready for his delectation.

His control snapped.

He spun her around and sitting on the chair, he pulled her down to straddle him. "As my lady wishes."

She gripped his shoulders, watching him through a heavy, lidded gaze. Her nipples were erect, flushed, and perfect. Each creamy globe of her breast called to him—begged him to touch.

Keeping his left hand behind her for support, his right played. He tested the weight of first one, then the other. She was small in his large hand, but she moaned in pleasure as his hand roamed. So sensitive, so... He groaned, and locking her gaze with his, he took one delicate peak in his mouth and sucked.

She let out a strangled sound and pressed his head to her breast.

She was so close all it would take was a little pressure. He freed one hand and pressed it to the junction of her thighs. With slow deliberate movements, he brought her to the edge.

She shattered. Her legs, clenching over his, sent waves of heat straight to his groin. The soft sound of her release was music to his ears, a balm to the beast within.

With a final shuddering breath, she collapsed against him. "Oh, my God."

He chuckled and held her. His body urged him to take her now, but his mind was content. His goal was to give her pleasure—to teach her intimacy. He reined in his desire and stroked her back. For now, with her, this was enough.

CHAPTER FOURTEEN

"Well, you were right about the ship still being here." Draven watched the solicitor leave.

"And now you'll need to find out where she is inside. You must interrogate men aboard that ship to learn where the girl is hiding."

Since leaving earth, Shadow had grown paler and paler until now he was barely discernible amongst the backdrop of crates in the darkened alley. Draven had to strain his ears to hear him.

"I could just lure her out."

"I need strength. Pushing that storm weakened me."

Draven's brows shot up. Weakened. He knew Shadow had faded but was it weakened to the point where he could escape?

"Nicholas?" Nora's wavering voice echoed through his ears.

"Not so weak as to have lost control of her," Shadow added. "I have held on for millennia and even at my lowest, I could control the souls of the departed. She will remain with me until the end of days if you do not comply with my wishes."

Draven gritted his teeth. "I need to prepare. I can't elicit the screams you require without drawing notice."

"Make haste. Her torment will only worsen as you delay. I must have strength else they will win." Shadow withdrew.

"Let who win?" Draven asked.

Shadow didn't answer nor did it reappear.

With a shrug, Draven returned to watching the ship. There had be a way to get inside.

A man with thinning brown hair sauntered down the gangway. Chin pointed high, he ignored the men around him.

Draven took note of how the other men looked at him with disdain and scorn on their faces. That was a man who didn't make himself popular with the lower orders.

The tilt of the chin was a common affectation amongst his peers, and several of his friends still used it. A heavy weight lifted from his shoulders and he smiled. He knew how to make friends with men like that and with luck, he wouldn't have to resort to unsavory methods to get the information he wanted.

It wasn't that he was squeamish about torture but he was beginning to see the benefit of a weakened Shadow. The storm unnerved him. What kind of entity could conjure up an aether storm so big it moved entire islands?

He shuddered and pushed the thought aside. He needed the book to save Nora and his son, but he had to do it in such a way that Shadow remained weak.

The haughty man walked passed, and Draven stepped out behind him.

It didn't take long before Haughty Man dipped into a tavern.

The scent of cheap ale and body odor assaulted Draven's nose from across the street. A man like that only entered such a low tavern for nefarious purposes. Draven's smile grew. It was his lucky day.

He had to duck to get through the door. The smoke hovering just under the low ceiling made everything in the room appear hazy. Still, it didn't take him long to find his quarry. Haughty man stood out like a dandy sore thumb in this place.

So did he, for that matter.

He walked into the bar and placed a coin on the counter. As if conjured by a magician, a mug of ale materialized where the coin had lain.

With a nod, he moved to the edge of the bar and waited.

Hunched in a back booth, his quarry looked like a frightened mouse in a room full of cats. This was definitely not his normal milieu.

A small wiry man in a black coat, a scarf pulled over his nose, and hat jammed down on his head slid into the booth across from Haughty.

Haughty didn't look up from his ale, just slid a package over the table. The wiry man looked it over and passed coin back to him. "Pleased to do business with you, Herr Galveson."

Galveson's head shot up.

Draven frowned. Galveson? As in the son of Baron Galveson? This day kept getting better and better.

All that was visible of wiry man's face were his eyes, and they twinkled with deviltry as he slid from the table.

Galveson had pocketed the purse, ignoring the rest of the bar.

This young man was definitely up to no good. Now how could he use that to his advantage? He slid into the booth next to Galveson.

The shorter man glowered. "What do you want?"

"I believe you can be of further use to me, Mr. Galveson." Draven leaned forward and steepled his hands.

"You got what you wanted. I said I was done." He fidgeted with his mug.

"We're done when I say we're done." Draven channeled Shadow, letting his voice drip with malice while remaining outwardly composed.

Galveson shrank back. "I can't get you more. I almost got caught the last time and now that blasted cyborg is on a witch-hunt. It's too dangerous."

"This should be a trivial task for you." Draven pulled out a coin and began flipping it between his fingers. "And I will see to it that you are well rewarded."

"What is it?" Galveson's eyes watched the coin's track, never losing it.

"Your captain recently hired a cook."

Galveson snorted. "Yes, just made her secretary."

"Excellent," Draven palmed the coin. "I need to speak with her."

"With the cook?"

"Yes."

"She's a nobody," Galveson sneered. "Why would you care?"

"That's my concern." Draven let the chill return to his voice. "Your concern is to find a way for me to do so."

"You're obviously an aristocrat." Galveson crossed his arms. "Just show your card on deck and you'll be fine."

"For reasons I will not discuss, I would rather not use my real name. You will introduce me as a friend of your grandfather's. I've come to pay a call on the captain. You will see to it that the captain is detained."

"Sounds overly complicated."

"Would you rather I inform your grandfather of your exploits?" Draven asked. He didn't know what Galveson was up to but he didn't need to. Galveson's imagination should provide enough incentive.

"You'd be implicating yourself." Galveson's started to shake.

"No, I won't." Draven chuckled. "What's that about boys who play with fire? You were careless. I never am."

Galveson's face went ashen and he clutched the ale mug tightly between his hands.

Draven rose. "Please, stay and enjoy an ale on me. I will come to call tomorrow. I expect everything to be arranged then."

Galveson only nodded.

Draven hummed to himself as he walked down the wharf toward his own ship. Who would have thought fate would be so kind to him. If his luck continued, he wouldn't have to make Shadow any stronger. That could only be a good thing.

CHAPTER FIFTEEN

"There. Done." Marianne put the final letters on her blotter. She'd been afraid the captain had been making work for but it was clear the woman needed help.

And she was happy to have the work. She needed the distraction. Her hands lifted to her chest. Her nipples puckered and she closed her eyes on a groan. Her body wasn't just humming, it was begging. Tavish had wrapped her in a spell and she only wanted him to cast more.

She was a wanton. No respectable girl wanted the feel of a man's hand on her naked skin. Yet, she craved it. It was a good thing she was no longer respectable.

She dropped her hand back to the blotter and sighed. Now if only she could find a time and place to be alone with him again. She was ready for the next lesson. Should she send a note or would that look too eager? Was visiting him too aggressive? Would it draw too much attention to her? She had no idea how these liaisons were supposed to work.

"Excuse me, miss." Carlsby popped his head into her office. "There's a right important chap here to visit the captain but she's off somewheres. He says he'll wait but she ain't here and Freddy doesn't think we should let the chap alone…."

Marianne smiled. "And he wants me to sit with him until the captain returns?"

"Yes, ma'am." Carlsby gave a shaky laugh.

"See that tea is brought up." She walked through the door connecting her office to the captain's and then through a second door into the sitting room.

A tall, well-built man rose as she entered. His great coat billowed at his feet. He had sable hair slicked back and a strong, clean-shaven jaw. His brown eyes smiled in welcome as she crossed to his side.

"My lord, please tell me someone offered to take your hat and coat?" She extended her hand in greeting.

"The steward offered, but I find I'm a bit chilled and would prefer to keep it on." He replied in a pleasant baritone as he took her hand in a firm shake.

"I'm Miss Lindstrom, the captain's secretary. I'm afraid the captain isn't here. I understand someone was sent to locate her. Can I offer you some tea while we wait?"

"That would be delightful." He smiled at her but it didn't reach his eyes. "I believe the steward is already procuring tea."

"Please have a seat." Marianne waved her hand toward the couch as she took a seat in the chair opposite. "I am sorry for the wait. With the repairs being so extensive, the captain is often needed in multiple places at once. Tracking her down can be difficult."

Freddy opened the door, baring a tray. He sat it down on the table. "Will there be anything else, miss?"

"No, thank you. This looks lovely." Marianne started to pour. "Cream or sugar?"

"Both please." His lordship took the offered cup, his fingers caressing hers.

She pulled back as if stung and looked for Freddy but the steward had already left. At least the door was still ajar.

She hid her discomfort by pouring herself a cup of tea. "What brings you to New Richmond?"

"Business." He sat back and crossed his legs.

Perhaps Freddy should have remained. She had the distinct impression she was sitting down to tea with a leopard.

"Well, I hope the trip out here has been worth your while." She sat on the edge of her chair and reminded herself she was on a ship surrounded by people.

He arched a brow. "Indeed."

Marianne understood her job as hostess was to keep the conversation going but if he was going to stick to one-word answers that was going to be difficult. "I hope it was an easy trip. As you must have noticed coming aboard, we ran into a spot of trouble."

"Yes, I had heard about the storm."

Silence spread over them like an oppressive blanket. It was a stark contrast to the comfortable silence she enjoyed with Tavish. This man, with his dark look and brooding appearance, made her want to crawl back to her office and lock the door.

She wished she understood her reticence. He wasn't doing anything outwardly wrong. He just seemed false somehow.

He uncrossed his legs and sat forward. "Actually, perhaps you can help me."

"In what way?" she asked.

"I'm looking for a family heirloom. I've managed to trace it to the Sheba but no further. I was hoping the captain would be willing to aid me in my search. But you are her secretary so you must see everything that goes through her desk. Perhaps you could help me locate it."

"I haven't been her secretary for long." She pinched her eyebrows together. "But I'll certainly try to help."

"It's a book my grandmother bequeathed to a friend. It's been in the family for years and I would rather not part with it. I'm willing to be generous in a settlement to get it back."

"A book?" Marianne's stomach turned. "Can you describe it?"

He grinned. "You're the friend, aren't you?"

"I did recently come into possession of a remarkable book but I'm not sure it's the one you seek. From what I was led to believe it was in fact an heirloom of my own family. My mother gave it to my godmother for safe keeping."

"Was your godmother Mrs. Attewater?" He leaned forward, his hands fisting on his knees.

"Yes," she hedged.

He sat back and chuckled. "She's my grandmother. I assure you the book was actually from my paternal line. It should rightly be mine."

"Your grandmother was my great aunt, so we are family." Marianne fidgeted with her skirts. "So it's still within the family."

"Yes, but I am the direct line. My grandmother was quite ill when she died and no doubt made a mistake." He folded his hands. "That isn't your fault of course. I am prepared to pay handsomely for the book, and as you are family, it only seems right for you to receive part of the estate."

Marianne remained silent. She didn't understand why he was being so insistent.

"Give me the book today and I will write you a bank draft for twenty thousand pounds."

Marianne's mouth dropped open and she snapped it shut. Twenty thousand pounds? She could live on that. Have a small cottage in the country. She turned her head and gazed out of the large window that filled the entire back wall of the room.

Small green bats flew outside, circling among the garbage and refuse floating along the dock's edge.

If she took the money, she'd have security, a house to call her own. But she would have to give this all up. She didn't have a choice but to accept the captain's generosity. If she could afford to live on her own she would be honor bound to leave.

She would miss out on seeing things like those small green bat-like creatures so alien to Earth yet so fitting here on this floating island. If she took the money she'd be relegating her life to simple domesticity.

Did she really have a choice?

She rose from her chair to pace before the window, taking in the universe she would leave behind if she took his generous offer. It was eternally dark. The sun, almost five hundred million kilometers away, cast a soft glow along the island's atmosphere, barely enough light to see one's feet while walking along the street. All along the wharf, lamps, gas here on the island, lit the way. It was as if a hundred twinkling stars were hovering around her.

"Miss Lindstrom, I need to return to London shortly. I need an answer now." He approached her.

She started. Why was he in such hurry? There had to be more to it than simply an heirloom. There was something special about that book. It was obvious to anyone who looked at it. Was it somehow worth more than the twenty thousand pounds he offered?

"Your answer?" he snapped.

It was her turn to arch a brow. "I don't see the hurry. It is, after all, the only gift my godmother gave me. I feel it deserves thought before I simply give it away."

"Simply give..." he ran his hands through his hair. "I'm offering a small fortune for that book."

"Yes, and if you can't wait to get it then I'm afraid you'll have to leave disappointed. I am not yet ready to part with it."

"Then you leave me no choice but to force you to give it to me." There was an edge of desperation to his voice as he prowled closer.

She backed up. "You need to leave."

"I... I'll force you to marry me." His face, no longer covered by the facade of the languid aristocrat, turned ugly. His brown eyes darkened and his face contorted in a scowl. He shoved her against the window.

"He—"

His mouth crushed over hers, silencing her. He wedged a knee between her thighs and slammed her head against the window.

She squirmed and pressed against this chest but he was too strong. Cool air ticked her ankles as he bunched up her skirt. Her head spun. Her struggles became frantic. She had to get away.

Her heart racing, she wrenched her hand free and beat against him.

He ignored it like they were insect bites. She twisted her head, beads of sweat tricked into her eyes but she opened her mouth and took in a gulp of air to scream. He slammed her body against the wall, pressing the air from her lungs.

Her skirts bunched up to her waist, he fumbled with his trousers.

No... No... No... God, not this! She gasped for air, but with his chest pressed against her, she couldn't breathe.

She had to keep fighting.

Blackness crept into her vision.

Suddenly, he grunted and stumbled back, clutching his side. She crashed to her knees, taking in lungfuls of air.

Her vision cleared just in time to see the captain slam his lordship's head into the desk. He crumpled to the floor.

Freddy hovered by her side. "Are you all right, Miss?"

Her body started shaking and Freddy helped her lean against the wainscoting under the window. "I'll get you some tea."

"Freddy," the captain walked over and draped a blanket over Marianne's shoulders. "I'll look after her. Get that pile of refuse off my ship."

"With pleasure, ma'am." Freddy's usual cheerful tenor dropped several degrees.

"It's alright, my dear," Ridgewell soothed, rubbing her back. "Take your time. When you're up to it you can tell me what happened."

An hour later, Marianne was safely ensconced in an armchair, covered in blankets, and cradling a cup of tea in her hand.

Tavish joined them shortly after three airmen had carried the still-unconscious lord from the room. He prowled by the window like an angry wolf. His lip curled up in one corner in a snarl that hadn't left since he'd seen her huddled and shaking on the floor.

Ridgewell had ordered him away but he refused to leave.

Marianne was glad he was there. His hulking presence made her feel safe, and she needed that if she was going to get through the coming interview.

"Start from the beginning," the captain said in a gentle voice.

"Carlsby came in and said there was someone important waiting for you and asked if I'd entertain him until you are found."

She took a deep breath. "One of the first things out of his mouth after the usual pleasantries was to inquire about a book I have just received from my godmother's estate."

"So, his real purpose was to see you?" Ridgewell asked.

Marianne nodded.

"I see." Ridgewell turned to Tavish. "Fetch Carlsby."

He didn't move.

"I'll look after her. Now fetch Carlsby. I need to know how Lord Draven got on board."

Tavish grunted deep in his throat but bowed and left.

"His card said his name was Lord Neville Dent." Marianne frowned.

Ridgewell shook her head. "So, false name and a false reason for being here. What was he up to?"

"He wanted the book."

"Clearly, but what's so special about it?"

"You have to see it to understand. It's beautiful, handcrafted, and written in a language I don't recognize."

"What foreign languages do you know?" Ridgewell asked.

"Latin, Greek, French, and German."

Ridgewell raised her eyebrows. "Impressive."

Marianne blushed. "I had an excellent education."

"May I see the book?"

"Yes, I'll get it." Marianne put down the cup and rose, wrapping her blanket tightly around her shoulders. No matter what she did, she couldn't get warm. When this interview was done, she'd take a hot bath to clear her body and her mind.

She walked through the office and into her own.

Ridgewell followed. The book, still wrapped in brown paper, sat on the bottom shelf of her bookcase.

The captain bent to retrieve it. Opening the brown paper, she gasped. "You weren't joking. It's remarkable."

"Twenty thousand pounds remarkable." Marianne said.

"Did he offer you that sum?" Ridgewell blinked.

"Yes. When I turned him down, he... " Marianne closed her eyes and swallowed back the fear. She didn't want to relive this. She couldn't.

Ridgewell eased her into the desk chair. "You're safe. He can't hurt you here."

Marianne willed herself calm. "I might need to be reminded of that from time to time."

"Carlsby, ma'am." Tavish crowded the doorway with a startled Carlsby standing in front of him.

"You let Lord Draven into my office?" Ridgewell asked, her voice unthreatening, as if she were soothing a startled child.

"Yes, ma'am." Carlsby nodded. "After I informed Mr. Argylle. Though, he didn't say he was Lord Draven. It was a different name on the card."

"And Freddy told you to get Marianne?" Ridgewell asked.

"Yes." Carlsby avoided looking at Marianne. "Mr. Galveson said he was a friend of his grandfather's and that you'd want to see him. I figured, as he was a Lord, Miss Lindstrom would know how to treat with him. Mr. Argyle agreed."

"Did Mr. Galveson confirm his identity?" Tavish growled.

The young airman jumped away and shook his head violently. "Not in name, sir. Just said that he was who he said he was and sent Miss Haversham off to find you."

"Thank you, Carlsby, you may go." Ridgewell shooed him away.

The airman avoided Tavish and ducked through the other door.

"Galveson." Tavish's lip curled up in a sneer as he shut the door.

"Didn't do anything wrong as far as we know." Ridgewell leaned against the wall. "Lord Draven's father was a friend of the First Lord's, or at least a close acquaintance."

"Won't he cause trouble for you then?" Marianne bit her lip. "You slammed his head into the desk."

"I should have done worse." Ridgewell's voice was soft, like the sound of a knife being drawn from a sheath.

"I would have," Tavish whispered, his voice all the more menacing for being quiet.

"I should have arrived sooner," Ridgewell berated herself. "But as for Draven, he won't make a fuss. He was caught attacking my crew and he isn't going to want to explain that to the admiralty."

"I doubt he was here on his lordship's orders. It was likely just a pretense to get on the ship," Tavish added.

"What do we do now?" Marianne asked, "I don't want to give the book to him now but I don't want to worry either."

"Repairs are just about finished." Ridgewell tapped the book cover. "I have a friend who might be able to translate it for us. Once we know more about it, we can make a better informed decision."

"I don't like this," Tavish muttered.

"I know, but we can't make a decision without knowledge. Set a course for New Alexandria. I'll keep the book locked in my safe."

"What about the thief?" The question was out of Marianne's lips before she could stop herself.

Ridgewell stiffened.

"She was the first person I investigated." Tavish shuffled his feet. "The disappearance started when she arrived."

"No, they didn't." Ridgewell shook her head. "They started before she arrived."

"Oh." Marianne's eyes went wide.

"The new safe was installed this morning. It's much harder to break into. Besides," Ridgewell shrugged. "We don't have many other options. We can't keep it here in Marianne's office. Anyone could come in and grab it."

"Agreed," Tavish said.

"In the meantime, Tavish, keep an eye on Marianne. I don't want her going anywhere without one of the crew watching her."

"That I can promise." Tavish looked resolutely at Marianne. "Attacks like this won't be happening again."

"Good." Ridgewell walked through the door into her office. "Take the rest of the day off, Marianne. You deserve it."

The captain shut the door and Tavish turned to her. "Are you sure you're all right?"

Marianne raced into his arms.

He held her, rubbing her back. "I thought I'd frighten you. That you'd want to avoid any memory of what... what happened to you."

Marianne buried her face in his chest, as if she could absorb his strength through the beating of his heart. "I feel safe when you're near."

He kissed the top of her head. "I'll have to give the order to leave and the new course needs to be set but as soon that's finished, I'll return."

She nodded.

"Will you be all right if I leave for a few minutes? I can have someone sit with you. Sam, maybe?"

Marianne swallowed. "Everyone has a job to do if we are going to get this ship moving, Sam most of all. I'll be fine on my own for a short time."

"Lock the door when I'm gone," he ordered.

"I will."

She watched him go, her heart heavy. They were going to investigate this book even though there was no profit in it for the crew. She had wanted stop being a burden and all she'd managed to do was become a bigger one.

CHAPTER SIXTEEN

"Nicholas!" Nora cried out from a prison of bone.

Draven shot up from his pillow. Sweat dripped down his face and his head spun.

"My lord, calm yourself." An airman eased him back on his pillow. "You've had a bad knock to the head."

Draven rubbed his temples and wished he could rub away Nora's screams. "What happened?"

"You were mugged and dumped in an alley."

"What was stolen?" He closed his eyes. His head pounded as if a thousand booted feet raced across his scalp.

"Your purse was gone." The airman pushed a cool cloth to his head. "But you still had your boots and coat."

Everything about the day was foggy. He was supposed to get something.

He grimaced. Something important lay just out of reach. "Why are we here?"

"I don't know." The airman stroked his eyebrow. "Can't you remember?"

"If I remembered I would have asked," Draven snapped.

"But you know who you are?"

"Yes, now where are we?" Draven clenched his teeth.

"Ah... New Richmond, my lord."

"New Richmond," Draven's lip curled. What the devil? The devil... His eyebrows shot up. Shadow and the book. He was here to get the book.

Someone must have stopped him from getting it. He remembered cornering Miss Lindstrom and then someone had attacked him from behind. He cursed under his breath.

"I need to send a message to my friend aboard the Sheba. He might have seen what happened." Draven sat up. "Fetch my writing desk."

"Aye, sir." The airman walked to the back of the cabin.

Returning, he set the desk on Draven's lap and propped his back with pillows.

Scribbling a quick note, Draven folded and sealed it. "Get this to Mr. Galveson aboard the Queen of Sheba. Wait for a reply?"

"Aye, sir." The airman removed the desk and left.

Draven leaned back against the pillows. His direct approach had failed. He needed another tactic. Somehow he had to convince the girl that keeping the book wasn't worth it. She'd be guarded now. He wouldn't get a second chance at her. Not unless she came out in the open somewhere.

"Where is it?" Shadow's insidious voice, caressed his mind like a snake slithering over rocks.

Draven swallowed and glanced around. Shadow was nowhere to be seen.

"Where is the book?" Two glowing red eyes floated in front of him.

"With the girl," Draven swallowed. Nora had haunted his dreams. He didn't need a further reminder.

"If you want to sleep soundly tonight you will feed me."

"How?" His voice quavered.

"You brought the machine."

"Yes, but I need time and a place to set it up. Even if I could soundproof this cabin, the crew will notice when one of them goes missing."

A deep chuckle glided over his skin. "I will show you how to turn the crew loyal to you. They will become as biddable as sheep."

"I don't understand."

"With your machine there is a way to limit a person's mental powers, yes?"

"I suppose so. Usually it kills them." Draven couldn't help but be intrigued.

"Yes, but if you stop just before?"

He sat up and put his feet on the floor. "I'd turn them into mindless drones. Capable of simple tasks and nothing else."

"Precisely." Shadow materialized. "And I will do what I can to cloud the rest of the crew's mind. The more men you give me, the easier that will become."

Draven blinked. Did he dare? If he took this step, there would be no turning back. He'd become more than a monster.

But wasn't he already there? Wouldn't he do anything to protect the woman he loved?

He looked into those floating red eyes and smiling conspiratorially, stepped fully into the dark. "Show me."

CHAPTER SEVENTEEN

Tavish scowled at his captain's back. He hated this whole thing. They should have just given the book over to the man who wanted it and left well enough alone. Instead they had changed plans, altered course and were diving head first into what was surely a fool's errand.

He glanced around, his eyes, both mechanical and natural, taking in everything. On board ship they could protect her. Out here?

The captain hadn't even brought along more airmen for protection. The only one protecting the two women was he.

At least the streets of New Alexandria were large, open boulevards that made it easy for him to keep an eye on things. No shadows for would-be assailants to hide in. New Alexandria was on one of the largest islands of the Lexicon belt. It was round, nearly a planet itself, with a day that was as bright as late dawn on Earth.

The vegetation was an unnatural purple. The fauna that had developed here looked more like something out of a Mary Shelly novel than what he would call animals, but they tended to avoid direct contact with humans.

"How much farther?" he grumbled.

Ridgewell laughed, not bothering to turn around. "It's just around the corner. Doctor Smith is a professor at Geldorf Hall."

"And she will be able to help?" Marianne asked.

"Smith has a knack for language. If anyone can figure out what this book is saying, it's her. She knows her business."

They turned a corner and Geldorf Hall came into view. It was a large, baroque building situated at the end of a boulevard lined with the white-blooming, purple-leafed Asinia trees. It was picturesque, almost postcard worthy, the beauty interrupted only by the shrill whistle of a steam bus as it trundled down the wide street.

Ridgewell led them down the sidewalk, passed students lounging out on the lavender-colored grass, studying or quietly chatting with one another. It was the picture of university life, and it was increasingly more difficult for Tavish to remain on edge. It was as if the serenity and peace of the surroundings lulled him to relaxation. He gritted his teeth and pushed the bucolic thoughts from his mind.

They stopped by the head porter's office. "Captain Henrietta Ridgewell here to see Professor Annabel Smith."

"Do you have an appointment?" the portly porter asked, frowning down at his ledger.

"No, but I'm sure she'll be happy to see me. I'm an old friend. If you could just ring her up." Ridgewell waved her fingers toward the small panel of lights on the porter's veemitter.

"Very well," he grumbled.

After a few minutes they were through. Professor Smith met them at the stairs leading up to the campus offices. She wasn't a remarkable looking woman. Her hair was neither blonde nor brown. Her height was average, her build slightly plump but not overly so. Her hazel eyes were her most extraordinary feature, changing between brown, green, and blue as the light flickered around her. He would have a difficult time describing her later should he be asked.

Professor Smith walked up to Ridgewell and kissed her cheek. "Good Morning, Henri."

"Anna, thank you for seeing us on such short notice." Ridgewell returned the embrace.

"Now, who are your friends and what can I help you with?"

Ridgewell smiled, waving a hand in his direction. "This is Mr. Tavish, my first mate, and Miss Lindstrom, my secretary."

"Nice to meet you both." The professor shook hands all around. "Would you like to speak privately? My office is a bit incommodious but I think we'll all fit."

"That would be wonderful, thank you." Ridgewell inclined her head.

"It's just up the stairs."

They started up the stone, spiral staircase. Geldorf Hall looked like it was trying to mimic its older and more prestigious cousins in Britain, but workmanship of the building was excellent.

At the top of the steps they walked down an arched walkway that looked out over the courtyard bellow. There were no windows in those arches. They didn't need them. The weather was always the same. Most of the water on the floating planetoid was underground, fed up to the topside vegetation by long roots that delved deep in the crust. When it did rain, it never stormed.

Add that to the fact that the large whale that fed the atmosphere of this planetoid created enough heat as a byproduct of its digestion of aether air to keep the temperature a comfortable 20 degrees centigrade and the buildings themselves became more of a habit then a necessity.

The professor opened a door and walked through. "I must apologize for the clutter." She began shoving piles of papers and books up against a wall, clearing space on the two seats in front of her desk. "If you'll take my chair, Henri. I'll stand."

Ridgewell waved her hand. "Nonsense, Tavish can stand. He'd be doing it anyway. "

"If you're sure." Smith shot a worried look up at him.

"Captain's right." He turned to shut the door behind them. Taking up a position beside the door, he turned his gaze on the doctor, while his other senses stretched outside the room.

A scratching sound had him frowning. What was that?

"So you have a thing for me?" Smith sat forward on her chair, her hands clasped in front of her, eyes sparkling. "Is it a book?"

He jerked his attention back to the professor. How had she known?

Ridgewell chuckled. "Always the same, Anna."

"Well, I do love to read. Why do you think I chose this line of study?"

He resisted the urge to snort as he took a quick glance around the room, full, from floor to ceiling in some places, with books. He relaxed back against the wall. The scratching continued. What the devil?

"I need your help deciphering the text of a book my secretary came into possession of. The language… " Ridgewell shook her head as she handed the book to the doctor. "I've never seen its like before."

With eager, twitching fingers, Smith grabbed the book. Her eyes became large round saucers as she took in the cover. "Fascinating," she muttered, flipping through pages. "Absolutely fascinating."

Tavish started lifting books, searching for the sound.

"What are you doing, Tavish?" Ridgewell asked.

"Can't you hear it?" he asked.

She shook her head. "Hear what?"

"That scratching sound."

"That's just Lang." The professor flipped through the pages of the book. "She's probably on her wheel."

"A pet?" he asked.

"Of sorts." She flipped back to the beginning. "I've never seen anything like it."

"Can you help us, Professor?" Marianne asked.

"I think so. Something about it is familiar. I'll have to consult my books."

Marianne shot a glance at Ridgewell.

The captain nodded. "We can't let you keep it here, Anna, but we might be able to give you a few hours to at least see what you can uncover."

"I wonder," Smith muttered. Not looking up from the book, she groped at a shelf behind her. Her fingers caressed the spines before stopping on one and pulling it out. She glanced at it. Then, nodding, she opened it.

Ridgewell smiled at her affectionately, then, shaking her head, she turned to him. "I imagine Anna will be at this for a while. Perhaps you two would like to explore the island."

Marianne bit her bottom lip. "I could use some more ink and pen tips."

"There isn't a better place to find such things then on an island devoted to knowledge. I'll stay and keep Anna company. I have some work to do of my own." Ridgewell held up her logbook.

Did he dare risk leaving the captain alone?

Seeming to read his mind, the captain rolled her eyes.

"Do you honestly think I could be in any danger here?" She waved her hand around the room. "We're inside a walled campus, with a door guard. Relax."

He took a deep breath. "Need I remind you, captain, that someone has already gone to dangerous and violent measures to get that book?"

Ridgewell rested a hand on her hip, the gleaming hilt of her sword evident against the dark navy of her trousers and jacket. "I am capable of taking care of myself. I think Anna and I can manage. Take Marianne and see the sights."

He crossed his arms and frowned.

"Don't make me order you." The tone of Ridgewell's voice hadn't risen, but that only made the ring of authority even more pronounced.

He bowed his head. "Very well, ma'am."

"Excellent." Ridgewell turned back to the desk and pulled out her log.

Marianne was waiting by the door, looking up at him expectantly. He stuffed any further protests. What danger could they get in while shopping?

"Does your head hurt?" Marianne asked.

Tavish looked down at her. "Hmm?"

She resisted the urge to roll her eyes. He'd been like this all afternoon, alternating between a simple frown and outright scowl. To make it worse, she'd had to frame all her questions carefully if she desired more than a one-word answer from him.

She wanted to stop in the middle of the street and shake him. "You're squinting," she said instead.

"The sun is bright," he muttered.

"Bollocks!"

He stopped walking and frowned down at her. "Did you just say... ?"

"You heard me." Marianne crossed her arms and faced him. "You've been acting ill-humored all afternoon."

He stiffened.

She didn't care. "What has gotten into you? What have I done now?"

"Nothing."

This time Marianne gave into the urge and rolled her eyes. "Petulant and sullen."

"I am merely irritated by the delay." He scowled at her.

"Really, and what would you have to be irritated about?" She crossed her arms. "This trip isn't affecting you in any way. The captain still managed to find cargo to ship out here, so you aren't down any money. The sailing was painless, no storms, no mishaps. In short, nothing to be irritated about."

"We are starting to attract notice," he growled.

Marianne shot a glance around. Students were still milling past but several of them had turned to stare. She shrugged. "I don't really care. I'm tired of this attitude of yours. I want explanations."

He grabbed her by the shoulder and hauled her behind a large tree.

Her senses immediately became a whirlwind. Every time he touched her, whether via flesh or metal, her insides turned to mush.

She shook her senses back under control and inhaled the deep scent of the white Asinia tree blossoms. Their faint odor of pumpkin spice calmed her.

Soothed her. She had to stay rational.

"That man tried to rape you." He said through gritted teeth. He was only inches from her, his voice pitched for her ears alone.

Marianne peered up at him, her lips tightening. "Do you think I'm not aware of that?"

"We need to be getting rid of that damn book, not investigating it further."

"Getting rid of it won't help. Draven's obsessed with it. He won't settle for 'We just lost it.'"

"Then give it to him and be done with it."

Marianne jabbed a finger into his chest. "Do you think that's wise? He's willing to go to some rather disturbing lengths to get that book. It's clearly valuable to him, and for more than just sentimental reasons."

"It's not worth the risk."

"We don't know that, and we won't know until we learn what the book contains."

He looked down at her, placing his large hands on her shoulders. "You could be hurt."

With that one sentence he took the wind right out of her sails. Her shoulders relaxed and she reached up and cupped his cheek, the scarred one. He deserved to be reminded every day that he was more than scars and metal. He was a good man.

"That's why I have you." She ran her thumb over his lips. "I won't be safe unless we know what's so important about this book. We can't anticipate dangers if we don't have the knowledge to make accurate assumptions."

"I know, it's just —" His head snapped up and he whirled her around, crushing her against the tree and protecting her with his own body.

Thunk.

Tink.

Tavish grunted.

Thunk.

"We can't stay here." He looked around, peering back over his head. "Come on."

Without waiting to ask, he picked her up. Cradling her against his chest, he ran toward a row of shops along the main street.

She tried to peer around his shoulder to see what was behind but he pressed her back against his chest.

"Stay down," he ordered.

Students screamed and ran, scattering like pigeons in their wake.

He ducked into a bookstore, only putting her down when the door had shut behind them.

The clerk behind the desk stared at them, but Tavish didn't wait to discuss things. He grabbed her hand and pulled her deeper into the store, between the shelves.

He huddled her into a corner. Pushing her behind him, he turned to face the way they'd come.

The door chimed.

He tensed and shifted, pushing her further into the shadows.

The movement forced him further into the light of a window, and the dull sunlight illuminated the short quarrels sticking out of his back.

She pulled her hands over her mouth to muffle her shocked gasp.

"Are you hurt?" she whispered, reaching up to touch the spot where one quarrel was imbedded. She felt the ridged leather, and metal of his mechanical shoulder. No blood; they hadn't hit flesh.

"Sshh," he hissed.

They heard voices near the front of the store.

"We need to find a way out of here," he said.

He grabbed her hand and darted down the line of books on the back wall until he came to a door, disguised as a bookshelf. He opened it slowly, the well-oiled hinges making not a sound.

Marianne strained her ears.

Soft, muffled steps.

Tavish touched her shoulder and motioned her through the door. He followed right behind her.

She looked around. They were in some sort of back stock room. A desk sat against one wall, a single unlit light bulb hanging from the ceiling.

They made their way through piles of boxes and books, past a shelf full of dusty volumes, to a door at the back.

He looked through and pulled her out into an alley. Without wasting to catch his breath, he dragged her deeper down the back street.

"Slow down!" She had to take three steps to keep up with his one. "Not all of us are six feet tall."

He grunted at her but didn't slow down. Checking doors until he found one unlocked, he opened it and shoved her in.

It was a small coal closet, thankfully nearly empty. As it was, they barely fit.

He locked the door behind him. Facing her, his large arms resting around her shoulders, he held her tightly against him.

She could hear the thudding of his heart as it raced in time to her own.

Seconds ticked by, then came the sound of pounding feet down the alley.

Shouts were muffled by the closed door and the roaring of her own blood filled her ears.

The door rattled behind them. She held her breath.

It rattled again.

More sounds, talking this time. Too faint to make out the words.

Footsteps leading away. More rattling doors.

She let out her breath. They were safe.

For now.

The sound of footsteps faded, yet still he didn't move.

Tavish tried to tell himself it was because the danger was still very real. Tried to convince his mind that it really was in control of his body.

It was futile.

His raging heart pounded in his chest. Those men had been after her. The quarrels in his back, aimed at her head. If he'd been only a few moments slower....

He stiffened, his body locked in protest. He knew this had been a bad idea.

He pulled her closer and held her.

The pounding in his chest eased. She was safe. They hadn't succeeded. He held her tighter.

"Are you hurt?" Marianne's soft whisper penetrated the haze of his troubled mind.

He looked down. Even this close, he wouldn't have been able to see her features without his bionic eye. It was pitch dark in the closet, but he could pick out even the smallest of light sources and illuminate an area. Her face was twisted in worry and concern.

"I'm fine," he soothed.

"They might have killed you."

"It wasn't me they were trying to kill."

The trembling started in her arms, traveling down the length of her body. She grabbed the lapel of his jacket and buried her face in his chest.

His good hand reached up and cradled the back of her head. What would he give to take away that fear?

"We're safe for now," he whispered. "We'll stay here until it's dark and then we'll sneak out."

She turned her head, resting her cheek against his shirt. "Why would they do this? What could they gain by it?"

"I don't know." He ran his hand over the back of her neck. "Do you still think keeping this book is a good idea?"

She tipped her head up. She would be blind in the dark but he schooled his features anyway.

"I think it's even more important to learn why it's worth killing for."

"You could die," he breathed.

She lifted a hand and cupped his cheek. "You'll be there."

His control broke. Unhinging like a door battered by a storm. How could she be so careless? How could she be so heedless of the risk? She nearly died today, and still she thought he could protect her. That she was safe with him. That he was safe at all.

"Are you mad?" He shook her.

She blinked up at him.

His mouth crashed down on hers, claimed her mouth in a savage kiss that held nothing back.

His shattered control was unable to cope with the onslaught of emotion that raged through him. The only balm was the haven of her lips and tongue.

He would frighten her, but he just couldn't fight it any longer. The more time he spent with her, the more he wanted her. The more he wanted to be the man she deserved, the more he failed her. Even now, as his tongue danced with hers, he failed her.

Marianne moaned deep in her throat and leaned in, matching him, fusing their mouths tighter. Her arms reached up and around his neck, and she rose up on her toes, pressing her body into his—molding against him.

He groaned, his hunger rising. He nipped her lower lip, his bionic hand reached behind her, bracing himself against the wall. He locked the mechanical arm, ensuring that he wouldn't lose control of his strength—ensuring that he wouldn't hurt her.

His right hand rose from her back slowly circling to the front to cup her breast. The rigid boning of her corset was rough underneath the soft cotton of her blouse, and it hid more than it revealed, but his mind didn't need the tactile sensation of flesh to know what it held. Her small, perfectly shaped breast pressed into his large hand and he squeezed.

The corset gave not a millimeter but Marianne responded all the same. Her lithe body shivered under his touch, and she broke from the kiss, gasping for air.

He dipped his head lower, caressing the soft curve of her neck with his lips and tongue. He tasted her pulse, felt the racing of her blood as her body responded to his. It was like the nectar of the gods. Nectar he could never have enough of.

The door rattled behind him.

His head shot up.

It rattled again.

He froze.

Marianne inhaled sharply, her hands dropping to rest on his chest. He could feel them pressed against his racing heart.

Voices, quiet, barely discernible through the door.

Barely discernible to a mere human ear but his were far keener.

Two voices arguing.

He pressed Marianne close, protecting her with the girth of his body. If they managed to get the door open... He pushed the thought away. He had to focus. He held his breath and listened.

"They have to be in this alley. There's nowhere else they could have gone."

"Are you sure you didn't miss them in the shop? They could have hidden, watched you walk by and exited through the front."

"We had people watching the front."

"We had people watching the alley, too."

"We need to start looking door to door."

"Don't be daft. If we start breaking down doors, we'll attract attention. The boss said no attention."

"We shot crossbows down a busy street." A snort. "How was that unobtrusive?"

"This is stupid. Let's head back to the ship."

The voices faded away. They were leaving.

"They—" Marianne began.

He pressed a finger to her lips and shook his head. Hoping she'd get the message in the dark. They couldn't talk. They weren't safe yet.

He would keep her safe. If she was determined to solve this mystery of a book, then he would have to protect her.

CHAPTER EIGHTEEN

Tavish knocked on the office door but didn't pause before opening it. He hurtled Marianne through and slammed it shut. The glint of a blade flashed in the corner of his eye and he turned to see the captain sheath her sword.

"I'm elated you've returned. We had started to worry." Professor Smith smiled at Ridgewell.

The captain crossed her arms and glowered.

Smith laughed and waved Marianne to a chair. "You look like you've had a run in with a coal cellar."

"Not far from the truth." Marianne sat and settled her soot-covered skirts.

"What happened?" Ridgewell demanded.

"Trouble," Tavish replied.

Smith's eyebrows rose. "Trouble? Here?"

He threw three small quarrels onto the professor's desk. Silence fell over the group as they stared at the small darts.

"Someone shot a crossbow at you?" Ridgewell frowned and picked up a quarrel.

"Several someones, we believe," Marianne whispered. "That's why we were late. We had to hide."

"You're both unhurt?" Ridgewell's right hand was fisted so tightly over her sword hilt her knuckles had turned white.

"Yes." Tavish rolled his shoulders.

Marianne looked up at him. "They hit Tavish in the arm."

"Is this true?" Ridgewell asked.

He pressed his lips together. "Two of the bolts hit the leather casing and did little damage but one managed to hit a gearbox. It's nothing Doctor Starrett can't fix."

"Hmmm... " Ridgewell gripped his good shoulder and spun him around to look at his back. Her fingers prodded the holes left in his jacket. "Anna, you're coming with us."

Smith's head whipped up. "I can't. I have responsibilities here."

"This isn't up for debate," Ridgewell ordered.

"But I'm just an academic." The professor protested. "I don't do field work!"

Ridgewell shrugged. "Someone just shot at a member of my crew. It won't take them long to figure out why we were here. I can't leave you alone."

Smith's face turned ashen and she sank into a chair.

"Don't start with histrionics." Ridgewell held up a hand. "We don't have time for them."

"I don't have histrionics."

"Good, so pack up." Ridgewell waved a hand over the cluttered office. "But only what you need."

"But... but... "

Marianne walked over and pulled the doctor up out of her chair. "Please, will you help us? Who else could translate this book?"

"I suppose. I did translate that bit in the beginning." Smith nodded. "And I'd like the chance to work on it some more."

"You what?" Tavish and Ridgewell said in unison.

Ridgewell shot him an irritated glare before turning back to the professor. "Why didn't you tell me?"

"I'd only just finished when they arrived." She waved at him. "The notes in the beginning, while written in the same language as the rest of the book, appear to have been added later. They looked like coordinates to me and I was right."

"And they are?" Tavish prodded.

Smith waved her hand in a throwaway gesture. "They lead to some backwater island on the far outskirts of the Lexicon Belt. Not sure why they're written, but they should help with translating the rest."

"Then that's just one more reason for you to come along." Tavish crossed his arms. "Speaking of which, we should leave soon. I can't promise we weren't followed back here."

"Yes," Ridgewell grabbed the book. "Grab what you need from this office. We won't have time to get to your apartments."

"But my clothes, my things?"

"We'll get you new things. Hurry." Ridgewell slipped the book into her satchel and slung it over her shoulder.

Smith crossed her arms. "I can't just leave."

"We are not having this argument again," Ridgewell snapped.

"Fine, but this is most aggravating." Smith stamped her foot.

"I'm sure it is, now grab what you need," Ridgewell ordered. "But only what you can carry."

Smith's jaw fell open. "How... I need all of my books."

"We don't have time for this," Tavish punched the wall.

Everyone turned to stare at him.

Marianne laid a hand on his arm.

He let her gentle touch soothe. "Please, professor, we have to hurry." .

"I don't even know where to start." The professor's voice sounded lost. She turned in a circle her arms wide as she took in the room.

Tavish saw the pile of books on the professor's desk. Most were opened and hadn't been there when he'd left earlier. He piled them all and shoved them at her. "Take these."

Smith flipped through them. "Yes, I suppose these will do for now."

"Good, let's go." He propelled her toward the door.

"Wait! What about Lang?" She dragged her feet and glanced over her shoulder at him.

Ridgewell popped behind the desk and grabbed the small metal cage with a white rat curled up inside. "I can't believe he's still alive."

Smith grinned. "He's getting on in years, but he's still with me."

"I'll carry him." Marianne took the cage from Ridgewell. "We should leave the fighters with their hands free."

Ridgewell gave her a crisp nod and made sure her sword was loose in the scabbard. "Hopefully, we won't need it."

Tavish could not agree more. The further they got into this mess, the more he hated it. He still wasn't convinced the book was worth it.

The streets of New Alexandria were still lit in the same late dawn glow as always, but the shadows that had earlier seemed bucolic now grew more and more oppressive as they made their way back to Sheba.

The wide boulevard was empty of people. It was dinnertime for the planetoid. Students and teachers alike were all down in their respective college dining halls partaking of a meal ritual as old as universities themselves. Even the shop owners had shut down their shops and headed home. No one was around to watch their small party make its way along the wide streets.

Or so she hoped.

The emptiness should have soothed her. They could see all around with plenty of time to react. Except the attackers used crossbows and the party was in the open.

Tavish looked like an avenging spirit. His bionic eye glowed red as he scanned the empty streets.

She knew that he had different settings for that eye. She didn't know what he could see with it but she knew it was more than anyone else in their party did.

Ridgewell was just as alert as Tavish, her eyes scanning for danger but without his advantages. She hurried them along the street, her long legs taking one step for Marianne's two.

Despite the tension they reached the ship unmolested.

"Tavish, report to the infirmary." Ridgewell strode up the gangplank. "Marianne, show Anna to my office. I'll join you as soon as we're underway."

"This way." Marianne motioned for the professor to follow. "What do you teach? Linguistics?"

"Yes," Anna smiled. "More specifically, I hold doctorates in sociolinguistics, discourse analysis, and semiotics."

"That's quite impressive, Professor." Marianne blinked.

"Please call me Annabel." She winked at Marianne. "Only Henri calls me Anna. I think she does it to irritate me."

Marianne grinned. "Then you must call me Marianne."

They walked into the captain's office and Marianne directed Annabel to a chair. "Thank you for agreeing to come with us."

"It's not like I had much choice in the matter." Annabel put her books down on the table and looked about the room.

"We aren't going to have to go through this again, are we?" Tavish grumbled.

Annabel jumped.

Marianne settled into a chair. "I thought the captain ordered you to the infirmary."

He stiffened. "I said I was fine."

Ridgewell walked into the office from Navigation. Noise rang through the room but was silenced as soon as she shut the door. Other than shooting Tavish an irritated glare, she didn't say anything about his presence as she sat down behind her desk. "We're off to Axel's Island as soon as Quinn finishes recharging the engine batteries."

Annabel sat down and started flipping through books.

"Are you sure we should go to all this trouble?" Marianne rested her hands in her lap and peered at the captain. "We know very little, and this island has nothing for us to deliver. How will we explain it to the crew?"

Ridgewell shrugged. "My curiosity is piqued. The crew won't be upset over a small detour."

Tavish snorted. "Some of the shine might rub off your goddess-like presence."

Ridgewell's lips pressed together. "I never wanted that attention. I won't miss it."

"I knew it was familiar!" Annabel exclaimed.

Everyone whipped their heads round to stare at her.

"Knew what was familiar?" Marianne asked.

"The language! I've seen it before." She moved Lang's cage to the floor and spread two books open across the table.

"Excellent." Ridgewell dragged a chair from before her desk and sat. "Where?"

"Everywhere." Annabel waved her hands in the air above her head, nearly bouncing out of her seat.

"I don't follow." Marianne frowned at the open tomes. One was written in Latin the other was completely foreign.

"It's quite simple, really," Annabel grabbed Marianne's book from the captain's hand and opened it. "Do you see this word?"

"Umpor?" Tavish leaned his hands on the back of Marianne's chair. "What does it mean?"

"I think it means 'to use' or perhaps 'I use' or 'you use.' I'm not sure on conjugation. The point is that it sounds a great deal like the Latin word for 'use.'"

"Are you saying Latin is formed from this language?" Ridgewell cocked her head and tapped the open book. "It's been a while since my Latin lessons, but that doesn't look anything like I remember."

Annabel shook her head. "Not exactly. Look at this grouping."

"Bilig Orka?" Marianne read. She leaned back and bumped her head against Tavish's chest.

He started to back away but she stopped him. "If you're going to ignore the captain's order about the infirmary then you had better take a seat."

He hesitated, and then with a sigh, sat. "Get on with it."

"'Bilig' could come from Turkish but 'Orka' sounds more like Greek." Annabel shook her head. "It's remarkable."

"You've lost me." Marianne squinted at her book, hoping something would come to her.

"Don't you see it?" Annabel asked.

"Anna, assume for the moment that we won't see what you see." Ridgewell leaned back in her chair. "Just tell us your theories."

"Oh, of course." Annabel blinked but then her face brightened. "I'm seeing evidence of nearly every Earth language here."

She turned a page. "In addition to Latin and several other European languages, there's Arabic, Incan, even Chinese. The list goes on and on."

"Incan?" Tavish snorted.

"Yes," Annabel beamed at them. "It's extraordinary. It'll take me years to translate it all."

"We don't have years," Ridgewell stated.

Annabel shrugged. "No way around it. I'm not fluent in all of these languages and some of them I've never even seen before. They could be some remnant of a lost language. I'll need to pour through books to figure it all out."

She frowned down at the small pile of books on the table. "These will do for now but I'll need access to the library at New Alexandria if I'm to finish it."

"We don't have years," Ridgewell repeated.

Annabel's lower lip quivered. "No one else could do it faster."

"No doubt." Ridgewell rose and walked to stand before her friend. Crouching down, she grabbed the professor's hands. "Anna, this book threatens to change the way we think about human history, and there are men, bad men, willing to kill for it. We have to know what's going on before we can protect it."

Marianne shrank back against the chair. She could still feel Draven's lips pressed to her own, his grasping hands.

Tavish squeezed her hand. "Perhaps we should call it a night," he said. "It's been a long day. We have a direction to travel and dwelling over what might happen won't help any of us."

Marianne took a steading breath. "I'm fine."

"But you won't be if we don't stop the idiot behind the attacks. I don't know what Lord Draven is playing at but my instincts tell me that it isn't good." Tavish's jaw clenched.

Ridgewell walked over to Marianne and rested a hand on her shoulder. "I have a secure place on Earth to store this book but it will help if I have more evidence of what it is before I bring it there. Hopefully, when we reach the coordinates Anna uncovered we'll learn more."

"And then back to Earth where we can get rid of the d—" Tavish grunted. "The thing."

"Yes, it will take several weeks to reach Axel's Island. Marianne, I want you to work with Anna to make an exact copy of the book. Miss Haversham is a talented artist. I'll attach her to you for the time being. Other than running the autochef you are to focus fully on this task."

Marianne rose from the chair. "My office is a bit snug but we should be able to fit another desk in there. I'll go find one in storage."

"Tavish, go with her." Ridgewell sat back down. "I don't want knowledge of this book to leave this room. As far as the rest of the crew is concerned, the book is just a family heirloom."

"Where do we store it in the mean time?" Tavish asked. "Can you trust your office safe?"

Ridgewell shook her head. "No, but I had a second safe installed under my desk. I'll give the combination to the three of you. The only thing in there will be the original of the book. The copy will stay in the main safe."

"Any questions?" The captain looked between the three of them.

No one answered.

"All right, dismissed."

Marianne exchanged a glance with Tavish as they left. She could see the fear etched on his face. It mirrored her own. She'd seen the danger first hand and had no desire to relive it, but the captain was right: They had to figure out what this was.

Tavish followed Marianne down the long corridor. The gentle sway of her hips and the swishing of her skirts at her ankles soothed him. There was no hesitation in her steps. No signs of lingering fear.

How could he have been so callous? He'd all but forced himself on her in that coal cellar. It hadn't occurred to him that she might be frightened, that his kiss might bring back unpleasant memories.

Now he had to know if he was still welcome. If she needed space, he'd have to give it to her. She had every right.

The pain at the thought of her leaving nearly sent him to his knees. He knew there was no future for them. He'd known that before he'd started down this road, but it hadn't anticipated how he would react when the road ended. How it would affect him.

"We don't need anything big. Freddy said there were some old school desks he put down here that were used for the deck cadet's classes." Marianne opened a hatch that led to the storeroom.

"Those are meant for twelve-year-olds," Tavish pointed out.

She grinned over her shoulder and lit a lamp. "Yes, but I'm not much bigger than a twelve-year-old."

"Ah, here it is," she sang out. Bending down to lift a box, her heart-shaped bottom pressed against her skirts. Outlining her curves to perfection. His fingers itched to touch.

She dropped a box and squeaked.

He rolled his eyes. "Let me."

She stepped aside.

Brushing past her he caught the soft whiff of lemons and the smile she seemed to reserve just for him. He took a deep breath, and inhaled her scent—letting it soothe him.

"Marianne, earlier today in the coal cellar… " He cleared his throat. "Did I…."

His voice caught. It was more difficult then he'd imagined saying the words out loud. "Did I frighten you?"

She stepped closer and ran a hand down his shoulder. "No, I was frightened but never by you."

The weight eased from his heart. "I was afraid that I might have… "

"That you might have reminded me of what that bastard almost did?" she asked.

He nodded.

Marianne closed her eyes and shook her head. "Tavish, how many times do I have to tell you before you believe."

Leaning up she kissed the scar on his left cheek. "You don't frighten me. You never have."

"But in the cellar, I didn't ask. I just took," he countered.

She grasped his upper arms. "You didn't have to ask. It was implied. We were both recovering from the excitement of our escape and we'd both been frightened. What happened was a natural extension of that. We needed to know that the other was well.

"We are lovers, aren't we?" Her lips curled back up in her secret smile and she stepped into him, her arms rising to wrap around his neck. "And lovers find comfort in each other."

"Are you certain?" He searched her eyes. "I couldn't bear the thought of hurting you."

"What Draven did was ugly and horrid." She traced his scar with a free hand. "What we share is beautiful. Comparing the two is like trying to compare ashes to flowers."

He kissed her forehead. "What did I do to deserve you?"

She took a deep breath, her breasts pressing into his chest. "You were yourself."

He pulled back far enough to look at her. "I suppose we should get this desk back."

Her grip around his neck tightened. "And miss the opportunity this semi-private room gives us? I've missed your lessons."

"The hatch is open." His whole body thrummed at her suggestion but he gritted his teeth against the onslaught. He had to be responsible for her sake, at least.

"And even I can hear anyone coming long before they reach this room." She rose on her tiptoes, her lips hovering just above his. "If you're worried, turn up your ear. I'm not letting you go until you kiss me."

How was a man to ignore that invitation? He settled his lips over hers and took what she offered. He kept it gentle this time, unwilling, even after her assurances, to frighten her.

She sighed in his arms, melting against him.

Boot steps echoed from down the hall.

"Do you see how the first mate follows the cook around?" An airman asked.

Tavish froze.

"Like he has a chance with a lady like her," another snorted. "Talk about Beauty and the Beast."

The other man chortled.

Tavish froze.

"Maybe she isn't that picky. Maybe we have a chance at her."

"You couldn't get a woman to look at you if you were a lady's hat."

Tavish ripped away from the kiss and pushed Marianne to the side.

She stared up dazedly at him.

God, he was a fool.

He picked up the desk. "Let's get this back to the office before I do something even more idiotic."

"Idiotic?" she whispered.

"Yes." He turned and left, checking only once to ensure that she followed. He was a fool. He'd let himself dream for just a moment that he was good enough for a lady like her. But in the end those airmen had been right. He had no business chasing after a lady at all. Beauty and the beast was a fairytale. It was best if he remembered that.

CHAPTER NINETEEN

"I doubt I'll ever get sick of seeing this." Marianne grinned over at Annabel.

White birds flitted about the ship's masts, orders were called, and the wind rushed through her hair. All these sounds reminded her of a wet-navy ship docking in a London harbor.

The professor bounced on her toes. "I will admit to being afraid of this journey but now that it's here, I can't seem to keep from smiling."

"Creating the map didn't hurt," Marianne chuckled. "It's like a treasure map. X marks the spot!"

"I just wish it had any resemblance to the known maps of Axel's Island." Annabel bit her lip. "I hope we don't get lost."

"We won't." Marianne patted her satchel. "I have maps of the island if we get lost."

Covered in jungle, with only a single human habitation no more than a logging camp, Axel's Island was an imposing prospect. A monstrous mountain rose up in the center, dominating the horizon. Purple tentacles waved in the air above the peak like a sea anemone.

According to their map, that mountain was their destination. The local loggers called it Lindenbrock Mountain and to reach it, they would have to trek through three hundred kilometers of jungle.

She glanced up at Tavish standing silent watch next to her. He hadn't said so much as a word to her since their meeting in the storage closet. He'd done nothing but stare at her, giving her no indication of his mood, not even a frown.

She wanted to scream at him.

"Are the weapons ready?" she asked instead. The jungle was populated with were-apes, six-limbed creatures with eight-fingered paws. They stood nearly two and half meters tall and weighed almost a thousand kilos. Worse, they hunted in packs. Just thinking of them made her shiver.

"Of course," Tavish replied, still not looking at her.

It was a good thing she'd been so busy this past few days, else she may have done him damage.

What did she have to do to get through his thick skull? He seemed to think she was some sort of innocent with no notion of how to do anything on her own. She almost wished he'd stay behind so she could prove to him that she wasn't useless. She was perfectly capable of determining the direction her life took all on her own.

She snorted. The odds that Tavish would stay behind were so close to zero that they might as well be nonexistent.

She let out a breath blowing tendrils of hair off her forehead. They fluttered in the air before coming to rest just off her face.

"What has you so bothered?" Annabel asked.

Marianne rolled her eyes upward toward the looming behemoth.

Annabel flicked her eyes in the same direction and grinned. "You picked him."

Marianne crossed her arms and eyed Tavish. "Don't I know it. Now if only I can get him to figure it out."

His lips firmed into a straight line and he fisted his hands but said nothing in reply, even though she knew he could hear them.

Marianne quirked her lips. "See what I mean?"

Annabel chuckled.

The ship lurched slightly as it came to rest alongside the dock. Ropes were swung over the edge, grabbed by the waiting dockhands and tied into place.

Sheba looked out of place on the small dock. The island didn't see the large barque vessels often and the ship didn't fit into the usual berth slot. The crew had had to swing Sheba around so she ran parallel to the island, covering all but one of the six docks the camp had for incoming aetherships.

"Ship's docked, captain," an airman said.

Ridgewell, standing a few feet away, rose from her relaxed position against the railing. "Very good, start unloading our supplies. I want to head out in less than an hour."

"I'll see to it, ma'am." Tavish bowed to the captain and Annabel, ignoring Marianne entirely as he left.

Ridgewell frowned after him, her brows pinched together. "He hasn't come around has he?"

"I wish I knew what happened. He won't even look at me." Marianne shook her head.

"Oh, he looks," Annabel teased. "Just not when you can see. I'm surprised you haven't felt his eyes boring into your skull."

"What a delightful image." Ridgewell shook her head. "He'll come around, Marianne."

"Maybe it's me. Maybe he just doesn't...." Marianne shrugged. "I should go make sure my bag is packed."

Ridgewell stopped her with a hand on her shoulder. "Give him some time. He's not used to beautiful women looking at him. He doesn't understand how handsome he is, or how much he has to offer a woman like you. You'll need to beat him across the head with that fact before it sinks in."

Marianne sighed. "I'm out of tricks."

"Then learn some new ones." Annabel shrugged. "We're about to undertake a weeklong voyage. You'll have plenty of time to come up with something."

Marianne looked back out over the vast jungle of Axel's Island. "I hope you're right."

Tavish rose from his seat by the fire to walk around the camp again. The camp was set up in a large circle, with the captain, Marianne, and Professor Smith in the center. Starting by the central fire, he walked in an ever-larger circle about the camp until he reached the outermost fire.

They were two Earth days out from port and they hadn't encountered a single problem since they left. That made him nervous. The tales about this island might be exaggerations, but tales usually had some basis in truth. He would feel more comfortable once he experienced what the island would actually threaten them with. It was hard to prepare for something you didn't fully understand.

A twig snapped behind him.

He whirled around, hands up and balled in fists. Only the fact that the sound came from the wrong direction kept him from swinging and hitting the person responsible.

Marianne stood in front of him, her eyes large saucers catching the flickering firelight.

He stared at her, horrified at what he'd nearly done.

"I didn't mean to startle you," she whispered.

He stood up from his fighting crouch. "You shouldn't sneak up on anyone in the dark. It's dangerous."

His heartbeat slowed but a vein in his forehead continued to pulse. How could she be so stupid? What was she doing here?

She walked forward, stopping just inches from him—seemingly oblivious to his rolling anger and confusion. "We need to talk, and you're making it difficult."

"We have nothing to talk about."

She grabbed his arm. "Yes, we do."

He tensed under her touch. It was his left arm. He looked down at her. Her hand was steady, her gaze direct. No matter how hard he tried to keep the wall up between them, she found a way inside.

"Miss Lindstrom, this is unwise."

She flinched, pain etched in her eyes.

He tried to warn himself this would happen, tried to protect them both, but even in this, he was a failure. He couldn't stop hurting people. When would he learn?

Marianne didn't let go of his arm. "We can't go backwards. We've come too far for that."

"You don't understand," he ground out.

"Then tell me." Her gaze entreated him to be honest, to explain.

If only he could.

"How can you deny what's growing between us?"

"There isn't anything there." This was hopeless. How could she not see it?

Her lips firmed and she took the small step to close the gap between them. Reaching up, she pulled his mouth down on hers.

He tried to fight it, to keep her at bay. Tried to protect her. But the chains he kept on his desire exploded at the contact of her lips. He hauled her closer, angled his head, and took her mouth in a kiss meant to sear, to burn.

She tasted sweet, sweeter than any dessert ever created. He savored that flavor, reveled in it. Took, with his mouth, what his mind refused to accept.

She pulled away abruptly, her chest heaving. She looked away. "Even you can't deny what's there. Not when you're stripped bare. Underneath, you see it too."

"I..."

She shook her head, held up her hand. "I don't want to hear it. I'm tired of trying. I should have known I wasn't good enough for someone like you. Your body wants, but your mind refuses."

He reached for her, wanting nothing more than to strip away the pain etched so deeply into her face. A pain he knew he put there.

She flinched back, her eyes once again large saucers. Only this time instead of surprise or shock, he saw fear.

God no, not that.

Please don't let her be afraid of him.

"Behind you!" she screamed.

He whirled around just in time to take a savage claw across his chest. His great coat took the brunt of the attack as he flew backwards into Marianne, pushing her to the ground.

As they landed, he took his full weight on his arms and rolled off her quickly. He turned to face danger.

The creature towered over him by at least half a meter and looked like something out of a nightmare. Red in color and hairy like an ape, it had a wolf's head, six massive limbs and wicked claws.

Strange calls echoed through the night, followed by a scream so unearthly it set his teeth on edge. No need to worry about the camp waking up. Nothing would sleep through that. He risked a quick glance to ensure everyone was rising all the same.

The camp was stirring. Men trained to wake at a moment's notice were already on their feet, weapons in hand. Marianne scrambled away, moving closer to the fire.

"Stay by the fire," he ordered.

The ape roared and swiped at him tearing the hat from his head.

The hat dangled from a claw and the creature shook it off.

He crouched down and drew his sword. The sound of metal on metal was music to his ears and he flipped the switch at the hilt. The sword hummed as electricity coursed up its length in beautiful arcs.

The ape took a step back, startled by the sudden appearance of the weapon.

It started to circle him but he kept with it, keeping it in his sights.

He lunged, whipping the sword out in a long arc, slicing through to the shoulder of the creature's uppermost right arm.

The sword bounced off the thick hide.

He cursed.

Around him the sounds of combat coalesced into a single buzz. He tuned it out, focusing his mind on his opponent. The sword hadn't cut through the creature's skin but it had seared the hair. He tried again, this time aiming for the creature's midsection.

It danced away, attacking with its powerful limbs.

Those wicked ten-centimeter claws came slashing forward from two directions.

MacTavish bent backwards at the waist, leaning away from the slashing claws. Twisting to his right he came under the creature's arm and swung up. This time the sword cut through, without resistance, and sliced through the limb.

It howled.

Tavish hit the switch on his sword again and the lightening crackled louder, sending a jolt of power straight into the creature through its open wound.

It stumbled back and fell, face frozen mid roar.

He stepped forward and aimed the tip of his sword under the creature's jaw. It slid in like butter and he sent another jolt of electricity right into the base of its skull.

If it wasn't dead now, there wasn't hope they could win the fight.

He looked back, taking in the scene, checking where he might be needed.

Ridgewell danced around a group of three apes. Her sword glinted as it caught the firelight. She was holding her own, but for how long?

He started for her, but an ape dropped from the trees, right in front of him.

He stumbled back, bringing up his sword.

A large airman jumped between them. He carried an Electro-Cannon in his large hands.

He fired. The ape fell to the ground, a gaping wound in its chest.

"The captain," Tavish ordered.

The airman nodded, the massive gun, turning in an arc to fire at another ape.

Tavish brushed past, running toward Ridgewell.

The airman with the gun was diverted by a second group of apes.

Tavish rolled under the guard of one ape, coming up just behind it, bringing his sword up over his head, to slice through the underarm.

He didn't have time to hit the button to send a surge of electricity through the wound before he was past the creature, and behind it.

The creature's mid-limb hung uselessly at its side. It howled in anger or pain as it turned to face the new threat.

"They're vulnerable under the arms," MacTavish shouted over the creature's shoulder.

"Got it." Ridgewell dodged another attack, bringing her sword up to block the claws before they hit her face. She rolled to the side out of the way, deflecting the claws to the ground.

Tavish danced to the left as the injured creature swung both of the limbs from his good side. The movement brought him behind another ape. He swung his sword upward slicing into the underarm of the mid-limb. He flipped the surge button and the electricity on the sword danced into the creature.

This time it didn't have time to even scream. It simply fell to the ground.

Two left.

Ridgewell lunged forward, slashing at the remaining uninjured ape.

The attack put her under the creature's guard, her sword pointed down and behind her. She whipped the sword up, slicing into it's arm.

Not giving the creature time to react, she drew her own Electro-Gun and fired point blank into the gaping wound her sword left behind. A small ball of energy shot from the gun, piercing into the creature. It jerked, and it, too, fell to the ground.

One left.

They circled it.

Its head darted around.

Then it gave a howl, similar to the unearthly sound he heard earlier, and leapt ten meters into the air to the overhanging tree above.

Calls echoed around them, and Tavish turned to see the remaining apes leaping to follow.

They'd won.

Ridgewell watched them go. Her chest heaved from exertion but the weapons in her hand remained steady. Her face was dirty, smeared with mud and blood. A long strand of her black hair had fallen out of its braid and fallen across her face. The right sleeve of her shirt had been ripped clean and blood seeped from a wound on her shoulder.

The rest of the crew remained on edge. He could see them all standing like statutes, weapons at the ready, staring up into the dark canopy.

As the last echo of the retreating apes faded into the dark, He flipped off and sheathed his sword.

"At least we know what to expect now," Ridgewell murmured. She walked up beside him, sheathing her own more mundane sword and holstering her gun.

"We'll need more than a one-man watch," he said. Guilt over what he'd been doing during his watch hit his gut like a sledgehammer. He should have been paying attention to his surroundings, not kissing Marianne. What had come over him?

Ridgewell laid a hand on his shoulder. "I'm not sure anyone would have noticed those things coming. They're damn silent for something so large."

He brushed off her hand. The captain could think what she would, but he knew the truth. He hadn't been doing his job. There was no excuse for it. He looked out over the camp. The survivors were moving about, checking on fallen comrades. It was time he did the same. "I'll go check the damage. See how many men we lost."

Counting up the dead would be a start to the penance he would have to pay.

One dead.

Several injured, but only one dead.

Tavish let out a deep breath. One was too many. He slowly walked the perimeter of the camp, eyes now turned to the trees. Who would have thought that the apes would attack from so many different angles?

He should have known. There were plenty of stories out there about these creatures and they had disregarded them. What a fool he'd been. The stories they'd heard had been exaggerated in the wrong direction.

A twig snapped behind him.

He whirled around.

Ridgewell stood five meters from him.

"I thought it was best to warn you I was approaching." Her lips were twisted in a wry smile.

"You should be resting." Tavish waived his hand at her bandaged shoulder.

Ridgewell stretched. "I keep rolling over on it."

A scream echoed through the night. It was an unnerving but faint echo, like it came from kilometers away.

He rubbed the back of his neck. "I doubt I'll ever get used to that noise."

"I have Sanders and Fitchum on the Electro-Cannons. They'll keep them off us."

"How much farther does the professor think we'll have to go?"

Ridgewell turned to look back at the camp. "She says another day."

"Why are we doing this?" he asked.

"I have to."

"Why?"

Ridgewell looked off into the darkness. "I can't reveal that information."

He blinked. Ridgewell had never hidden anything from him before. What was she hiding?

"Ma'am, this is endangering the crew."

"I'm sorry, but I can't tell you." She sighed. "But I really wish I could."

"Ma'am?"

"You should get some rest. I'll stay up and watch." She pointed toward the fire.

He looked at the uncompromising tilt of her chin and shook his head. "Very well, but wake me in two hours."

"We'll see." Her voice was soft, a faint echo of the cool soprano she usually used. The lines etched in her face were deeper, and she sat down on the stump as if the weight of the world was on her shoulders.

What threat loomed that could reduce the captain to such a state? The strong, proud woman he'd grown to admire had never shown her worry so openly before.

He walked back to his bedroll. There was more to this than a simple treasure hunt and more than mere danger to the crew from local wildlife.

He glanced down at Marianne, sleeping restlessly next to the fire. How was he going to keep those he cared about safe if he didn't know what he was facing? He had to get the captain to tell him what it was.

He laid down on the bedroll and let his mind wander over possibilities. He would keep everyone safe one way or another. If his monstrosity allowed him anything it was the ability to fight for those he cared for. He wasn't going to let them down now simply because he didn't know what the threat was.

CHAPTER TWENTY

Sweat dripped down Marianne's forehead, landing in her eyes. She wiped it away with her handkerchief. God, it was hot here.

A canteen was shoved in her face. She looked up to see Tavish standing next to her. He hadn't been far from her since the attack by the wereapes.

"You should drink," he said.

She took the canteen and took a sip. The cool water dripped down her throat, taking away the oppressive heat. She licked her lips and handed the canteen back to him. "Thanks."

"The Professor says we shouldn't be far from the cave now."

Marianne nodded. "Hopefully, it'll be cooler in there."

Tavish walked with his hands behind his back, and stared straight ahead as he walked beside her. "How's your head?"

"It's fine. The heat isn't helping the headache but I'll manage."

"I'm sorry, if—"

Marianne rubbed her throbbing temple. "Stop with the apologizing."

He reared back as if slapped.

"You aren't to blame for every mishap that happens in my life." She clenched her teeth.

He rubbed the back of his neck. "I fell on top of you."

"I tripped over a log." She rolled her eyes. "Why do you insist on taking the credit for everyone's pain?"

"Because I am usually the cause of it," he bit out.

"It's not 'usually' your fault. In fact, it's rarely your fault. You are not responsible for everyone's mistakes."

"You don't understand," he said through gritted teeth.

"You're right. I don't." She sighed and rubbed her arms. "I doubt I ever will."

"What is that supposed to mean?" he snarled.

"It means that until you stop with the 'woe is me' attitude you'll never be happy and I can't be around someone like that." She lengthened her stride and walked closer to Annabel, her heart sinking with each step.

He grabbed her arm.

She gasped and whipped around to face him. "What do you think you're doing?"

"Trying to —"

Twigs snapped. Lots of them.

Marianne froze. Tavish pushed her behind him. The soft smell of ozone assaulted her nose as his sword hummed to life.

She peered around his shoulder. Everyone around them was alert, ready for anything.

An airman stumbled out of the brush and froze, eyes wide as he faced the muzzle of the Elctro-Cannon. His lips moved, though no sound came out. .

"Stow the cannon, Sorenson." The captain's crisp command cut through the battle haze.

Tavish sheathed his sword. "Aiden, you should know better than to run up on this group."

Aiden swallowed as the cannon was lowered. "I found the cave entrance. I was so excited, I forgot."

"Where is it?" Marianne stepped out from behind Tavish.

The airman seemed to shake himself. "Just a kilometer or so to the east. Entrance is large. We can't miss it."

"How do you know it's the cave we want?" Smith asked.

"There are these markings on the cave wall that ain't natural, ma'am."

"So, you're saying this trail doesn't lead to the entrance," Tavish loomed over the airman, a dark scowl crossing his face.

Marianne resisted the urge to roll her eyes. When would he learn to stow his anger? She placed a hand on his arm and shook her head at him.

He relaxed. Even when he was being obtuse and difficult she could calm him. If only he would notice, maybe he could pull out whatever thorn had gotten into his head and realize that he cared for her.

"How far off trail are we?" Ridgewell's voice broke into her thoughts.

Aiden scratched his head. " I don't know what this trail leads to or not, but the mountain is east of us. We're circling it now."

"Thank God for flankers," Tavish grumbled.

Ridgewell walked over to Smith and conversed with her quietly as the professor consulted her books.

After a few moments, the captain raised her head and looked at the now calm airman. "All right, Mr. Vann, show us the way."

He nodded and turned back into the brush.

The group followed, making slow progress through the thick foliage of the jungle. The trail Mr. Vann had made returning to the group was haphazard, narrow, and difficult to follow.

Marianne stumbled over a bush. Tavish's steely hand caught and steadied her. Her legs ached and her head had gone from an incessant throb to stabbing pain. She leaned on Tavish's arm as he helped her over a fallen log.

It may have been only be a kilometer of travel but it felt more like ten. She rubbed her temples. "How much longer?"

"Nearly there, ma'am." Mr. Vann cut through another swath of jungle, clearing a wider path for the group to follow.

Finally, they were through the thick underbrush and the group stepped out into a large clearing. They'd lost sight of the mountain when they entered the jungle, but she remembered what it had looked like from aboard ship, rising above the tops of the trees, looking like a man walking on a grassy plain.

Up close, the mountain was even more intimidating. She tilted her head back, but the mountain continued up above what she could see.

"I wonder if its peak is even within the Space Whales atmosphere?" she muttered.

"I remember seeing several tentacles waving around up there, so my guess is no." Ridgewell was standing next to them. "It's a mighty impressive mountain. Makes Everest look like a foothill."

"That it does, ma'am." Marianne said.

"The cave entrance is just up ahead." Aiden stood in front of them, waving his hand toward the mountain.

"Onward, Mr. Vann." Ridgewell locked arms with Marianne and dragged her after the retreating airman.

"I'm right behind you," Marianne laughed.

Ridgewell tossed Marianne a grin, her violet eyes gleaming with excitement.

They stopped just inside the cave entrance. Marianne immediately felt the temperature difference. The cool air of the cave caressed her skin and she breathed deeply, letting it whisk away the heat from her blood. Her headache eased and she ran a finger along the intricate carvings on the wall. "They glow."

"They do. How strange." The rest of the crew remained outside as Ridgewell stepped in deeper. She also put her hand on one of the markings. The light seeped through her hand. "Anna, what do you make of these?"

Before the professor could answer, a deep rumble echoed through the cave and the ground shook. Marianne fell forward deeper into the cave.

A rock dislodged from the ceiling, crashing to the floor inches from where she had been standing.

She scrambled back as more rocks began to fall.

"Marianne!" Tavish bellowed.

She couldn't see him. The dust was too thick. A large hand came down on her shoulder and hauled her up. "This way, miss. We have to go deeper."

Mr. Vann pushed her, propelling her before him.

Her feet slipped along the rocky floor as the ground shook beneath her.

More rocks fell. Larger ones crashed around her.

Ridgewell grabbed her hand and they stumbled together.

Marianne coughed and put her handkerchief over her mouth to protect her lungs from the dust.

The rumbling eased and they both fell against the wall, chests heaving as they took in the pile of rocks in front of them. It looked like the side of the mountain had collapsed on them.

"Oh my God," Marianne whispered.

"At least we have the book. Should help us navigate," Ridgewell said.

"But Annabel was the one with the map. All we have is the untranslated original. I can't read the language, can you?"

"No." The captain's voice sounded strained.

Marianne looked down.

The captain was kneeling before the edge of the pile, her head bowed.

A hand stuck out from the rock.

"Mr. Vann?" Marianne laid a hand on the captain's shoulder. "Had he been with you long?"

Ridgewell nodded. "Yes, since the beginning. He was a good airman."

"Do you think the others got out?"

"I hope so." Ridgewell looked down at her fallen airman. "I'll take care of your family, Aiden. I promise."

The captain rose and looked into the depths of the cave. Air rustling her hair, she sighed. "We should move on. We have to find another way out."

"How?"

"We walk and we consult the book. Maybe something will look familiar. There were pictures in there, if I remember correctly."

"What if this isn't the cave we came to find?" Marianne's voice quavered and she clutched her arms around herself.

"Come now, Marianne?" Ridgewell twitched her lips into a half smile. "The cave is lit by some source we can't identify and the air that blows through it is cool and moving. If this were a real cave we would have to be worried about our air supply and the fact that neither of us brought a torch."

"Right." Marianne blushed and looked deeper into the cave. It seemed to stretch on endlessly. She raised her hand to her throat. "Well, we're not going to get out by standing around."

Wishing her rolling stomach would relax, Marianne started walking. Whatever lay ahead, she would face it. After everything else she'd faced so far, how could it possibly be worse?

Sweat dripped off his forehead and Tavish reached to wipe it away. He had to get to her. He had to make sure she was all right.

He couldn't hear anything coming from the other side, but that didn't mean they were dead. He wouldn't allow for that possibility.

He lifted a rock.

A rumble began from above him and he quickly backed away. Just in time. A cascade of rocks, the largest one bigger than his head, fell over the small gap he'd made.

"Damn it!"

"Mr. Tavish, we'll never get in this way. The entrance is too unstable." Doctor Smith rested a hand on his shoulder.

He brushed it off. "I won't fail her."

"There's another way."

"I shouldn't have let her go ahead. I should have protected her better."

Smith grabbed him by the shoulder and shook him. "Mr. Tavish, you have to listen to me. This isn't helping."

He tried to brush her aside but she remained firm.

She took a deep breath. "Look, I don't think I was wrong about the direction we were headed before. There's another entrance."

He wanted to believe. He really did.

"We can find them. We just have to be smart about it. If we try to dig in, we risk another cave in. This one could hurt someone."

Another rumble.

More rocks fell.

Dust danced out of the cave mouth and men came out coughing. They carried another behind them.

Tavish hurried over. It was Sorenson. Damn, he was needed on the cannon.

Sorenson groaned and opened his eyes.

"Can you stand, airman?" Tavish asked.

"I think so, sir." Sorenson rose. He was a bit unsteady on his feet, but his eyes were clear. "I've got a thick skull, sir. I'll be fine."

He nodded. The professor was right. He might not like it, but at this point he had no choice but to let her lead. He looked at the cave entrance. Loosing crewmen wouldn't help. "All right Professor, we follow you. Which way do we go?"

"They must mean something." Marianne traced her finger on one line of an intricate carving that spun out along the wall like dancing waves.

Ridgewell nodded. "I agree, but we won't know until Anna gets a look at them."

Marianne stopped and turned to face her. "Why are you doing this?"

"Doing what?"

"Helping me."

Ridgewell stared at the wall and avoided Marianne's gaze. "You're a member of my crew."

Marianne crossed her arms. "You risked the lives of half your crew or more just to reach this place. I... " She looked down at her feet. "I'm not worth it."

Ridgewell rested a hand on her shoulder. "You shouldn't be so hard on yourself. You are a valuable member of the crew."

Marianne snorted. A very unattractive sound but she didn't care. "Be honest, I'm about as effective as a door jam in a crisis."

"You keep a cool head." Ridgewell tipped her head up. "Don't discount that. All you lack is knowledge, and that can be learned."

Marianne bit her lower lip. "Would you teach me how defend myself?"

"Of course," Ridgewell grinned and patted her on the back. Then her smile turned serious. "I won't turn you into an expert fighter overnight. If we end up in a scrap, no heroics."

"Yes, ma'am. Frankly, I'll be happy if all I manage to do is learn how to run away." Marianne rubbed her throat.

"Don't underestimate running away." Ridgewell leaned against a wall. "Sometimes that's the best answer to a difficult situation. Only fools charge in all the time. Even well-trained fighters find themselves in untenable situations."

"Really?" Marianne asked. "What if they have a gun?"

"Pray they don't hit you and keep a large object between you and them."

"Not very helpful." Marianne looked at her feet.

"But the best advice I can give you. Odds are, if they plan to use a projectile weapon you won't know they're there until you're unconscious or dead."

Marianne's legs went numb and she leaned against a wall. "Then why do I even bother learning this stuff?"

"Because it might save your life. Not everyone fights with guns these days. They're expensive."

Marianne stood straighter. "All right, what should I know?"

"If an attacker comes from behind and grabs you around the waist, you drop. Becoming a dead weight will force the opponent to readjust his grip that will give you time to run away." The captain came behind her and grabbed her around the waist.

Marianne sank to the floor and broke free from her grasp. "That seems easy enough."

"Once they pick you up, you're pretty much helpless. You need to break away before they have a complete hold on you." Ridgewell grimaced. "Women as a general rule are physically weaker than men. I hate to admit it, but even I would be in trouble if a man picked me up."

Marianne sobered, remembering her encounter on the streets of London. If Tavish hadn't arrived, she'd have been raped and likely killed. She hadn't fought the brutes at all. She'd just stood in place like a helpless fool. "I see what you mean."

"As a last resort, using your elbow or the heel of your foot, aim for the attacker's instep, their nose, or stomach." Ridgewell demonstrated each move as she described it.

"What about... You know... ?" Marianne blushed and pointed downward..

"Only after you've hit somewhere else painful like the instep or nose. Men are instinctively protective of that area. It won't do any good to go there first." Ridgewell placed a hand on Marianne's shoulder. "Don't forget that you aren't meant to fight. All these skills should only be used to run away."

Marianne stood taller and looked the captain in the eye. "I'll remember."

They continued down the hall in silence. There were no bends or turns in the corridor. It was just a straight path that led them deeper into the mountain.

Eventually, the rough, uneven pathway turned into perfectly worked stone. The markings changed too. The soft swirling patterns becoming ridged geometric designs with sharp angles and few curves.

They paused just inside the new passageway. The worked ceiling was about five meters from the floor and all sides, floor and ceiling included, were covered in the new pattern.

"What do you think it means?" Ridgewell asked.

"I'm not sure. These look more like symbols then the others do, and they look familiar." Marianne ran her fingers along the wall, wisps of memory pulling at her mind.

Ridgewell turned from examining one of the designs. "What do you mean?"

"Here, look at this." Marianne quickly flipped through her book. Stopping on a page, she walked over and showed it to the captain.

The page was covered in designs similar to the markings on the walls. Each design had a brief description in the foreign tongue that no one but Annabel seemed to be able to decipher.

"Well, at least we know we are in the right place." Ridgewell looked around, frowning. "I wish I knew what was causing the light."

"Me too." Marianne bit her lip.

The same light that had permeated the previous cave worked its magic here. Still, there wasn't a single light source to be seen, not a sconce nor light fixture anywhere. A soft, yellow glow, like that given off by a candle, continued as far as she could see, no brightening.

She glanced down at her feet. "It bothers me a bit that we don't cast a shadow."

Ridgewell shivered. "I was trying not to think about that."

They reached a "T" intersection and Marianne turned her head to look down both paths. "Which way?"

"Left."

"Why left?"

Ridgewell shrugged. "When in doubt, go left."

"Is that a rule in the Captain's Handbook or something?" Marianne chuckled.

"No, just a rule I follow. Leads to consistency and I don't dally over the choice between two seemingly equal things."

"You're the captain."

Ridgewell smiled. "Yes, I am."

They turned left.

Nothing really changed.

The corridor remained glowing at the same level. Nothing jumped out to attack them, and the floor and ceiling remained the same distance apart.

Ridgewell turned to Marianne. "Do you have any paper on you by chance?"

"Of course I do. I'm your secretary." Marianne reached into her bag and pulled out a small notebook and a pencil. She handed them over.

"Excellent." Ridgewell went over to the wall and began sketching the path they took. "I figure we should at least have an idea of where we came from. We can map the turns we make so we can backtrack if we need to."

Marianne nodded.

The two moved onward, coming to several intersections. On each one, Ridgewell took the left path.

"Do you think Tavish will find another way in?" Marianne asked, after the third turn.

"Anna has the map you both drew. If there's another way in, she'll find it."

Marianne reached up and rubbed her throat as her stomach churned. "This is the first time since I boarded Sheba that he hasn't been near."

"Have you managed to deal with your differences?"

Marianne's fingers stiffened at her neck. "One moment I think I have him figured out, and the next he's gone and done something stupid again."

"Well, he is a man." Ridgewell's lips turned up in one corner.

"It's not just that. I'm not sure he even knows what he feels, let alone how I feel."

"Have you made your feelings clear?"

"As plain as I can." Marianne threw her hands in the air and paced ahead. She whirled around. "I've all but declared my feelings in words."

"Do you love him?" Ridgewell asked, trying to make her voice as gentle as possible.

"I don't know." Marianne whirled around. "All I know is that I feel wonderful when he's near and terrible when we're apart. I know that the sound of his voice is more welcome to me then the sound of beautiful music. I know that I… " She shook her head. "I know that I miss him already."

"I'm no expert on love, far from it in fact, but from what I hear, I think you might be."

"And if I am, how does that help me?" Marianne asked.

"I don't know." Ridgewell's expression turned inward and a single tear dripped down her cheek. She wiped it away. "Like I said, I'm far from an expert. My experiences… well…. Let's just say they've left me ill equipped to answer you."

Marianne's expression softened and she laid a hand on her friend's shoulder. "I see."

"No, you don't." Ridgewell shrugged her hand away. "How can you expect Tavish to understand his feelings for you, if you don't understand your own?"

Marianne's eyes grew wide. "I hadn't thought of it like that."

"Have you actually told him your feelings, said the words?"

"No, I uh…." Marianne blushed.

Ridgewell took a deep breath and smiled. "When we get back from this adventure, corner him and let him know."

"If you think it's best."

"Trust me, you don't want to leave it for later. Sometimes later…" Ridgewell's voice caught. "Sometimes later isn't an option."

Marianne's eyes grew round. "Captain, I—"

Ridgewell waved her hand. "My past is in the past and not up for discussion."

Marianne shrank back. "Yes, ma'am."

The captain took a deep breath and laid an arm around Marianne's shoulders. "I'm sorry. I just don't like thinking about it. We should focus on finding a way out of here."

Marianne shot her a half smile. "All right."

They reached another intersection.

"Is it just me or does it look lighter coming from the right?" Ridgewell asked.

"No, I see it too." Marianne peered at Ridgewell. "You'll have to make a turn other than left here."

"Don't be smart."

Marianne chuckled as the two women walked down the corridor toward the light.

CHAPTER TWENTY-ONE

"This should be the last one." Draven dropped the contraption over Captain's Pierce's head.

Pierce fought against his binds.

They always did.

How could anyone miss the changes that had crept over the crew? Surely Pierce had noticed the way the men ate in sync or how they performed their assigned tasks perfectly, never deviating.

Just more evidence that Pierce was an arrogant sot. He probably didn't notice anything beyond his own ego.

Draven snorted in contempt.

"Are you certain you can make the ship run smoothly without him?" Draven asked the being hovering behind the captain.

"Yes." Shadow was now almost black in color. "I have had enough time to learn what he knows. No one will guess he is under my command and not his own."

Draven suppressed a shudder. The entire crew, captain on down, would be under Shadow's control.

His hand hovered over the switch. He looked into Pierce's terrified eyes and his stomach churned. How easy would it be for Shadow to have him placed here?

Too easy.

The being had plenty of opportunity to learn what he knew. He could easily get someone else to set the machine up.

If he flipped the switch was he dooming himself to Pierce's fate? What use to his beloved would he be if he were a puppet on Shadow's string?

"I would never turn you into such a creature," Shadow purred. "You are far too useful to me as a thinking man. Just look at this machine you have created. What a marvel."

A chill slithered down his spine.

With every passing day he saw the creature he'd bargained with in a clearer light. Yet, he was in too deep to back out now. When you dealt with the devil you didn't leave. Had he doomed Nora to a fate worse than death?

He was beginning to suspect that even when he got the book, he wouldn't be free of Shadow.

He shook his head. He'd made his choices. He had to see them through.

There was no way out for him now. No way he could leave Nora behind.

He flipped the switch.

Pierce screamed as whirling blades sliced into his head.

Waves rippled through the man-shaped cloud of smoke and Shadow moaned in ecstasy. "I will never grow tired of that sound."

"We'll get you more once we return to London." Draven stepped back and let the machine do its work. After the first hundred victims the screams ceased to affect him.

"You are certain the girl will return to London?" Shadow asked over Pierce's screams. "I am not pleased that you let her slip free of our trap."

"It couldn't be helped." Draven pressed his lips together and frowned. "The men we hired did the best they could with the information we gave them."

"They failed," Shadow hissed."

"And they were punished for it." Draven shrugged. "Where the girl goes isn't important. We know where she'll end up. Sheba is based in London and will have to return. Once it does, we will have her."

"And if they hide the book somewhere in the meantime?" Shadow asked.

"Then we get the location from Lindstrom the hard way." Draven checked a dial on the machine. Pierce's screams hadn't died a decibel. With the careful administration of certain drugs, Draven could keep a body from going into shock or passing out. As torture went, it was very effective.

"And in the meantime you will build me an army." Shadow reached out a hand and caressed Pierce's shoulder. "This one is nearly ready."

"Yes, but I think we'll leave the machine on a little longer. He's irritating."

Shadow answered with a deep chuckle.

Draven sat down at his desk and wrote out a summons. "I'll have a message waiting for my contact aboard Sheba."

"When this is all over, you will be well rewarded." Shadow's dark purple shape materialized beside him.

Draven nodded his head in acknowledgment.

Yes, he'd made his bed and now he'd lie in it. After all, wasn't it better to own the debt of such an evil being than the other way around? Nora would be his once again, and who knew? Maybe Shadow was serious. Maybe it would be generous. After all, there would be an army of mindless drones when Draven was finished. Wouldn't that army need a general?

CHAPTER TWENTY-TWO

"I could really go for some sunlight right about now," Marianne muttered.

They'd been walking for what felt like hours with nothing but that soft glow to light the way. It was unnerving not knowing where a light source came from. The strange symbols, at first delightful, where changing. What had originally looked like intricate and playful designs had turned sinister, each sharp edge a dagger, each long line a knife. How much longer would they have to walk?

"At least the glow is getting brighter." Ridgewell took a sip form her canteen. She paused. Frowned. Tipped it upside down and shook it.

Empty.

Just like hers.

Ridgewell ran her hands through her hair.

"We can't be far now," Marianne said, hoping she sounded surer then she felt. She swallowed, her throat already feeling dry. It was as if the mere thought that they were out of water made her mouth parch

"I'm not sure I've ever been this tired."

"We've walked quite a ways. How long have we been in here?"

Ridgewell pulled out her watch. Blinked. Turned to stare at Marianne, then back at the watch. "Over a day now," she whispered.

"How is that possible?"

"That's what my watch is telling me."

Marianne rubbed the back of her neck. "No wonder we're so tired."

Ridgewell nodded. "We could camp here in the hallway."

Marianne shook her head. "I'd rather wait to do that until we're so exhausted we can't move any longer. I want out of this cave."

"Me too." Ridgewell blew hair from her eyes.

They trudged on. Heads bent, exhaustion evident in every step and each breath. The light in the corridor had grown in brilliancy. It was as light as a bright, sunny day on Earth.

Ridgewell leaned against the wall, and closed her eyes. "I'm not sure I can go much farther."

Marianne rested next to her. "Just a few meters more?"

"I'm not sure I can." Ridgewell's lips were dry and cracking. "What I wouldn't give for some water."

Marianne wasn't in much better shape. The hallway was eerily quiet without the sound of their boot heels clicking on the stone floor.

"Let's rest for a few moments. Then we can move on," Marianne said.

Ridgewell caught her hand. "Do you hear that?"

Marianne shook her head. Everything was foggy. All she could hear was the pounding of her heart in her chest, the soft thud of her pulse.

"It's water, Marianne!" Ridgewell stood up, pulling Marianne with her. "Water!"

Marianne strained her ears but heard nothing. "There isn't water, captain. It's nothing, just more hallway."

"No, it's water. I'm sure of it."

Ridgewell started forward. "Come on, Marianne. We have to find it."

Marianne reached for her but the captain ran away, down the hall. The excited sound of her cheers echoing after her.

"Fantastic." Marianne rolled her eyes and started after her. "Now we've split up. This will end well."

She found Ridgewell collapsed on the floor in front of another intersection. Marianne collapsed next to her. Felt for a pulse. It beat steadily but soft.

Another "T" intersection, they could go straight or turn right. The hallway was brighter going straight, but Marianne sat staring down the darker passageway.

Memory stirred.

She looked at the small map they'd been drawing. Something hard and solid hit the bottom of her stomach.

They'd been going in circles the entire time.

How were they supposed to get out?

She pulled the book from her bag. This thing had started it all, had gotten so many of her new friends in trouble, and now this? She slammed it against the wall behind her.

"Damn you!" The book fell from her fingers to her lap.

Tears of frustration welled in her eyes. She was too exhausted to fight them—too exhausted to even try. They fell from her cheeks in silent rivers, dripping onto the book on her lap. The tears coalesced, formed rivulets inside the carvings on the cover.

The book began to glow.

Marianne wiped her eyes, entranced by the glowing book before her.

Was she seeing things?

It started off a soft blue, but changed colors before her eyes: blue, to violet, to blue again and then all the colors of the rainbow. When it reached red the glow intensified, lighting the entire chamber.

The book shook in her hands. It was all she could do to hold on to it.

The sound of stone grinding on stone echoed through the cavern and dust began to fall from the ceiling.

Marianne looked up in horror. Was the ceiling collapsing?

She blinked.

Rubbed her eyes.

Looked again.

The wall behind her was rising. A large chamber opened up before her and the soft sound of water, more beautiful to her ears than music, filtered through.

She stood up on shaking legs, grabbed Ridgewell around her shoulders, and dragged her into the room. Collapsing inside, she tried to find the source of the water.

A small spring tricked its way through the cavern, winding its way along channels carved into the floor.

Marianne put the book down next to the captain and ran toward the nearest channel. She dipped her hands in and drank.

The water tasted sweet, like honey water.

She dipped her canteen into the water and carried it back to Ridgewell. Cradling the captain's head in her lap, she poured the life-giving liquid into her mouth.

The captain drank. Her eyes fluttered open. "Where?"

"You were right. There was water," Marianne giggled, relief making her giddy. "We just had to figure out how to get to it."

Marianne bounced and held up her book. Though no longer glowing her tears were somehow still flowing between the channels carved into its cover, held there by some magical force.

Ridgewell reached up and touched the cover. "How?"

"I don't know." Marianne got up. "I'm going to explore the cavern a bit. You should rest."

"I'll go with you." Ridgewell began to rise but Marianne pushed her back down.

"Captain, you need to rest. You can't push yourself like this. I won't go far."

"I'm coming with you," Ridgewell ordered.

"Yes, ma'am."

The cavern was huge. It would easily fit three Shebas and still have room for a person to move around. Marianne started toward the nearest rivulet. Each channel was about a meter wide and filled to the edge with cool blue water. A pedestal sat in the center of the room.

Marianne walked the perimeter until she found a pathway across the first channel. The channel wasn't wide but Marianne wasn't sure how deep they were and she didn't want to risk falling in.

The path led to a dead end. No way forward except jumping. She glanced down at her feet. She was tired. She could slip.

"What about the book?" Ridgewell held it up. "It looks like the carvings on the floor match the design on the cover. Maybe it's a map."

"That's a great idea." Marianne took the book and searched for the point she'd started on. Using that as a guide, she quickly solved the maze. "Okay, we have to go this way."

The pathways were no wider than the water channels, and they had to squeeze together to allow Marianne to pass. Once back on the outside ring, Marianne made quick work of the maze. The book cover was indeed a map, and they soon found themselves standing before the pedestal.

The designs on the floor continued in smaller scale up the sides of the pedestal. Made of a blue stone so brilliant it sparkled, the pedestal stood a little over a meter from the ground. It tapered open at the top to reveal a ledge slightly larger than the book in Marianne's hands, with a bowl-shaped indentation in the center.

"Water, do you think?" Ridgewell dipped her hand in the pedestal bowl. "We could dump some canteen water in there."

"I'm not sure that's it." Marianne looked at the pedestal opening and at her book. They weren't quite the same size. The opening in the pedestal was a circle; the book was rectangular. "What about the book?"

Ridgewell arched a brow. "That might work."

With a deep breath, Marianne put it into the opening.

The room shook. Marianne grasped the pedestal for support. Ridgewell grabbed her shoulders.

Wind hallowed through the cavern, blowing her hair into Marianne's face, obscuring her vision. Her tears flowed from the book into the space around it. More water joined it, flowing upward form the channels by her feet. Soon the book was surrounded by water. Yet it wasn't wet.

A light pierced down from the ceiling hitting the book dead center. The light shattered, heading in several different directions.

The rays bounced off walls, bathing the chamber in brilliant white light.

The light coalesced into a single beam that traveled the length of the water channels. It rose through the pedestal and then shot out, piercing Marianne in the heart.

An earsplitting sound like a steam whistle reverberated through her. She grabbed her head and collapsed. It was as if something was trying to rip her apart from the inside.

"Make it stop," she cried.

"It's been over a day since the cave-in. How much farther will we have to go?" Tavish wiped his forehead.

Smith consulted her map and compass. "We're still on the right path."

"You mean we're lost," Tavish grumbled.

"We're not lost. We've kept the mountain to our left the entire time. All we do is turn around and we'll find our original trail." She glared at him, her hands, still holding the map and compass, sat on her hip.

"I don't want to find our original trail. I want to find the entrance of this cave."

"I want to find it as much as you do."

Tavish snorted and rolled his eyes.

She stomped up and shot him an irritated gaze. "Henri is my friend."

"I'm sorry." He sighed, rubbing the back of his neck. "I'm just worried."

She patted him on the arm. "We all are, maybe if we—"

A scream ripped through the air. Everyone froze. The scream had come from the mountain.

Marianne!
All of Tavish's instincts screamed for action but he had no idea where to start. No idea where he should even begin.

The entrance, it had to be near. He ran toward the mountain, his hand moving along the rock, desperate to find something, anything that would tell him what to do.

Damn it, he couldn't fail her!

Another scream, this one louder.

"I'm coming, Marianne!" he bellowed, pulling at the rocks with his bare hands. "I'm coming."

The sound was gone. Left in its place, peace.

Soft hands shook her. "Marianne."

Marianne slowly opened her eyes. She was on her back, cool stone beneath her, darkness surrounding her.

The light was gone.

"Marianne?" The captain peered over her. "Are you all right?"

Marianne's head was in the captain's lap. She reached up and rested her hand on her forehead, rubbed her face. "Yes, I think so."

Ridgewell helped her sit up. "What happened?"

"I don't know. There was this sound in my head. It felt like someone was trying to dismantle me." Marianne glanced up at the pedestal. It still glowed with a soft blue light, but the book was no longer resting on its surface. "Where's the book?"

Ridgewell handed it to her. "You were in agony. I wanted it to stop. All I could think of was to remove the book."

"Did it work?"

Ridgewell shook her head. "No, it stopped the light but you screamed for a long time."

Marianne glanced down at the book. The cover still held the swirling rivulets of her tears.

"Daughter of Water?"

Marianne sat still, her eyes glued to the pedestal. It started to shift in form. It grew, melted, transformed.

"I'm really not enjoying this," Ridgewell whispered.

"Me either."

The shifting form solidified, the blue stone now looked like water. Streams fell from its head to the floor and back up again, constantly in motion.

It opened its mouth.

Ridgewell fell forward screaming, holding her hands over her ears.

Marianne held her friend. "What are you doing to her? Stop!"

Music filled the air around her. Whispered words caressed her ears as if they came from many directions. "She must be tested."

"You're hurting her."

"It will only be a moment."

Ridgewell relaxed. Tears streamed down her dirt-stained face.

Marianne squeezed her shoulders. "Are you all right?"

Ridgewell swallowed. "I think so."

Together they struggled to their feet.

The being of water bowed. "Daughter of Air."

Marianne shook her head. "What's going on here? What do mean, Daughter of Air and Water?"

"You are the Daughters of Air and Water. Long have we awaited your arrival."

Other beings coalesced from the water surrounding them. There were hundreds, all looking like blue stone rivers.

The being looked around. "Do you have the Sons of Fire and Earth with you?"

Marianne shook her head. "No, what do you mean? Who are they?"

"Oh." The being deflated, shrinking several inches back into the stone. The others sank back into the water. The pedestal being, its eyes barely recognizable in its face, peered at them. "You must find them. We cannot fully awaken until all are here."

"Awaken from what?" Ridgewell asked.

"You will see. The book will guide you." It slowly sank into the stone, transforming back into the pedestal. "Good luck, daughters."

The room was silent and dark once more.

"Well, what do we do?" Marianne asked.

"Look for a way out?" Ridgewell suggested.

Marianne flipped open the book. This time no strange voices assaulted them. The book simply opened. She turned the first page, then another.

"Oh my God," she whispered.

"What?" Ridgewell leaned over. She inhaled sharply.

The intricate designs and the foreign language were now as clear to her as her native tongue.

"Atlantis," Ridgewell whispered.

CHAPTER TWENTY-THREE

"Were did the exit go?" Marianne glanced around her. The cavern walls were covered in a single, unbroken geometric pattern that gave no indication that there was a door present. If she hadn't seen the door open herself, she would never have believed it had existed.

Ridgewell ran her hand along the wall where the door had been. "It must have shut while we were dealing with the pedestal thing."

"How do we get out?"

Ridgewell brushed dust off her hands. "We aren't going to find the exit by standing around here. I'll head left, you head right, and we'll meet in the center."

Marianne nodded. "Very well."

They circled.

Marianne examined every crevice and design, trying to match it to something she'd seen in the book. Nothing came to mind. The designs never broke, and there was no hidden door, not even a hint of where one might be.

She rubbed her temple. Resting her forehead against the cool wall of the cave, she closed her eyes.

"Head hurt?" Ridgewell came up behind her.

"Yes." Marianne fought back the urge to slam her fists against the wall. "I didn't find anything. Did you?"

"No." Ridgewell slouched next to her.

"Is it just me or is it getting warmer in here?"

Ridgewell fanned herself with her hat. "The air isn't moving anymore."

"Does that mean our air will run out?" Marianne couldn't keep the panic from her voice.

"I sure hope not."

Marianne turned her back to the wall and sank to the floor. She pulled out her canteen and took a sip. "At least we won't run out of water."

"True." Ridgewell crouched next to her and accepted the offered canteen. A piece of hair fell from her braid and she blew it out of the way. She chuckled.

"What's so funny?" Marianne pinched her lips together.

"I was just thinking it was too bad I couldn't blow some air around here like I blew away my hair." Ridgewell shrugged. "I mean, they did call me Daughter of Air."

Marianne sat up and blinked. "Have you tried?"

"You're not serious?"

"Why not?" Marianne's pulse quickened. "What could it hurt?"

Ridgewell stared at Marianne. "Move air with my mind? That's nonsense."

"Up until a few minutes ago would you have said a blue stone man appearing before you would make sense?" Marianne asked.

Ridgewell bit her lip. "So, if I were to try this, how would I go about it?"

Marianne flipped through the book. Stopping on a page she frowned. A woman stood leaning over the pedestal bowl. "Hmm... There is this image."

She handed the book over.

Ridgewell looked down at the picture. "Is she blowing into the bowl?"

Marianne shrugged. "That would be my guess."

Slapping her hands on her knees, Ridgewell rose. "As you said, what could it hurt?"

Marianne laughed and followed her. Wincing, she grabbed her head. "Don't make me laugh. It hurts."

"No promises." The captain reached the pedestal. Copying the image exactly, she leaned over and without touching the bowl, took a deep breath and blew. The water in the basin stirred and so did her hair.

She stood up; the breeze died.

Ridgewell looked toward Marianne. "I can't stand here blowing at this thing. I'll pass out or hyperventilate."

Marianne looked down at her book again, turned a page, and frowned. "Try saying 'Entu Iritui Me.'"

Ridgewell leaned over her shoulder. "How do you know that's the right pronunciation?"

"I just do, and so do you."

"This whole having an entire language dumped in your head thing is going to take some getting used to," Ridgewell muttered.

"I know. Now, are you going to say it or not?"

"Fine." She stood before the bowl again. "Do I need to blow into the bowl again, do you think?"

"Couldn't hurt."

Ridgewell rolled her eyes. "Thank God no one else is here to see this."

Marianne smiled. "I won't tell."

"You better not." Ridgewell took a deep breath, leaned over the bowl, and let out her breath. "Entu Iritui Me."

This time when she stood up, the breeze didn't stop.

It ruffled Marianne's hair and caressed her damp skin. She shivered. "I can't believe that worked."

"I really don't want to think about it." Ridgewell's face had turned ashen and she clutched her arms around her.

"Magic," Marianne breathed. Her heart raced and her head spun. It was almost too much to take in. "Do you think it will work outside of this cavern?"

Color returned to Ridgewell's face. Her cheeks turned a brilliant red. "I doubt it. And no, I'm not going to try, either."

Fighting for levity, Marianne wiggled her brows. "I would pay good money to see you do that in public."

"Not going to happen." The captain crossed her arms and glowered.

Marianne sobered "We have the problem of our oxygen supply covered, but we still haven't addressed how we are going to get out of here."

"At least we won't roast before we do figure it out." Ridgewell looked down at the pedestal and then at Marianne. She smiled.

"I'm not sure I like the look of that smile." Marianne took a step back.

"If I, as the Daughter of Air, can make wind, why can't you, as the Daughter of Water, make a passage out of the cavern? Isn't water known for cutting channels in the earth?"

Marianne opened her mouth, but then shut it again. She regarded Ridgewell seriously for several seconds and then she grinned. "I think you're right."

She flipped through the book. "There must be something in here."

She paused on a page and frowned. The only thing she'd found was picture of a woman leaning over the water.

"What is it?" Ridgewell asked.

"Well, I did find something that might work, but I'm not sure how much help it will be to us."

"What do you mean?"

Marianne bit her lip and looked back up at Ridgewell. "It won't be as simple as open sesame."

Ridgewell's shoulders slumped. "I didn't expect it to, but I'd hoped."

"You and me both." Marianne frowned down at the page again. What use was touching water? She squared her shoulders and shut the book. Only one way to find out.

Kneeling next to the flowing water, she laid a hand on it, and in a clear voice, belted out the words she'd seen written under the image.

"Ubi mòd amech."

The music of water filled Marianne's ears. She focused on her breathing, calming her heart and quieting her nerves. The sounds of the wind disappeared. The sounds of her friend at her side disappeared as well. Soon, all that was left was the water. It churned and gurgled, singing.

She listened.

The music became words. The water was talking to her.

"We're near the south side of the mountain," Ridgewell whispered.

"What?" Marianne blinked, pulling herself from her water trance.

"We are on the south side of the mountain," Ridgewell repeated.

Marianne blinked. "You can hear the wind?"

"I can command it to blow. How is hearing it any harder to believe?"

"I mean, did you have to say any words or anything, or did it just talk to you?" Marianne crossed her arms.

"No, I just concentrated on it."

Marianne bit back her resentment. She'd had to say words to make the magic happen. Ridgewell could just listen. It was Stupid to feel jealous over this. She blew the hair out of her face. "The water was talking to me to. I know where it leads to."

"What do you mean?" Ridgewell asked.

"This stream feeds the entire island. It's why the forest is so lush despite the distance from the sun."

"How does that help us?"

"I can tell you're tired. Or you'd have figured it out by now."

Ridgewell's face brightened. "It has to exit the mountain somewhere."

"Exactly. If we find the exit, we can leave." Marianne tipped her chin up.

"And you found it."

"I did." Marianne waved the captain to follow. She stopped in front of a wall.

Ridgewell looked down at her feet and back up at Marianne. "I don't see it."

"It's beneath us." Marianne waved back toward a channel. "We have to swim."

"We what?" Ridgewell stepped back. "I don't know how."

"I'll help you." Marianne tugged the captain toward the water. "I am the Child of Water, after all."

"We don't know how far we'll have to go. Or how long we'll have to hold our breath," Ridgewell protested.

"It's the only way out for us, and holding our breath won't be a problem." Marianne tucked the book into her knapsack and muttered a few words before jumping into the nearest water channel.

The water soaked through her clothes but it was bathwater warm. "Come on in. The water's great."

Ridgewell took a deep breath and joined her in the channel. She gripped the edge so tightly her fingers turned white. "I hope you know what you're doing."

"We'll be all right." Marianne grabbed Ridgewell's hand. "Èlieno."

A tingling sensation traveled around her neck. Marianne reached up and felt gills. She glanced at Ridgewell.

The captain was staring at Marianne in horror. Her hands were resting on her own neck. "If I wasn't seeing this with my own eyes, I wouldn't believe it."

Marianne grinned. "I told you breathing wouldn't be a problem."

"This is pointless." Tavish fell against the side of the mountain, sinking to his knees.

"Digging the rock with your bare hands?" Smith nodded. "Yeah, that's pointless."

"Do you have any better ideas?"

"We could try blasting it with the Electro-Cannon."

Tavish shook his head. "That won't work. It'll just melt the rock and make it harder to get in."

Pain ripped through his heart. He'd lost her. "I never should have let her out my sight."

"You can't keep me glued to your side forever. What will people think?"

Marianne walked out from behind a rock.

Tavish stared. She was a ghost. She had to be.

"Then again, it might be rather amusing to see him try." The captain followed Marianne as the two women stopped right before him.

"Marianne," he croaked.

She cupped his cheek. "Yes, I'm all right."

Bedraggled though they were, they were still the best sight he'd seen. He scooped Marianne up in his arms and swung her around.

He buried his face in her hair and inhaled the scent of her. Water dripped down the front of his shirt. "You're soaked."

Marianne giggled and patted his back. "We swam to get here, but we're whole."

Ridgewell laughed. "Put her down."

He let go, and Marianne slid back to her feet. He turned and glared at the surrounding crewmembers. They were all several meters away tending to camp.

Good.

"Marianne and I will need to rest before we head back to the ship," Ridgewell said, staring off at the line of trees in front of them. "Will we be safe to camp here?"

"The wereapes seem to avoid the mountain. We haven't encountered any sign of them since we arrived at its base, not even the sounds of them moving about." Smith said. "We've been camped out here for a day or so with no problems."

"Then another day should be fine." Ridgewell stretched her back. "I haven't slept in…" she looked at her watch, and closed her eyes. "Far too long."

"Did you find what we came for?" Tavish asked.

"Yes, and quite a bit more." Ridgewell walked toward the center of camp, heading toward a bedroll.

"What do you mean, 'quite a bit more'?" Smith followed behind.

"I'll tell you after I've slept. I'm exhausted."

Marianne handed her book to Tavish. "Keep an eye on this. It's important."

Tavish looked at the book. It was different somehow. The cover looked almost alive. Rivulets of blue meandered through channels of silver and gold. When he'd last scene that cover, it looked like a leather book, with fancy engraving. Clearly something had changed.

"Of course," he reached for it, taking it from Marianne's hands.

The cover changed.

Went inert.

"Ummm…. Marianne?" He held the book away from his body. "Something happened."

Marianne turned back, looking at him with confusion.

He flipped the cover over and showed her.

She hurried over. "What have you done?"

"I just took the book like you asked," he snapped.

"Sorry, I'm tired." She sent him an apologetic smile before taking it back.

The book returned to life.

"That's strange," Tavish said.

"Strange doesn't even begin to describe what my last two days have been." Marianne turned her head toward the camp. "Captain, you're going to want to see this."

"Two more seconds, two more, and I would be asleep." Ridgewell mumbled as she trudged back, the professor at her heels. "What is it?"

"Watch." Marianne handed the book to Tavish.

The book became inert.

Tavish handed it back and it sprang to life.

"Let me take it," Ridgewell ordered.

Marianne handed it to Ridgewell.

The cover still flowed with blue rivers. Marianne grinned. "That's it. That's how we find the Sons of Fire and Water."

"Sons of what?" Tavish asked.

Ridgewell waved her hand. "We'll talk about it when we get back to the ship. Tavish, keep that book safe. No one but the four of us is to know that the book is more than simply old."

"Yes, ma'am." He tucked it into his pack.

"We rest for a few hours then we head back. It's going to be a forced march but I won't feel comfortable until that book is locked up in my safe."

He watched Marianne as she trudged after the captain to her bedroll. The sight of her soothed the raging beast. He'd almost lost her. That put things in perspective.

Now that he had her back, he wouldn't let her go. He'd been a fool to let her go the first time. He wouldn't make that mistake again.

"I agree that we have to keep it locked up, ma'am. I'm just not sure your safe is the best place." Marianne held on to her book, looking between Ridgewell and the open safe.

"She's right, ma'am," MacTavish added. "The captain's safe is the most logical place to put something of value. Anyone skulking about is going to look there first. And you've already had someone break into it once."

Ridgewell pinched her lips. "Do you have any other ideas as to where we keep it? Surely you aren't suggesting we just leave it on a book shelf somewhere."

"Actually, Henri, that might be the best option." Annabel smiled at the captain. "No one would expect it and we do have a diversion." She pulled out a book; save for the inert cover, it looked identical to the one held by Marianne.

"So we put the fake one in the safe and put the other one on my bookshelf?" Ridgewell asked.

"No, we put the original on Tavish's bookshelf." Marianne added. "Of the four of us, he has the least interest in the book."

"Do you have a bookshelf, Mr. Tavish?" Annabel asked.

"Of course, I do. It's full of nautical books and reference material but I imagine this book will fit in the shelf nicely." Tavish grinned at her.

"Especially if we disguise the cover first," Ridgewell stated. She walked over to one of her bookshelves and pulled a book from the shelf. She pulled a knife from her belt and cut the pages from the spine, then made slits in the cover. "Here, Marianne, give me the book."

Marianne held the book closer to her chest "How are you going to keep the new cover on? Please tell me you're not going to glue it."

"Of course not!" Ridgewell snorted. She grabbed the book from Marianne and slipped it into the pockets made in the fake cover. When finished, she placed it on the table.

From far away it was indistinguishable from other books.

"It's not going to pass a true inspection, but it will work for the kind of cursory look Tavish's room may warrant form a thief." Ridgewell smiled at her handiwork.

Marianne reached for it and the cover glowed, the flowing rivers seeming to appear on the new cover as if they were originally put there. She pulled her hand away and the rivers died.

Ridgewell reached out. The same thing happened. "Okay, so Tavish or Anna will have to be the ones handling the original if we don't want anyone to know it's not an ordinary book on navigation charts."

Tavish picked up the book. "I'll put it in my cabin after we're done."

"I think we are done," Ridgewell said.

Marianne looked up sharply. Was the captain serious? They hadn't even scratched the surface of what they'd learned.

"I trust the new information you have will lead in some way to a profit for the crew." Tavish asked. "Not that I care, but the crew will ask questions. We are a merchant ship after all."

Ridgewell nodded. "If what we uncovered is even half true, the crew will be well rewarded."

"That's enough for me. I'll put this away and check on our readiness for departure."

"Find Quinn. I want the engines fired for the entire trip to London." Ridgewell sat down behind her desk.

"We'll blow through power that way," Tavish warned.

Ridgewell's leaned on her desk and frowned down at her hands. "I know, but I want to reach London as soon as possible. Plot a direct course and get us there as fast as the engines will take us."

"We'll have to keep the crew below decks. The aetherwhale won't be able to maintain an atmospheric bubble large enough for us to breath up there."

"I know. See that it's done."

"Yes, ma'am."

As the other two filed out of the office, Marianne stayed behind.

"Is there something I can help you with, Marianne?" Ridgewell asked.

"Why didn't we tell them more?"

Ridgewell sighed and rubbed the bridge of her nose. "It's not that I don't trust them. I do, especially Tavish. I just don't feel comfortable talking about something so sensitive where so many ears can hear."

"I thought that was why we waited until we were aboard ship to discuss it."

"I feel too exposed. Too many chances for eavesdropping, not enough ways for me to protect the flow of information."

"How will going to London help with that? I'd expect that to cause more trouble, not less."

Ridgewell turned her chair around to look out the large window. "I have people I trust there. People who can keep this book safe until we figure out what it does."

"Who are you, ma'am?" Marianne asked.

"I'm the captain."

"With all due respect, you're more than that."

Ridgewell took a deep breath and exhaling slowly, turned to face Marianne again. "I can't tell you."

"Whether we like it or not, we're connected somehow. You can't deny it, and neither can I."

Ridgewell rubbed the bridge of her nose. "It's not solely my secret to reveal."

Marianne pinched her lips and narrowed her eyes. Then, sighing, she forced her mind to calm. "All right, I won't press you but if we're going to London, I should get your correspondence in order."

"Marianne—" The captain's voice was so quiet, Marianne had to lean in to hear. "Please know that if I could tell you, I would. I do trust you."

"Thank you." Marianne left, her heart both lighter and at the same time heavier. She was honored that the captain trusted her, but what secret could be so powerful the captain wouldn't even share it with Tavish? The gravity of the idea was almost enough to pin her in place.

The captain would never be part of something nefarious.

But if not that, then what? She shut the office door and closed her eyes. It was just one more mystery about a woman who had many. It shouldn't bother her so much. Opening her eyes she started toward her own office when movement caught her eye.

Galveson ducked his head back behind a door.

Why was he skulking around here? He didn't have an office in this section of the ship. Had he heard anything about the book? Should she warn the captain?

She shook her head. She was just tired and jumping at shadows. Galveson was second mate. He had every reason to be walking about in the captain's hallway.

Opening her office door she shut it and sat down at her desk. She couldn't tackle the mystery of her captain. Perhaps she could figure out Tavish. He'd been attentive since she'd returned from the caves. In fact, this was the first time he'd left her alone since then. Was that indication of his feelings? Did she have to tell him the words?

She stared at her desk, seeing his face before her. His actions could be explained as guilt. She had to know unequivocally that he had feelings for her. And if that was going to happen she'd have to tell him how she felt first.

It would have to be her and she had to accomplish it before they reached London. After that, everyone would be too busy.

His usual haunt would be inaccessible until they reached their destination but that didn't mean she couldn't corner him somewhere else. She leaned back in her chair and planned. One way or another, she was going to know whether she had a future with Tavish. Her heart belonged to him. Time to find out if he would break it.

CHAPTER TWENTY-FOUR

Tavish swirled the amber liquid in his glass. He normally didn't indulge. He needed to have his wits about him to handle his added strength. But tonight he needed the liquid fortification. He hadn't seen Marianne since they'd returned to the ship.

He took a drink, and the fiery liquid burned all the way down his throat. He'd pushed her away. How could he expect her to take him back? He'd hurt her. Again.

There was only so much a body could take. He knew he needed to apologize, even beg for her forgiveness; but coward that he was, he couldn't bring himself to do it.

It wasn't the apology that he feared but her rejection. If he begged and she turned away… He took another swallow of the whisky hoping it would burn away the regret.

He closed his eyes, focused on breathing.

When they reached London, he'd leave. He wasn't fit company. Maybe it was time he took his own advice and removed himself from the equation.

He'd buy an old shack somewhere in the Americas and disappear to the West. He could live a life alone and separate from the outside world. Somewhere where he wouldn't hurt anyone else.

His door opened.

Or at least he thought his door had opened. He couldn't be sure. His vision was a bit fuzzy. How many glasses had he had? Two? He couldn't remember.

A white angel stood in the doorway, her wings draped around her shoulders. Smaller then he'd thought they'd be, the angel stepped into the room and shut the door.

"Angel, have you come to take me away."

"No, I've come to talk some sense into you."

Marianne's voice… Maybe it was a dream. That would be nice. One more heavenly dream before he left all hope behind and fled.

Marianne stepped closer and rested a hand on his shoulder. "I wanted to make sure you are all right. I haven't been able to get away until now."

Tavish reached up and gently tugged on her hand. She fell into his lap. There was too much talking in this dream. He didn't want to talk. He wanted to taste, to feel, to experience.

Marianne's hands fluttered on his chest. Her face, now mere inches form his,

was in focus. She bit her lower lip.
He wanted to bite that lip. He drew her mouth down on his, took her lip into his mouth and sucked. Nipped.
A soft moan escaped her lips. Now that was the sound he needed to hear. He drew her deeper into the kiss. His tongue was ready to dance. In moments, he had the fires lit. She was willing, and wanting.
She shifted, startled him. Brought her hands up to cup his face as she angled her head and kissed him back.
Red-hot desire raced through his veins, pumping blood to his groin. He was hard and aching for her in moments. Such was her power. He reveled in it.
Tonight, for this one night, his mind would let him dream. He'd brush aside his misgivings. In this dream world he couldn't hurt her. Everything would be perfect. Just a man and a woman making love.

Marianne wouldn't lie. She'd been hoping something like this would happen.
She'd come to say she loved him.
She still intended to.
But with his lips so hot and needy, and his hands so demanding, she could do nothing but follow along.
He tasted of fire and cinnamon, and she lapped it up—drank the intoxicating essence of him.
Through lovemaking, she intended to make him see and understand what she felt, no ambiguities, no hidden agenda or meaning. He either accepted her love or he rejected it.
There was no turning back.
If she wanted something she needed to reach out and take it.
She let her hands fall to his neck, felt the blood pounding through his veins as her hand rested on an artery.
The ridged metal of his artificial limb gave not a millimeter as her hand dropped further to rest on his leather-covered shoulder. Her right hand fell too, grabbing his arm, squeezing.
She moved to the front of his shirt, tugged. It came loose. Reaching down she forced her hands beneath the soft linen, and touched the hot, rippled muscles of his abdomen.
He tensed and he groaned. Tilting his head, he took her mouth in a savage, aggressive kiss that left her gasping for air.
He was hard everywhere. It was nearly impossible to tell where the man ended and the machine began. But it didn't matter. To her, in this moment, he was just a man, she just a woman. Together, they could be ever so much more.
His hands roamed over her back, caressed her through the thin silk of her robe. They circled forward, starting at her hip he brought the hand up, gently massaging her waist, her ribs, then finally, when she was all but aching, he cupped her breast.
The sensation of his large hands over her delicate flesh, protected only by her

thin nightgown and silk robe, sent a shiver of anticipation through her. What would it feel like for him to kiss her through that cloth? Would the fine linen tease?

He squeezed.

She broke form his kiss, tipped her head back, and gasped for air.

"God, Marianne, you're perfect." He kissed her neck, licking, sucking on the base, and tasting her pulse.

Desire flew.

"Take me to bed." She tipped her head back.

He stood up, taking her with him. Pivoting on one foot he dropped her down on the bed, her hair spilled out over the pillow, and she smiled, Madonna-like, up at him. Opening her arms, she welcomed him.

The look of pure bliss that crossed his face was enough to warm her heart anew. If she'd had any doubt of what she was doing, if she'd even thought of hesitating, that look would have washed away all resistance. How could a woman ever ignore a man who so obviously cherished her?

He ripped his shirt off and crawled into bed, his large legs straddling her. He dropped to his elbows, one hand reaching up to brush hair form her face.

"You are so beautiful," he whispered. "May I worship you?"

"Yes." Her reply was barely a whisper as anticipation raced through her blood.

His hands traced her cheek. Light fingers trailed down her neck, her throat, dipped down between her breasts.

His fingers were an artist's brush, her skin a canvas. Warmth spread from his fingertips into her, heating her blood, sending her heart racing.

He untied her robe, and spread the halves wide, up over her shoulders, pinning her arms and opening her up to his gaze.

The heat of his gaze seared her as his touch had. Everywhere he looked, she was exposed, opened, devoured with eyes hungry for more.

Her white linen nightgown was no barrier to his delectation. Her nipples puckered and brushed against the soft linen. The fabric rubbed, tweaked. Her nipples hardened further.

He stared at them. He gaze locked on each soft peak, each round mound. As if in a trance, his hand reached out, cupped her, squeezed.

A shiver of anticipation spread down her spine. She arched her back, pressing her breast more firmly into his hand.

He dipped his head, and leaning on his elbow, he took one puckered nipple into his mouth. The sensation of his hot, wet mouth, over the cool cloth was like nothing she'd experienced, nothing she dreamt possible. Spikes of pleasure radiated from her breast, penetrated her core.

She was torn between tearing her breast away and pressing it closer. From easing the hard peak in his mouth and cooling it with the night air.

He seemed to understand. Sitting up, he unbuttoned the front of her gown. Opening each button until she was bared to her navel.

The cold crisp night air hit her hot skin, but instead of cooling her, it sizzled.

The air heated.

He grinned down at her, and with slow deliberate movements, he brought his mouth within an inch of one tight peak. "Do you know what you taste like?" He asked.

She couldn't speak. Couldn't form words. She shook her head.

"You taste like a morning sunrise, like dew on a flower petal." He took her nipple into his mouth and sucked.

Her back arched. She threw her head back, opened her mouth gulped in air. The pleasure was so intense it was painful, and left her dripping, needing, wanting.

Tavish lavished attention on her breasts, and it was all she could do to hold on to reality as he ripped away her senses and laid waste to all conscious thought—turned her into a wanton.

"If I had my way, I would strip you bare. I would taste every last inch of you." He kissed her sternum, kissed his way up her chest to her neck and then kissed her chin before pulling her mouth into a blistering kiss. "I would demand your complete surrender."

He rose and stripped naked. He stood before her, a bronze god.

He leaned over her. Spreading her legs wide, he kneeled between and positioned himself at her entrance.

His gaze locked on hers. She couldn't look away—didn't want to.

She wrapped her legs around his waist, reached up and took his mouth in a kiss.

He eased in.

Her world splintered as he stretched her.

His body locked in tight control, he opened her, took her.

The pain was sharp but faded with his slow penetration. Deeper. Until he was seated fully. Their bodies joined.

He nuzzled her neck and kissed her nose. "Did I hurt you?"

She cupped his neck. "You'll never hurt me."

"I do it all the time."

"Not in any way that matters. I love you." She pulled her body off him, down his long length.

He hissed, his body shaking with effort.

"All of you." She pressed up, taking him back in, in a single fluid movement.

He growled, deep in the back of his throat. Buried his face in her neck and took the reins.

Each thrust sent her higher, toward a bliss she'd never knew existed. Gripping his shoulders, she held on for the ride.

A tight ball of pleasure grew and built, until finally, her world came apart.

"Marianne!" He stiffened, followed and followed her over the edge.

Together, they floated down to oblivion.

Tavish trailed a finger down Marianne's face and watched her sleep. So much had changed.

She loved him.

Just thinking of the words was enough to lighten his heart. She'd seen the worst of what he was capable. She'd witnessed the strength and the monstrosity of his body. Yet, still she remained.

Could he offer her a future after all? Did they have a chance for happiness?

She shifted, curling her face into the crook of his neck. She fit there like she belonged. He wrapped an arm around her and squeezed.

With Marianne he had a chance at happiness he'd never had before. Here was a woman who loved him, not despite his flaws but because of them. He'd been a fool to fear her response to his apology. How could he have ever let himself doubt her affection for him?

He would tell her his own feelings. Say the words aloud that he'd held in his heart.

A strand of her strawberry blonde curls fell across her face.

He reached and brushed it away.

Her eyes popped open. Pools of green, they looked like the heath after a storm. She reached up and touched his cheek, trailing a finger along his scar. "What happened?"

He took her hand and kissed her palm. His emotions were too raw for words. He wasn't even sure he could speak.

"Tell me," she whispered.

"It doesn't matter." He nuzzled her neck until she tipped her head to the side. He'd distract her from questions he wasn't ready to answer. He doubted he'd ever be able to answer them.

"It does matter." Her words were like arrows, each one finding its deadly mark.

He pulled away, sat up and stormed to the porthole. His room was on the port side of the ship, but all that greeted him was a blanket of stars and the occasional glimpse of an aetherwhale tentacle. They hadn't arrived at London yet.

"Tavish?" Rustling came from behind him but he ignored it.

A hand, delicate and small next to his massive mechanical arm, pressed into the leather casing over his wrist.

"Arthur." She kissed his shoulder.

His breath caught. It was the first time she'd used his given name.

"Arthur," she continued. "It does matter what happened to you, but not for the reasons you seem to think."

She ducked beneath his let arm and wrapped it around her shoulders. As she snuggled against his chest, one small hand lifted to rest over his heart.

His heart thudded in his chest and he couldn't help but reach up and cover her hand with his. He'd always been careful to keep her on his right side, the human side. The side he could more easily control. "Marianne I— "

She pulled her hand free and pressed it against his lips. "You need to hear what I have to say."

He nodded and she dropped her finger.

"You are the man I love because of everything that's happened to you. We are each of us the sum of our experiences and our actions based on those experiences. The choices we make, as it were."

She snuggled deeper and ran a hand down his abdomen chasing the scar that crisscrossed his body.

He stiffened, not in anger or pain, but in shock, as he realized how much he needed her touch. It was going to be a night of surprises, and here he was, naked before her. Naked not just to his skin, but also to his soul.

She understood him. The realization rocked him. It was all he could do to remain standing. She said she loved him, and he wasn't going to question her on that, but until this moment, he hadn't realized how well she knew him.

He turned her so she stood in front of him and tipping up her head, he kissed her. He poured every last ounce of love he had for her into that kiss. Then he picked her up, and carried her to the chair.

If he was going to open up so much of himself, he had to be sitting and he had to be holding her. He adjusted her on his lap so that her head was cradled against his heart.

"I joined the army at eighteen. I was brash and young, headstrong really, and I craved adventure." He chuckled. "I used to hate my father. He was dictatorial, opinionated, and severe. I thought he understood nothing about me, but in retrospect, he probably knew me better than I knew myself. He never argued with my chosen career. He could have. I was his only heir, but all he did was see to it that I had a commission.

"I did well in the army. I was strong, and while the army had rules, they made sense to me, and I thrived.

"We were at peace for so many years that the battle for the Suez Canal came as surprise. Seemingly out of nowhere, the Ottoman's attacked and we were at war."

Marianne squeezed him tightly and placed a kiss on his chest. "Were you frightened?"

He rested his chin on the top of her head. "No, I should have been, but I still had the sense of immortality that only the young have, and I thought war would be glorious fun.."

"Most young men do, or so I'm told." Marianne ran her hand up and down his arm and squeezed.

"Two months in, it was clear that the Ottoman's meant business. They were tenacious and wouldn't back down. The fighting got dirty and I saw so many friends fall that I was beginning to be numb about it all."

"I couldn't imagine." Marianne murmured, continuing to massage his arm.

"It's impossible to imagine without having been there." His voice broke and he closed his eyes. "I was guarding an ammunition bunker. I'd managed to rise to the rank of Lieutenant of an artillery squadron."

He held Marianne, using her as an anchor to keep him in the present. He didn't want to relive that awful day, but she was right, she deserved to know. "I had two men inside the bunker and several more spread out in a perimeter around the arsenal. I was checking on the rear guard when it happened. One moment the bunker was there, the next thing I knew I was flying through the air. I woke up in the hospital tent, a monster."

Marianne didn't say a word. She tipped her head up and kissed his throat, her hand continuing its slow, soothing motion on his arm.

He swallowed. "Three of the twenty men guarding that bunker survived. I was one of them. None of us remained unscathed, and the other two committed suicide after returning to England."

"Did they ever find out what happened?" she asked.

"No, there was an inquest but all they could determine was that something had set off the arsenal. The official report listed it as an accidental discharge. To this day, I wonder if there was something I could have done differently. Was there anything that could have stopped so many good men from dying?"

Marianne shifted so she was straddling him. Staring into his eyes, she trapped him with her gaze. "There was nothing you could have done differently."

He opened his mouth to speak but she stopped him with a quick, hard kiss that left him breathless.

"I know you. If there had been anything you could have done, you would have done it. You say you woke up a monster but you're wrong. You woke up a man. You may have mechanical parts, but in the end, you never let it define you. You strode ahead and forged a life for yourself. You never gave up."

"How can you say that? I ran from life. I hid away I... " He ground his teeth together, hating the pain he heard in his voice, hating the weakness.

"The only thing you've let define you is your guilt. The mechanical parts, they're an excuse." Marianne grasped his head between her hands and pierced him with a determined gaze.

He blinked. Was she angry with him?

"If you think for one second that I'm going to let you wallow any longer, you have another thing coming."

She hadn't wagged her finer at him; but suddenly, the image of Marianne, naked as the day she was born scolding him with wagging finger and tapping foot, made him smile.

It made him laugh.

She was right of course. He was hiding from the guilt; but somehow, with her, he could forget and be a man. He wasn't sure he could ever fully let the past go, but for her, he would try.

"Why are you laughing?" She sounded so disgruntled he couldn't help but laugh harder.

"I love you." He kissed her forehead.

"Oh," she breathed. "You do?"

He took her mouth in a searing kiss, ravaging her mouth. "I do."

And then, he showed her with his hands, his body, with all he was, and everything he wanted to be. He was hers and nothing would ever take that away.

CHAPTER TWENTY-FIVE

A knock rapped across his door, waking Tavish from a sound sleep. He rolled out of bed and still naked, opened the door a crack. Seeing the deck cadet on the other side, he hid his body. "What do you want?"

"Captain needs you in her office, sir." Miss Haversham rubbed her eyes and yawned.

"I'll be up as soon as I've dressed." Tavish shut the door, and grabbed clothes.

As he threw on his trousers he looked at Marianne, sleeping like an angel. He'd go see what the captain wanted and then he'd move her. Let her rest a bit longer.

He was still raw from the emotion he'd shared with her, but he also felt whole for the first time in far too long. Smiling at her sleeping form, he grinned..

She'd earned her rest.

He found the captain in her office, pacing before the window. Her long black hair was pulled into a braid, and her uniform was neat.

He knocked on the open door and walked in. "You asked for me, ma'am."

She looked over her shoulder at him. "Tavish, have a seat."

"What has you up at this ungodly hour?" He looked at the clock and cringed. It was the middle of third watch, barely past three.

"We'll reach London in an hour or so and I want to depart as soon as we dock."

He arched a brow. "That fast?"

Ridgewell's lips turned up at the corner. "I'm not sure Sam is ever going to talk to me again. I made her work the engines hard."

"I'd say. This trip should have taken us three weeks and it took, what, three days?"

"About that…" Ridgewell looked down at her feet. "This book has me worried."

"So I'd gathered."

She held her hands behind her back and started pacing again. "The book is dangerous to have on board, and I need…" She swallowed. "I need permission to continue to explore the possibilities it presents."

Tavish frowned. "Permission from whom?"

She closed her eyes. "Whitehall."

"Whitehall?" He sat up straighter and squinted his eyes. "Who are you, ma'am?"

She gave him a wry smile. "You're the second person in a week to ask me that."

"And?"

"I'm the captain." Ridgewell shrugged. "I may have a few other titles but that's the only one that matters for now."

Tavish crossed his arms and glared at her. "With all due respect, ma'am, I disagree."

"It's better this way."

"Are you a —"

"Don't say it." Ridgewell held up her hand as she spoke over him. "If you don't know, you can't say anything. It's safer for everyone if I keep my past a secret."

He scowled. "Fine, we'll play it your way, but I can't look after you if I don't know the danger you're in."

Her face softened and this time her smile reached her eyes. "You do well enough."

"Humph." He wasn't appeased but he sat back and waved her to continue.

"I feel too exposed with this book in my possession. Will you escort me to Whitehall?" Ridgewell cocked her head. "Under the circumstances, my conscience won't let me order you."

"Of course I would." His shoulders slumped. "Why would you think I wouldn't?"

"I'd hoped." Ridgewell stopped pacing and leaned against the window. "But I couldn't force you. This is dangerous, and you have other interests to protect now."

Tavish's cheeks heated. "Ah... Is it that obvious?"

"Tavish, it's been obvious for weeks now. I'm just glad you're now admitting it."

"I was thinking I'd ask her... " He cleared his throat. "Well, it wouldn't bother you, would it, ma'am? I mean, would you let a married couple work onboard your ship?"

Ridgewell walked over and laid a hand on his shoulder. "Do you think I'd let the two of you leave after all we've been through?"

He chuckled. "I guess not."

"Good. Have you asked her yet?" She squeezed his shoulder and stepped away.

"Not yet. I want to find a gift first."

"A ring?" she asked.

"No, it needs to be something special. Do you mind if I take detour once we're done at Whitehall?"

"I won't need you in the meeting. You'll have time to go shopping while I'm sitting with... " she shrugged her right shoulder. "Just get me to Whitehall, I'll be fine after that."

"Yes, ma'am."

"I'm happy for you." Ridgewell's voice mellowed, her soft soprano sounding almost wistful, like she was a young girl dreaming about her future.

"Thank you," he smiled. "Now if only I can get her to say yes."

Marianne stretched, pulling muscles she didn't know she had. Sighing, she opened her eyes.

Sunlight, filtered by the curtains, poured into the room. She smiled at the fitting wake up. Sunlight shining into her room after such a momentous night was surely a good sign.

They must have made port. There was no discernible sunlight in deep space.

And she was in her own room. She sank into the covers. Tavish must have carried her here. How had he managed to do it without waking her?

She chuckled and sat up.

The clock on the stand by her bed showed half past four.

She had time to change before breakfast was due.

She stretched again. Maybe a bath as well.

One of the benefits of being so close to the kitchens was the ready supply of hot water. She opened a spigot on the side of the autochef and filled a bucket. It was heavy work carrying hot water pails but at least she could be clean.

Marianne settled herself in the hot water and relaxed into its warmth. Her body thrummed as if newly awakened. She giggled, picking up her sponge. Awakened wasn't so far from the truth. Grabbing her soap, she paused.

Lemon soap.

His gift.

She couldn't keep from smiling. It was as if everything reminded her of him.

He said he loved her. Sighing happily, she dried off and pulling clothes out of her trunk at random, she got dressed.

What happened now? They both had duties on board the ship. Something they'd have to consider as their liaison continued. They'd have to come up with a system that worked best.

Someone pounded on her door. She opened it and took a step back. "Mr. Galveson, what are you doing here?"

His skin was flushed and sweat dripped down his forehead. "It's Tavish. He's been hurt."

Her stomach plummeted. "What? How?"

"Hurry, he's asking for you." Galveson reached into the room and grabbed her cloak off a hook. Then he tugged on her arm. "No time to explain."

The blood drained from her face as she followed behind him. He led her topside and down the plank to the platform below. "Where is he?"

"In London, he left with the captain earlier." Galveson pulled her onto a shuttle. "The man who attacked you earlier got to him."

"No," she breathed. She took a seat and closed her eyes and prayed. *Please God, don't take him. Not now that I've found him. Don't let him die because of me.*

How hard could it be to find a pawnshop? Tavish ducked down an alley. It had been only two months since he'd saved, and yet, the warren of alleyways and dilapidated buildings had him going in circles.

He returned to Commercial Street and approached a street seller.

The woman held out a brown speckled orange. "Fresh oranges, gov?"

"Yes, thank you." He handed her a coin. "I'm looking for a pawn shop."

She cackled, her free arm gripping her side. "Lots of them 'ere, sonny."

"I need a specific one. A friend of mine sold something and I want to buy it back for him," he lied.

"Ah, and he don't remember where he sold it, eh?"

Tavish shook his head.

"Well, your best bet is to ask at one along this street." She waived her arm down the road. "They might know."

"Is there a shop further into the neighborhood?" He remembered having to navigate the alleys to rescue Marianne.

"Aye, a few." The woman narrowed her eyes at him. "You ain't gonna get 'em in trouble are ya? You really do just want to 'elp a friend?"

"Yes, ma'am."

She cackled again. "Imagine the likes of you, ma'aming me."

"Please, ma'am," he asked again.

"Down the way there's Sokolof's and then there's Mercher's." She tapped her finger on her chin and started listing names.

He'd never find them all on his own. "If I were to buy all of your oranges would you be willing to take me to these pawnshops?"

She glanced down at her basket, full to the brims. "All of 'em, sir?"

He pulled out his coin purse and handed her two sovereigns. "Will this do?"

Her eyes grew into round saucers and the coins disappeared into her hands in a flash. "Aye, gov, that'll do."

She started handing him her oranges but he held up a hand. "You give those oranges to the children down the street. I couldn't possibly eat that many before they went bad."

She grinned. "Mighty fine treat for the young'uns that'll be."

She flagged over a lad no taller than Tavish's knee. "Jimmie, go fetch yer brother?"

Jimmie darted off down the street but returned soon enough with a larger lad in tow.

"Frank, hand these out to the young'uns." She handed him the basket. "Mind you don't lose any?"

"Really, Gran?" He took the basket, grinning from ear to ear.

"Aye," she shooed them away and motioned to Tavish. "Follow me."

She darted into an alley, moving far faster than he'd expect of a woman her age. He lengthened his stride to keep up. The sounds of the working streets echoed in his bionic ear but he kept he dial turned high. She seemed an honest woman but then they all did before you were led to a trap.

She stopped by a thin building smashed between two larger ones. The sign on the door read "Ogleman's."

"Here's the first." The old seller pointed to the sign.

He stepped inside, ducking under the doorframe. The ceiling was so low he couldn't stand up fully even once inside. The dim lighting made it difficult to see but the crowded room looked like a closet, stuffed to the brim with curios and odds and ends. How the devil did anyone find anything in here?

"Hello, good sir, how can I help you?" A thin man with oily hair approached, his hand outstretched.

"Don't touch me, to start," Tavish barked.

The woman cackled in the doorway.

He arched a brow at her but she only grinned back.

Turning back to Ogleman, he crossed his arms. "I'm looking for something a friend of mine sold to a pawn man here in Spitalfields."

The man's gaze danced gleefully over Tavish. "What was it that he sold to me? I'm sure I have it here."

Tavish scanned the display cases by the register. "I'll know it if I see it."

"But I have some things in the back. Perhaps it's not here." Ogleman slid closer.

Tavish held up a hand. "Stand back by the register, please."

The glass on the display cases looked like it hadn't been cleaned in years. Black muck dripped down the glass, obscuring anything in side.

He leaned closer. One case held a small necklace that looked like a snake. "What's that?"

Ogle man brightened. "Ah, a lovely piece sir. It's a mechanical."

Tavish scoffed and waved his hand around the room. "A mechanical here?"

"Ah, yes." Ogleman preened. "Best piece I have."

"Prove it." Tavish nodded at the device. He wouldn't know if it was Snake until he got a look at it.

Ogleman pulled it out and laid it on the table. He touched the base of its neck and it uncurled to its full length. He hit the spot again and it curled back into a necklace.

"Could be a spring," Tavish sneered. "That's not much of a mechanical."

Ogleman's face reddened. "Are you calling me a liar?"

"No," Tavish shrugged, "merely an exaggerator."

"It's a mechanical, I tell you." Ogleman huffed.

"I think you got taken." Tavish scanned the room. It had to be Snake but he couldn't let the man know he wanted the thing. "Looks like you don't have what I want."

He turned back to the entrance and smiled at his guide. "You said there were others along this way?"

"Oh, aye, sir." Her eyes lit up. Just follow me."

"Wait!"

Tavish turned back the pawn man. "Yes,"

"I'll sell it to you for half-a-crown."

Tavish snorted. "That's not worth a farthing."

"Three shillings?" Ogleman offered.

Tavish considered the thing lying on the table. "Two and a half."

"Done."

Tavish reached into his pocket and pulled out the coins. Tossing them on the table, he picked up Snake.

"Blasted girl took me to the cleaners she did. Next time I won't be so generous." Ogleman muttered as he picked up the coins.

Once outside, he dug in his coin purse for another sovereign. "Thanks for your help."

"Ya wanted that lump o'metal?"

"That's what I wanted." He handed her the coin.

Once again it disappeared before he could blink. "For that, I'll get ya back out o' the warrens."

"Much appreciated, ma'am."

She cackled again and started off.

Tavish's heart felt light. He had Snake. He was sure of it. The small little mechanical felt heavy in his pocket and he couldn't wait to give it to Marianne.

She wasn't the kind of girl to want a ring or bracelet. She appreciated things with real value.

He tipped his hat to his guide once they reached Commercial Street. "Again, I thank you."

"You ever need help 'ere again, you just ask fer Maddie."

"Will do, ma'am." He checked his watch. He'd been gone for just over two hours. Hopefully, the captain had finished her business. He wanted to get this necklace to Marianne. He could already picture her face and how it would light up when she saw it.

Ridgewell was standing just outside the building as he approached. Her large mouth was drawn into a firm line.

"Ma'am?" Tavish asked, his heart sinking into his stomach.

"Tavish." She looked up. Her violet eyes were dark with anger. "It's Marianne."

The world crashed in around him. "Is she hurt?"

"She's missing."

He shook his head. "I don't understand."

"Neither do I." She shook her head. "I just know she's missing, and Galveson is involved somehow."

"Why would she leave with him?" Tavish choked.

"I don't know."

He reached into his pocket and curled his real hand around Snake. To be so close and then to lose her. No. He wouldn't let it happen. He wasn't going to let go of his dream because of this. He would find her and bring her home. "Then we had better find out where he's taken her."

CHAPTER TWENTY-SIX

Marianne gripped her hands so tightly together they turned white and kept her gaze locked on Galveson. "Why won't you tell me what happened?

"I don't know." He growled. "All I know is the captain sent word that you should be delivered to Tavish's side."

"Can I see the message? Maybe there's something in there for me," she pleaded.

Galveson shifted in his seat and gazed past her head. "It was addressed to me."

Ice crystals barreled through her blood. "There was no note, was there?"

He jumped in his seat and darted his gaze around their small compartment. "What! I don't know what you are talking about. Of course there was a note. Why would I make something like this up?"

She sank into her chair. "I don't know."

When they'd boarded the small shuttle, Marianne hadn't worried about the lack of windows but now the small space closed in on her like a coffin. She rose and went to the door.

The handle rattled but wouldn't open.

"Why is this locked?"

He sneered at her.

"Let me go!"

"You might as well sit down, you aren't going anywhere until we get to our destination."

She sank onto her seat. "Why are you doing this?"

"Because I'll be rewarded. I shouldn't be serving under a woman." His lip curled up.

"So, get a different job." Marianne squeezed her hands together again.

"After I deliver you, I won't have to work again." He leaned back in his seat and crossed his legs.

"Where are we going?" She tugged on the collar of her shirt, gulping in air.

"You know."

"That man isn't to be trusted. He won't pay you a dime." She laid a hand on her neck. "He's evil."

Galveson snorted. "Don't care."

She curled into herself. A fool, that's what she was. Tears welled in her eyes but she shoved them away. She didn't deserve her own tears. She walked into this with her eyes open. No wonder her father thought her worthless.

She was just a witless girl.

Tavish paced back and forth in the small room Ridgewell had hired a little ways from Whitehall. The room was so tiny he could only make two steps before he had to turn again. "We are wasting time."

"Stop pacing. You're making me dizzy." The captain, with legs crossed, leaned back in her chair, a cup of tea steaming next to her. "Going all the way back to Sheba is foolish. It's faster to send word via pigeon. We stay put until Freddy and the crew get here."

He stopped and stared at her. "You're sure she's gone?"

"Yes." Her voice was barely a whisper.

"How? If no one from the ship told you, how do you know?"

She rose and poked her head out of the small snug. The noise from the bar was loud at this time of day. Men, having their breakfast before heading to work, babbled inanities at each other while they ate.

Ridgewell shut the door. "Stand in front of it and hold it shut for now."

He pinched his eyebrows together but did as she asked. "What's going on?"

"In the cavern… something happened to us." Ridgewell paced to the window and peered out. She closed her eyes and stood still.

"What happened?" Tavish growled after she'd been staring for several minutes.

"We're connected somehow."

"What? You can sense where she is?" Tavish scoffed.

"No, nothing like that." She faced him. "This is going to sound ridiculous, and if it hadn't happened to me, I'm not sure I would believe it."

"Spit it out!"

Ridgewell arched a brow at him.

"Sorry, ma'am." He bobbed his head.

"There was this rock that rose out of a pedestal. It called me Child of Air. Marianne was the Child of Water. We're supposed to find two others."

"Ma'am, you're not making much sense."

She rubbed her palms on her thighs. "I know, but it's the truth. Ever since that night in the cavern, I can hear the wind."

"It talks to you?" Tavish asked. He didn't want to believe it but that book was something he'd never seen before. It wasn't that far a stretch to assume the captain and Marianne had encountered something unusual in that cavern.

"Yes, and it told me Marianne was in danger." She looked straight at him. "Then I felt it."

"Then why doesn't it tell you where she is, so we can rescue her?"

Once again, Ridgewell stood still and closed her eyes. "She's still moving."

"Well, just keep listening." Tavish crossed his arms. "I'll wait for the men you sent."

Fifteen minutes later, there was a knock on the snug door. Tavish opened it and let in Freddy and Carlsby. Both men were small and easily fit into the room.

"What do you know?" Tavish asked.

The men looked at the captain, who hadn't moved from her spot since she started listening. "She's busy," Tavish said. "Talk."

Freddy shook himself. "Carlsby saw her leave this morning. It was shortly after you'd left. The rest noticed she was gone when they went for breakfast and she wasn't there."

"Why didn't you say something when she was leaving?" Tavish glared at Carlsby.

The airman took a step back. "Uh... like Freddy said, I noticed her leaving this morning. I was in the crow's nest, cleaning the spyglasses. She left with Galveson. I thought it strange but she didn't look like she was in trouble."

"What did she look like?" Tavish asked. His stomach was a hard lump in his gut, a heavy weight that threatened to drop him.

"It was hard to see from so high up, but I did use one of the clean spyglasses. She looked worried. Like she'd gotten bad news."

Tavish frowned and glanced at Freddy.

The gnomish little man only shrugged. "There wasn't anything disturbed in her room. Her bath water was still in the tub; cold by the time we got to it. Her cloak was missing. That's all I know."

"She's stopped." Ridgewell blinked out of her trance and frowned at the three men. "Freddy, Carlsby? When did you get here?"

"Just now, ma'am." Freddy replied.

"Hmm." She turned to Tavish. "She's nearby. You'll need to be Baron Summerfield for a bit."

"What?"

She reached into a pocket of her coat and pulled out a stack of cards. Rifling through them she grabbed a stack and handed them to him. "I kept this in case. I figured you wouldn't have any."

Tavish took the cards and looked at them. Baron Summerfield of Summerfield Grange stared back at him in an austere print. He nodded. "She's somewhere in Mayfair, then?"

"Yes, and we don't have much time." She hurried to the door and opened it. "Freddy, hire us a good-looking hack."

"Yes, ma'am." He ducked out.

She shut the door and turned her gaze to Carlsby.

Tavish didn't hear what she said to him. He couldn't look away from the lines of his name. Could he do it? Impersonate a lord. He'd turned his back on this life for a reason. It no longer held any allure for him. He fisted his hand around the card, careful not to crush it.

For Marianne he was willing to walk across hot coals. Picking up a name that belonged to him shouldn't be so hard.

Freddy returned. "Hackney's waiting, ma'am."

"Then let's go. Tavish, when we get to the address, bluster your way in."

"Yes, ma'am." Tavish followed Ridgewell and the other two men. He stood taller, deliberately filling the space around him. Men scattered out of his way but he ignored them. He was on a mission. Marianne needed him. He wouldn't fail her again.

Tea, the British answer to everything. No matter how tense the situation, a cup of tea was always offered. It was as if that brown liquid, no more than leaf juice really, could solve the world's problems.

Marianne held her cup in her hands but refused to drink it. There were some situations that even a good cup of tea couldn't fix.

"You're not drinking, my dear," Draven drawled.

Lord Draven, the man who'd tried to rape her.

She closed her eyes. God, she was a fool. She'd blindly walked into this trap and now she had no idea how to get out of it. She raised her eyes to stare at the other occupant of the room. Why had she trusted him? She closed her eyes. She was stupid—no, worse than stupid—foolish. There was no getting around that.

"Is the tea cold? Shall I have another pot brought in?"

She shivered. The lurching steps and vacant eyes of the maid... "Please, no. I'm fine."

Galveston snickered into his cup.

Draven gave an exaggerated sigh and put his cup down. "No time like the present, then."

She couldn't help but watch him rise and walk behind his desk. He moved like a dancer, as if each step was carefully choreographed. After raising the glass case and fiddling with something inside, he returned to her side

She heard a sound like the whoosh of air when a door opens. She looked toward the glass case, but couldn't see anything past the desk.

Draven grabbed her arm and pulled her to her feet.

The teacup tumbled from her fingers, crashing to the ground in splintered porcelain and cascading tea.

Tucking her hand in his arm, he patted her arm. "No matter, my dear. The maids will see to it."

He tugged her toward a large opening in the floor. "I believe I promised you a reward, Galveson."

The second mate put down his cup and rose. "Yes, you did."

"Do follow along, we'll get that settled first thing." Draven stepped down the stairs.

She met his gaze. They were hollow, without even the flint of hunger she'd seen earlier. Her heart slowed and it became difficult to breath. Where was he taking her?

They stepped deeper into the dark, the only light coming from the opening above. Draven pulled a lever and even that light disappeared, as with a swoosh, the floor swung closed.

Forced to cling to his arms, her breaths came in short gasps.

"Don't fret, I won't let you fall," Draven soothed. His voice was unmodulated, almost emotionless.

"Where are we going?" she asked.

"My laboratory," he replied. "I think you'll like it. At least I hope you do. I'd like you to visit me there often."

His voice rose in pitch until he sounded almost giddy.

"You make it sound like I'll be able to leave."

He patted her arm. "Nora, my dear. I would never keep you prisoner here."

Her stomach churned and she fought down bile. "I'm not Nora."

"You're not?" He hesitated on the steps and then laughed. "Of course you're not. But you will be."

Her mind froze. Before she could bludgeon her wits back, they reached a landing.

"Galveson, lend the lady your arm while I get the door open."

The second mate tugged her close, nearly ripping her arm off in the process.

"Gently, gently." Draven patted her shoulder. "Don't damage her. She's a lady after all—my lady."

Galveson snorted, but he did wrap her arm around his own in an almost gentlemanly way.

Draven hummed to himself several feet away stopping just as blood red light spiraled out from a spike on the wall. It ricocheted like shattering glass, making the shape of a door.

The sound of stone grinding on stone rattled her senses as the door rose up to the ceiling. She bit down on her lip to keep from cringing at the noise.

"Come in, come in." He ushered them forward into a well-lit room. It lacked the ambiance of a mad scientist's lair. Oh, it had the right tools, the right kind of tables, but despite the odd assortment of gadgets, the room looked almost cheery.

Draven grabbed Marianne's hand. "There's a chair just over here where you can wait. I'll get my business with Galveson out of the way, and then we can deal with our own."

He shoved her down into an armchair and cupped her cheek. "Such soft skin. I'll have to be careful not to mar it."

She squirmed out of his grasp.

"Tsk, tsk." He pressed a button above her head. Clamps slapped over her ankles and wrists. "None of that my dear. You need to stay until the end."

She struggled, but the clamps held tight. "What are you going to do with me?"

He patted her head like she were a child. "Nothing yet. Nothing until your friends deliver what I want."

Galveson came to stand next to them. "Isn't she what you wanted?"

"No," Draven shrugged. "Well, yes and no."

"My reward?" Galveson asked.

Draven grabbed Galveson's arm.

The second mate winced and tried to pull free.

Draven's grip held true. He brought a needle from his coat pocket and shoved it into Galveson's neck.

He crumpled to the ground.

Draven watched him fall and grinned. "To think he would walk so blindly into this."

A deep, violent chuckle echoed through the chamber. "You will do with him what I will?"

A visible shiver erupted through Draven. "Yes, master."

Smoke billowed from the lamps overhead, swirling down around Marianne. The air turned frigid.

The smoke coalesced into the shape of a man. It was tall, with a grotesquely long face and arms that hung below his knees.

"So this is the girl we've been chasing."

"Yes, master." Draven's eyes glowed with purpose. "I don't know why I didn't see it before, but you are right. She'd make the perfect host body."

"Not host." The deep chuckle returned. "Replacement."

It reached up and caressed her chin. "Do you think she will provide adequate entertainment for me?"

Draven walked closer. "How could she not? She's young and full of hope."

"My only regret is we must wait to do the transfer. They may ask to speak with her before delivering the book." Draven sulked.

Dizziness threatened to overwhelm her, but she bit down on her lower lip. Hard. Blood seeped down her chin.

Draven dabbed at the blood. "Careful, my dear. We mustn't injure ourselves."

"You won't get away with this."

He chuckled. "I already have."

"You sent the note?" the smoke being asked.

"Yes, shortly after this idiot brought her here." He pointed to the slumbering second mate.

"Good. In the meantime, the idiot will give me entertainment." Its cool hands covered her face. "*Ogho Apartó*"—eyes open.

Marianne's eye's popped open wide. She couldn't even blink. Her pulse raced and her breathing came in short, sharp gasps.

"May I put him in the machine?" Draven asked. "He may prove useful to us if he is still alive."

"Alive?" It nodded. "Yes, the machine will do nicely. I can easily control another."

Draven's eyes dimmed but he nodded. "I had no doubt, master."

Draven dragged Galveson to a large, gunmetal black contraption. A cage, with layers of wicked looking blades jutting out in several directions, hung over a seat in the center.

Galveson was planted in the seat and strapped down with metal clamps. After lowering the cage over the second mate's head, Draven tightened a few bolts. Reaching over to a nearby table, he grabbed a syringe and injected something into Galveson's arm.

The second mate's eyes flew open. "What... Where... ?"

Draven laughed and flipped a switch.

The blades whirled to life, spinning so fast they looked like whirling disks.

Marianne wanted to shut her eyes, but they wouldn't budge. She'd have to watch as those blades sawed into his head. She'd see the blood.

She turned her head away but she could still see the machine, the blades, and the pallid, wide-eyed Galveson.

Panic burbled in her gut. *"Ogho Wavólia"* —eyes shut.

The shadow being turned to regard her. "Interesting."

Her eyes remained open.

Blood spurted from Galveson's head, and the man let out an inhuman scream.

"Talligu," she muttered, in desperation.

Instantly, her eyes filled with water. Tears fell in rivers out of her eyes and down her face, clouding her vision.

"Maoutu." The shadow hovered over her.

She kept crying.

"Maoutu," it said again.

Still she kept crying.

Nothing could block out the sound of Galveson's screams, but at least she didn't have to see it.

"How can you fight me?" Its voice deepened.

Marianne said nothing. Modulating her breathing, she pulled her thoughts from her surroundings, from what was happening to Galveson.

No matter what happened, she had to find a way out of this. If Draven got her in that chair, it was over.

"You will answer me?" Shadow laid its hands on her shoulders.

Ice trickled down her arms but otherwise she felt no pressure. It couldn't actually touch her. She ignored it.

While the tears fell, she focused her mind, brought up Ridgewell's advice and planned her escape.

CHAPTER TWENTY-SEVEN

Tavish pounded on the door with his swordstick, his greatcoat swirling about at his feet. It had taken them fifteen minutes to get here; most of that time was wasted in what Ridgewell called necessary stage dressing. Tavish called it tomfoolery.

The monocle, walking stick and top hat made him feel like a blundering idiot. The kind of coxcomb he'd scorned since his schoolboy days.

He pounded on the door again.

It swung open, to reveal a small wiry man in the trappings of a butler. There was something off about him, but Tavish couldn't place it.

"May I help you, my lord?" The butler droned.

"I'm here on a matter of some urgency. I must speak with Lord Draven immediately."

"Of course," the man bowed him in.

Ridgewell, Freddy, and Carlsby followed behind him. The butler didn't even bat an eye at their addition. He merely moved farther down the hall in a lurching gait.

Tavish's frown deepened. "There's something odd about him."

Ridgewell walked just a step behind him. "Did you notice the footmen?"

Without moving his head, Tavish glanced around him. The footmen stood staring at the wall, each one moving a dusting cloth in circular motions, each of them in sync with the other.

"Keep your eye out. There's something very wrong here," Ridgewell muttered.

The butler bowed them into a parlor. "If you'll wait here, I'll fetch the master from his study."

Tavish drew back his shoulders and raised the monocle. "I do not appreciate being kept waiting. You will take me to the master immediately."

The butler stood staring at the door, his left eye twitching. "Must show you in to parlor... parlor... parlor."

"Is it a broken mechanical?" Carlsby asked.

Tavish pushed against the butler with the end of his stick. It sunk in a good two centimeters—flesh, not machine.

"Not a mechanical, but acting like one. What the devil is going on?" Freddy muttered.

"The study is this way." The butler turned around, walking away in the lurching gait that still puzzled Tavish.

They followed him, eyes darting around them. The maids were also acting oddly and cleaning in sync.

Tavish's stomach rolled and he clutched the swordstick tight.

Ridgewell laid a hand on his. "Relax. You'll break it."

He glanced down at the cane. The metal casing was dented. He shifted the stick to his right hand. "This makes me uneasy. What if something's happened to her?"

"We'll get to her. I promise." Ridgewell patted his shoulder as if to soothe, but the rigidity of her posture belied her calm.

"The master's study." The butler held a door open.

Tavish nodded and entered. The room was empty but a serving of tea sat used on a low table by the fire. "Where is he?"

The butler didn't let go of the door handle as his left eye ticked like the shutter of a signal lamp.

"Answer me," Tavish demanded.

"He is here." The butler retreated.

Ridgewell rubbed her upper arms and looked around the room. "Is it just me or is it colder in here?"

"The tea is still warm." Freddy pulled his finger from a cup. "Less than an hour, I'd say."

Carlsby held up a cloak, his hand shaking. "Is this Miss Lindstrom's?"

Tavish ripped it from the airman's hands. The velvet felt like sandpaper. He'd hoped—it had been a foolish one, perhaps—but he'd hoped that Marianne wasn't here. That she and Galveson had gone elsewhere, that the captain was wrong.

He closed his eyes and squeezed the fabric.

Reaching into his pocket he felt for the small mechanical he'd brought back. "Please be alive, Marianne. Please let me find you alive."

"What kind of man has three copies of the Bible in his study?" Freddy asked.

Tavish looked up and saw Ridgewell peering over Freddy's shoulder into a glass case. "They're all first editions. Valuable."

A blast of cold air sent ripples through his great coat. He flipped on the heat sensor of his bionic eye. There was a draft, but where was it coming from?

The floor underneath the captain and her steward was a dull, grey blue that stood out from the heat radiating from the two people and a third source in the glass case.

"One of those books is giving off heat?" he muttered.

Ridgewell looked up. "What?"

He rushed over and flipped open the case. "The middle one is glowing with heat."

He flipped open the cover to reveal a number pad. "My guess is that there's a secret door somewhere. Probably under our feet."

"Why do you say that?" Ridgewell asked.

"The draft is coming from there."

"How big is it?" She looked down at her feet.

"A circle, about a meter and a half in diameter."

"All right, we need to find the code that opens it." Ridgewell moved to the desk. "Carlsby, take the right side of the room, Freddy the left. Tavish look with your other sight."

Ridgewell rummaged through the desk while the men spread out.

Tavish focused on the number pad. He could see the indentation, the worn places where a finger had touched. The problem was all the numbers had been used, some more than others. "It's at least ten digits long, probably longer."

Ridgewell looked at him. "How do you know?"

"All the numbers show use."

The captain's lips pressed into a firm line, then she took a deep breath. "Keep looking, all of you. Tavish started digging in the desk. I'll try my own means."

Tavish nodded as Ridgewell walked to the window and opened it. He had no idea what she was going to do but he'd seen some odd things happen with her and wind, and he had no desire to question her about it. Not if it got him to Marianne.

"Talligu Juile," Marianne whispered—stop crying.

Her eyes cleared of tears. She took in a ragged, exhausted breath as her vision cleared. The screams had stopped. All that was left was the silence. A silence so intense it seemed to suck in sound, as if even the air was afraid to move lest it disturb the quiet.

Draven hovered over the body of the second mate, thankfully blocking her view of the body. Blood splattered across the walls, the floor, the ceiling. More blood than she thought could be held in a man's body.

"They're here," a deep raspy voice echoed around that room, cutting through the quiet like a broadsword, excessive and brutal.

"I heard you the first time." Draven picked an object out of a bowl on a nearby table. It dripped with a viscous green fluid that obscured the object's shape. "This is delicate work. Can you delay them?"

The being of shadow shifted before her. Its shadowy bulk seeming to suck in all the light in the room. "Not for long."

On a sigh, Draven dropped the green object back in a bowl. "Then it is pointless to continue this. Compared to the others, this fool is a minnow in a goldfish tank."

Shadow's head swiveled. Glowing, red eyes bored into her. "The tears have stopped."

Draven whirled around, gloved hands dripping with the viscous, green fluid from the bowl. "That was an interesting trick you played, my dear."

Marianne said nothing.

"Care to enlighten us as to what you did?"

She remained silent.

Draven stripped off his gloves and threw them into the bowl. They landed with a plop, sending liquid squirting upwards.

"I could make you." He approached her.

Her eyes darted between Draven and Shadow. *Stay focused. Remember your lessons.*

"I will admit to curiosity about you." Shadow shifted, smoke rippling through him like a vibrating violin string. "How is it you speak Atlantian?"

"Atlantian?" Draven whispered. He crossed his arms, the pointer finger of his right hand tapping a rhythm on his left elbow. "She's read the book, then."

"So it would appear." Shadow floated closer. "I will repeat myself. How do you know Atlantian?"

Marianne kept her silence. They didn't need to know. She had no idea who this being was, but it made her cold, just looking at it. Whatever it was, it was dangerous, and she had no intention of giving it more information than she needed to.

Shadow's color deepened to nearly black. "Tell me what it is you know!"

She shook her head.

"Draven, you will extract this information from her."

"I... can't hurt her. I need her for Nora."

Shadow whirled around. One arm reached out and closed around Draven's throat. "Nora is dead."

"No, you promised. I saw her." Draven gulped in air. "You tormented her."

Shadow laughed, an unpleasant sound so evil it made Marianne feel as if blood were dripping down her skin. "You are a fool Draven. An easily played fool."

Draven's eyes went huge and he clutched at his throat. "Why tell me this? Nora was the only reason I agreed to help you."

Shadow pulled him closer. "You have come too far to back out now. I no longer need your fear. I have you in my power."

Shadow let him go.

Draven fell to the ground, his skin a deathly pale. He bent over taking in lungfuls of air. "You were never able to touch me before."

"I grow stronger as your work continues." Waves floated through the smoke.

Draven stood up, shock and calculation dancing across his eyes. "You are that strong that you can manipulate things?"

A chuckle was his only response.

Draven closed his eyes. A visible shudder rippled through him. "Very well."

Marianne locked her jaw and glared at Draven. The moment her binds were off her, she was going to run. Ridgewell had taught her that much. All she had to do was get away and stay out of Draven's reach until Tavish got here. He wouldn't be far.

Her heart lightened at the thought. She wasn't alone, and she wasn't helpless —not anymore.

Draven busied himself with a contraption. It was a large platform with an archway over the top that stood larger than a man with a chair bolted directly under the arch. Lights ran up the side of the archway and peaked at a multifaceted glass ball that dangled from the center of the arch.

Like many of the objects in the room, Marianne had no idea what it did. She just knew she couldn't let herself be caught in it.

Shadow hovered nearby. "What does this do?"

"It's an electric current and cellular reorganization device. In theory it should change her into the shape I desire. I had hoped to test it on another before using it on her, but she can be the test subject as well as another, and if it works… " He winced. "If it works, she'll look like my Nora.".

Shadow floated around the device and then turned its grotesque head her way. "Perhaps you wish to talk now that this device is in your future?"

Marianne said nothing.

Draven snorted. "Stubborn girl."

"I need to know what she knows before she dies," Shadow hissed.

Marianne kept her mouth clamped shut.

"Oh, she'll talk. This is a very painful processes." Draven walked over and started to unbolt her arms.

Just a few more minutes and she'd be free to run.

Before flipping open the restraints, Draven grabbed her wrists. "Don't be a fool, girl."

He squeezed hard and Marianne had to clench her jaw to keep from screaming.

The last bolt flew open and Marianne leapt from the chair but his hold on her wrist was tight and he pulled her back against him.

She stomped on his instep and tried to wrench herself free.

He scooped her up and flung her over his shoulders. "Damn it!"

Shadow leaned over them. "Having trouble?"

"Nothing I can't manage." He limped toward the archway.

Marianne beat her fists against him but it did no good. He ignored her like she was an insect, or a worm. She screamed into his ear and wiggled but he only locked his arm around her tighter.

He'd have to put her down, and then she'd run.

The moment she hit the chair she was up and pushing against him, frantically trying to get away. She wanted to live, and she couldn't risk them finding out about Atlantis, about their search for the other Children of Elements.

A heavy metal arm fell across her lap and chest, pinning her to the chair.

She kicked and scratched at Draven.

He stepped back and straightened his coat. His hair was askew and so was his cravat. He adjusted the rest of his clothing and brushed the hair form his face. "That was tedious."

He turned his back to her, still standing on the platform, and flipped a switch.

The room went dark.

Marianne's hair stood up and the air had that sharp, clean smell that followed a storm.

The hiss of gas escaping a pipe was all the warning she had before the globe above her lit up, sending cascades of multi-colored lights drifting down around her and Draven. Outside that bubble, lightening crackled around the room, but other than the flashes of light she couldn't see anything through the brightness that surrounded her.

A howl rent the air.

"I will never submit to you again," Draven screamed. His back was to her as he stared out into the void of dark and lightening. "You lied to me. You used me."

Marianne was bolted to a chair but her feet were still free. With all of her might, she kicked out, hitting Draven in the back of his knees.

He started to crumple and she followed the kick with another to his lower back.

He toppled and stumbled, a startled cry escaping his lips before the black void swallowed him.

His screams mingled with Shadow's, and Marianne did her best to block them out as she wiggled to free her arms.

The chair was built to hold a woman, but she was petite, and with a cry of her own she managed to free a hand. That was all she needed to release the catch on the bars holding her down.

She took in a deep breath and calmed her racing heart. Draven's screams had silenced but she didn't dare step off the platform. How did she turn the machine off?

There were three switches on the machine but two of them were too high. She flipped the only switch she could reach.

The lights in the laboratory flipped on and Marianne stared out into a scene of smoldering ruin.

Tables and chairs that had once looked clean and orderly were now scattered about, like broken pieces of crockery. Smoke wafted from the floor, the walls, the ceiling. And in the center, bent over and still breathing, was Draven.

She froze.

He wasn't dead.

Her gaze darted about the room desperately searching for a way out. She had to get out. With all that had happened she'd forgotten where the door was. She ran to a wall and began to search. It had to be here somewhere.

"You little wretch," a shrill, female voice called out.

Marianne slowly turned to see Draven rising to his feet—or rather, to her feet.

Draven still wore the lab coat and cap, but was shorter now, about Ridgewell's height, with long, curly blonde hair and piercing, blue eyes that stared at her in despair.

"What have you done?" Draven whispered.

"I believe the correct question is, what have *you* done?" Marianne set her chin higher. "Now how do I get out of here?"

Draven's face twisted into a scowl. "After what you did, I won't let you live."

Marianne swallowed back the shaky laugh that burbled to the surface. "You're hardly in a position to threaten me. Besides, look what happened the last time you strapped me to a chair."

The other woman's face turned red. "I saved you."

Marianne shook her head. "No, you merely killed Shadow or banished him or some such thing. I saved myself."

Lightness infused her and she smiled. *I really did save myself.*

"What am I to do now?" Draven's hands fell helplessly at her sides. "I'm useless now."

"As a woman, I take exception to that." She felt along the wall behind her. *Was that a door?*

Draven collapsed to the floor. "The door is on the other wall. Behind the brain extraction device."

Marianne looked over to where Galveson, former second mate of the Sheba, lay slouched and quite dead in his restraints. She swallowed.

Blood laced across the floor, headed to drains spaced like a star around the room.

She lifted up her skirts and hopped over the streams, staying well away from Draven.

She pulled the lever down. The sound of grinding stone had her heart racing. She scrambled through the opening and felt her way up the stairs. Half way up, she found the lever that opened the other door.

Light spilled in from above and she pressed her hand to her mouth to keep from calling out.

"It's opening," Freddy called out.

Shuffling, then pounding feet followed the exclamation. Marianne had only taken a few steps before Tavish, large and imposing, blocked the light.

"Marianne," he shouted. Grabbing her up in his arms, he buried his face in her shoulder. "Marianne."

"Bring her up here, Tavish," Ridgewell commanded.

Tavish turned and carried her the rest of the way. Not letting her go, he sat down on a chair.

Tears fell down his face.

She wiped the tears away. "I'm safe."

He shuddered and closed his eyes.

"Where's Draven?" Ridgewell asked.

"Down below," Marianne said. "There was an accident. He is a 'she' now."

"Wait, what?" Ridgewell shook her head.

"There was this machine. I think he intended to turn me into the physical resemblance of his wife." She glanced between Ridgewell and Tavish. "I'm not sure about that. I'm not sure he's entirely sane."

"Something went wrong with his experiments, then?" Ridgewell stared down into the dark stairwell.

Marianne cupped Tavish's cheek. "Take me home. I want out of this place."

Tavish looked up at the captain and she nodded.

"Go. Freddy and I can take care of things here." Ridgewell ran a hand down her long braid, brushing down the stray hairs that had come loose. "Not that I have any idea how I'm going to explain this, but I can manage."

"Do you need me, ma'am?" Tavish hugged Marianne closer. "I can get her safely back to the ship and return."

Ridgewell laughed. "Tavish, take the lady home. I'll be fine."

He nodded, and only shifting her slightly, he rose and headed toward the door. He stepped over a mound on the floor.

Marianne gasped. Bodies littered the floor of the hallway. Some were hanging half out of rooms; others just sprawled out like discarded dolls. "What happened?"

"We don't know. They all just dropped." Tavish put her down, but he held her hand as he opened the door and led her outside.

Her hand looked so tiny in his large one, but it fit like it belonged. Warmth spread through her. She was going home.

CHAPTER TWENTY-EIGHT

Tavish paced back and forth behind the captain's desk, his gaze rarely leaving Marianne. He'd almost lost her. God's teeth, he almost lost her. He wanted to wrap her up in a cocoon and hold on to her. Keep her safe.

He knew that wasn't practical but the desire was there.

"Draven is being held by the authorities," Ridgewell continued. She was lounging back on the couch in her office.

Marianne and Annabel sat across form her, each sipping the tea that Freddy had brought earlier.

Like the good steward he was, Freddy had disappeared the moment everyone arrived back at the Sheba, only to reappear fifteen minutes later with a tea tray. He stood to the side and waited by the door, guarding the small party from unwanted intrusion.

"Is that wise?" Annabel put her tea down on a saucer. "He seems the mad scientist type. Will the authorities keep a close eye on him?"

Ridgewell shrugged. "I don't know. At the moment I think we're fine. Draven is still recovering from the fact that he's been turned into a woman. For a man like him, that has to be galling. He went from one of the most respected Lords in the land to a female."

"I agree with Annabel," Marianne whispered. "You didn't see what he was capable of. He's a monster, and even as a she, he could do damage."

Ridgewell crossed her legs. "Short of shooting him then and there, I didn't have any other options."

"Bloody good idea if you ask me," Tavish grumbled.

Ridgewell cocked an eyebrow. "Would you have me commit murder, then?"

"He's a threat as long as he lives," Tavish pointed out.

"Shoot him for what he might do? Shoot a helpless man before he's had a fair trial? That's not the country I serve." Ridgewell's voice reverberated around the room like the crack of a bullet. "If that's the sort of government you want, join the Ottomans."

Tavish hung his head. "I'm sorry, ma'am. You're right."

Ridgewell put down her tea and rose. "Well, I'm glad this is over. Freddy, in the morning I'll want you to post a notice that we need a new second mate. Shouldn't be too hard to find someone interested in the position."

She turned and regarded Tavish. "While he's doing that, I want you to scrounge us up a cargo. I'm afraid you'll have to do two people's jobs for the time being. I don't have anyone else to handle it."

Tavish nodded.

"I also need a course ready for New Alexandria. You can get Mr. Owens to handle that, or better yet, have Miss Haversham do it. She'll need to learn if she's to become a sailing master someday. Mr. Owens can supervise."

"As you wish, ma'am," Tavish replied.

"Why are we going to New Alexandria?" Annabel asked.

"To take you home." Ridgewell arched a brow. "Unless you'd rather travel on a liner. I brought you into this mess, the least I can do is get you home again."

"But I thought I could stay until we discover what this book is about."

"Annabel, I'm not going to go harrying off across the universe searching for two people. Especially when I have no idea where to even start. You need to be back at your university, and the Sheba needs to get back to being a merchant ship. I have to make a living."

Annabel slumped in her chair.

"Marianne," the captain continued. "My correspondence is starting to pile up. I understand you've had a trying day, but I'd appreciate it if you could see to it. I'd like to have a clean desk before departure."

"Of course, ma'am." Marianne put down her teacup.

"Well then, people. We have quite a bit to do. I suppose we should get to it." Ridgewell rose and walked to her desk.

Annabel moved to sit in front of it.

Likely to argue.

Tavish shook his head. The captain wasn't an easy woman to sway. He wished the professor luck. He stopped Marianne before she turned into her office. "Wait for me on deck tonight?"

Her pale green eyes, usually so easy to read, were inscrutable "As you wish."

Tonight he would open his heart. The danger was past yet he wouldn't feel whole until Marianne agreed to be his. If wrapping her up in a cocoon wasn't an option, he'd settle for having her as long as God allowed.

Marianne stared out over the railing inhaling the soft smell of peonies. The soft blossomy scent soothed her.

She would never forget the look in his eyes when he'd scooped her up in his arms. Cherished, loved.

She sensed him the moment he stepped foot on deck. It was a subtle shifting of the air, a change in scent, ever so slightly.

He stepped up next to her and laid a hand on hers. "I love you."

Warmth spread through her and she opened her mouth to reply.

Tavish stopped her with a hand on her lips. "Please let me finish."

She nodded.

Taking both her hands in his, he turned to face her. "I wasn't sure I could. I wasn't sure I'd..." He shook his head. "You remind me that I'm a man, not a monster. You ground me when I feel overwhelmed and soothe me when I feel agitated. I..."

He stared off over the ship and took a deep breath. Then reaching one hand into his pocket he turned back at her. "I wanted to give you something special. Something just for you."

He turned her hand over, and placed an object in it.

Snake!

Tears welled in her eyes and she squeezed the tiny mechanical to her chest.

Snake heated in her hand, purring in welcome.

"How did you find it? How did you know?"

He pulled out a handkerchief and wiped her eyes. "You talked about it. I found it just before..." his voice broke and he swallowed. "Just before I learned you were gone."

Marianne wrapped her arms around him and squeezed. "Thank you so much. I never knew that I could find such happiness. I never felt I deserved—"

He squeezed her back. "You deserve so much more than me."

Pulling back from the hug, she cupped his cheek. "Oh, Tavish. You are everything and more than I could ever want. Kind, gentle, compassionate. I've been in love with you so long. It's hard to imagine a day without it."

"We'll fight." He murmured into her hair. "I might hurt you."

Marianne sighed into his chest. "You will never hurt me."

"Marry me?" he asked.

She pulled back from the embrace and smiled at him. "Yes."

He kissed her. A hot, demanding kiss that pulled her deep into the passionate inferno he alone could ignite. Everything else washed away. Her fears, the book, Atlantis. All that mattered was this man, this night, and his arms. She'd found her happily ever after.

The End

Follow Kathryn Kohorst on Facebook and Twitter.

Join her newsletter by visiting her website at www.kathrynkohorst.com

Made in the USA
San Bernardino, CA
24 March 2016